I0645365

Praise for

Touch Me In The Morning

"*I love a story that immediately grabs your attention and keeps you involved 'til the last page. I enjoyed that the book included romance, family, and real issues. Good read.*"

—Mary Lee Robinson, Myrtle Beach, SC

"*Loved the characters and story line, which kept me guessing what was going to happen next.*"

– Pauline, an avid reader.

"*Ms. Jeffries characters are real life and enable the reader to eagerly ride along with them on their adventure.*"

– Abraham Leib, Critic.

"*Ann Jeffries puts so much into a book [and] pays special attention to characterization so that by the time you finish reading one of her stories you feel you know the characters.*"

– Janice Sims, best-selling author, *Thief of My Heart*

"*[Ann Jeffries] is as dynamic as her characters are in the book. As I read, I became a part of the book. She knows life and can take you places you have [never] been. Excellent book.*"

– Danny Keith

Ask Me No Questions…I'll Tell You No Lies

"*A very absorbing story with true-to-life characters and an explosive ending. A great read!*"

— Abraham Leib

"*This book is for all women who put their lives on the line for their man, only to find they have been set aside. What a great story of a woman coming into her own at a later age. Way to go, Ms. Jeffries!*"

—J. A. Meinecke, Author of *A Woman to Reckon With.*

"Never a traditional ending with certainly non-traditional characters, makes this page-turner a must read. [A] heart tugging, emotionally driven read."

—L. S. Casey, Author, *Alma Mater*

"Leading us on a journey of loss and reclamation, Ann captivates the readers early on and keeps them riveted to the very end."

—Bella Fayre, Author, *Maelstroms of the Silent*

"Ann Jeffries did a wonderful job weaving the characters' stories together to create a satisfying tale and ending. Once I started reading, I couldn't put it down."

—Nancy Engle, Author, *Reunions Can Be Murder*

Walking On Uneven Ground

"Ann Jeffries describes her settings so well I felt like I was living the story not just reading it. The characters seemed so real I wanted to meet them and congratulate them on their successes."

—Rebecca Bridges, President of Coastal Authors Network, Secretary of Lowcountry Romance Writers Association, and member of Carolina Forest Authors' Club

"Walking on Uneven Ground will keep the reader engaged from the first page until the last with action, intrigue, and, of course, Ms. Jeffries' own brand of romance."

—Nancy Engle, Author, *Image of Perfection*

"Ann Jeffries delivers another engaging read! Walking on Uneven Ground captures heart and soul, to the very last page! A dynamic presentation by a highly gifted writer!"

—Bella Fayre, Author, *Maelstroms of the Silent*

"Walking on Uneven Ground captures you from the initial paragraph and keeps you enthralled throughout. Fast paced and witty, a definite must read!"

—Barb Ryan, Carolina Forest Critique Group

"*In* Walking on Uneven Ground, *Ann Jeffries writes a compelling tale that supports the benefits made possible from those working for the greater good.*"

  —Carole O'Neill, Coastal Authors Network, Founding Member

The Better Part of Valor

"*Ann Jeffries has done it again! Intrigue, greed, power, and romance all combine to make this a real page turner!*"

  —J.A. Meinecke, Author, *A Woman To Reckon With*

"*Ann Jeffries never disappoints! Once again, she has the reader hooked and wanting more!*"

  —Bella Fayre, Author, *Maelstroms of the Silent*

"*Ann Jeffries takes the reader on a ride filled with twists that will leave you wanting more. In this case she leaves you with unanswered questions that keep your head spinning as you wait for the next novel.*"

  —L. S. Casey, Author, *Alma Mater*

"*Once again Ms. Jeffries captivates the reader with characters and plot that demand complete attention. She weaves a story full of intrigue, but leaves plenty of time for romance. This book is a must read.*"

  —Nancy Engle, Author, *Reunions Can Be Murder*

Moments to Remember

"*Ann Jeffries, once again, puts us on the edge of our seats, delivering a compelling storyline, complete with drama, intrigue, and romance! Jeffries takes no prisoners! A must read!*"

  —Bella Fayre, Author, *Maelstroms of the Silent*

An Unguarded Moment

"I love a story that immediately grabs your attention and keeps you involved 'til the last page. Good read. Highly recommended."
—Gayle A. Hopper, MD

"Ann Jeffries does an excellent job of weaving her characters' stories together and keeping the reader captivated."
—Nancy Engle, Author, *Murder at Mount Joy*

"Ann has a terrific voice for romance—it [is] light, readable and the characters were a lot of fun."
—Kara Cesare, the Richard Curtis Literary Agency

"I loved the story line! A little suspenseful, which I like. The story flowed and it felt like I was reading a movie. I enjoyed the book."
—Gina, an avid reader

"I really admire Ann's smooth writing style and the appealing premise of this project."
—Mavis Allen, Associate Senior Editor, Silhouette Books

"This [is] a book I couldn't get enough of. I read at night to fall asleep and this book had the opposite effect...I didn't want to put it down...Very well written with enough spice to keep things interesting. Never a dull moment."
—Terri Hershey

Uncommon Choices

"Ann Jeffries has given us a great adventure and a terrific love story together with characters who immediately come alive and involve us in their searing passion and heartbreaking dilemmas."
—Abe Leib, Esq.

"I truly loved and enjoyed the book. I haven't read a book expressed the way Ms. Jeffries explained the characters and their lives. Very entertaining, easy to read, [and] it [drew me in]. Great job!"
—J. Babey

Northern Exposures

"Ms. Jeffries never writes a slow read. Her novels are impossible to put down."

—Trisha Moriarty, Author, *The Secrets She Kept*

Another Point of View

"Ann Jeffries has done it again! Once you start reading you won't be able to put the book down!"

—J. A. Meinecke, Author, *A Woman to Reckon With*

Southern Exposures

"Loved the way [Ann Jeffries] described the activities...I felt as though I was there witnessing everything [that she was] describing. [She] immediately got my attention with the colorful...attention to details. The book is very warm."

—Brenda Irons LeCesne, Esq.

"I thoroughly enjoyed...this [novel]. I think [Ann Jeffries'] ability [to] create emotion is a true talent. [She] did a great job creating suspense. The [characters'] stories seemed most authentic and entertaining. Language and dialogue [o]ver all...is a strong area for [Ann]."

—Karen R. Thomas, President, Creative Minds Book Group

"I always like a happy ending and being the romantic that I am the ending makes me want the continuation to be available for me to see the two characters Vivian and Benny to have the happy ending like KJ with the respective characters Chuck and Stacy."

—Sharon Jarrett-Brown, Aurora Reading Group

Copyright ©2016 by Ann Jeffries
www.annjeffries.net
All rights reserved
Printed and Bound in the United States of America

Published and Distributed By
New View Literature
820 67th Avenue N, #7603
Myrtle Beach, South Carolina 29572
www.newviewliterature.com
annjeffries@newviewliterature.com

Cover and Interior design: TWA Solutions.com

ISBN: 978-0-9915003-8-3 Paperback
ISBN: 978-1-941603-59-8 eBook

Library of Congress Control Number: 2014909734

First printing August 2016

This is a work of fiction. Names, characters, business, places, events and incidents are either the products of the author's imagination or used in a fictitious manner. Any resemblance to actual persons, living or dead, or actual events is purely coincidental.

No part of this book may be reproduced, stored in a retrieval system or transmitted in any form or by any means without the prior written permission of the publisher—except by a reviewer who may quote brief passages in a review to be printed in a newspaper, magazine, or journal.

For inquires, contact the publisher.

Ask Me
No Questions...

I'll Tell You No Lies

Another Family Reunion Novel
In The Wisdom of the Ancestors Series

Ann Jeffries

Acknowledgements

I bow in humble appreciation to:

The Creator

The Ancestors

Jessica Tilles, again, your ability to create the perfect cover is second to none and the right fit to guide me on this literary journey;

Eleanor Shelton, a BFF. This one is for you, kid;

My fellow authors in the Carolina Forest Authors' Club. You made this one better and possible; and

To those of you who are in my dash—the ones who have been there since the beginning of this journey in my northeast Washington, DC, neighborhood, through Allen High School in Asheville, North Carolina, Anacostia High School in Washington, DC, Maryland University, College Park, Maryland, professional careers and beyond. To faithful family, friends, and fans everywhere, thank you for your unqualified support.

The journey continues and the struggle for literary perfection will never end.

Thank you all! I remain faithfully yours,
Ann Jeffries

If I told you I don't mind

Would you believe me

When I say to you you're not my kind

Do I deceive you with this fragile disguise?

Ask me no questions

And I will tell you no lies

If you could read my heart I would not deny

But I pretend

Prologue

It is the worst possible night to be out and about, Justin Willis McCoy thought, as a hurricane skirted the East Coast, bringing torrential rains, high winds, and rising ocean tides to his little slice of the South Carolina coastline. He stood inside the rear French doors of the still fragrant first-floor kitchen of the first resort hotel he ever purchased. He surveyed the furious Atlantic Ocean, as it surged, churned, and crashed against the shore like a wild thing hell bent on destruction. If the weather predictions were accurate, this hurricane could wreak more havoc, destroying his property, as Hurricane Sandy did, devastating the New Jersey and New York coasts.

This grand old lady, Oceans Inn Resort, his first foray into the hotel business, withstood many such storms since her construction in the early 1800s. She was an architectural wonder, built to last with her three stories of antebellum mansion located on forty acres of beachfront in a small southern community of Atlantic Beach along the Grand Strand. The Intracoastal Waterway was less than a mile away to the west and rising under the deluge of the heavy rains. With the Atlantic to its east, the Intercoastal to its west, and the water rising, the Grand Strand could cease to exist.

He could hear the creaks and moans, as the house fought to withstand the gale-force winds tugging at her hurricane shutters installed years ago on the windows and doors. Those shutters were among the best investments he made in the property. If this storm proved as dangerous and disastrous as predicted, his lady would again need an infusion of capital to restore her to her former glory. As his first and favorite resort, she would have anything and everything she needed from him. He loved her more than he loved any woman, except maybe one he never met.

He arrived from his Washington, DC, headquarters to assess the property hours before the storm shut down the airport. His Head of Major Projects, Michael Rodgers, suggested Oceans Inn Resort had seen better days and it was time to give up and sell this property or rebuild. Justin wasn't convinced. He rolled up his sleeves and helped his longtime, faithful employees close up the empty Inn in preparation for the harsh weather. Once everything was secure, most of the employees left to tend to their own homes. However, a few of the older women, who worked in the kitchen, stayed to make sure the food and supplies in the pantries were taken to a high floor in the Inn for storage in case of flooding. That task completed, his workers were now preparing for bed on the upper floors of the Inn to ride out the storm.

Because he was keeping vigil on the weather reports, and the Atlantic Ocean's surge now less than one hundred feet from the resort's foundation, he hadn't planned to get much sleep. There would be an incredible amount of beach erosion. Dredging would definitely have to begin to reclaim the beach.

His mind was on not only the storm, and the damage it would wreak on his ladylove, but also on the real threat David Delaware leveled against him earlier that day. The man was a criminal. According to investigative reports he received from Richardson

Investigation and Security, many times, Delaware had killed without malice or forethought. Never indicted for any crime, law enforcement agencies in several countries had Delaware and his Mafia family on their radar.

Justin knew, before entering a business deal to purchase the Delaware Group Hotel and Resort chain, that it was a dicey proposition at best. He tried making it a simple, clean acquisition as he had done before with other deals and then move on. However, the not-so-veiled threat of retribution from the Delawares had him concerned for his own safety and those close to him.

The raging storm outside wasn't the only thing that could possibly end his life.

"Justin?"

"Yes, Miss Nettie?" He turned from his troubling thoughts and vigilant attention to the ocean to regard his head cook's diminutive stature in her plain, cotton, nightclothes, and fuzzy, pink slippers. "I thought you were already asleep. It's late."

"I was about to turn out my light and close my shutters because I need to leave early in the morning, but I saw a car sitting out on the road near the front gate. The lights are on, but no one seems to be moving inside."

Justin tensed at the thought Frank Delaware might already be making good on his threat. "You're concerned about it?"

"I am, yes. I know it's a mess out there, Justin, but someone could be sick or injured. I won't rest until I know whoever it is will be all right. Maybe you could have a look?"

"Okay."

He donned a rain slicker, though it wouldn't be much protection against the elements. Still, if someone were after him, he wouldn't want harm to come to anyone in the Inn. He would go out into the storm and meet his fate head-on. He made his way to the front door of the Inn, taking time to close and lock it behind him.

Indeed, there was a late model, black, SUV Escalade parked, blocking the property's front gate. He would be royally pissed if someone were just looking for directions, but for Miss Nettie Baker, he would do nearly anything she asked of him. She was the oldest and among the most faithful of his employees. She was a sous-chef of sorts when he was still a boy, working his way through college as a waiter and kitchen helper at the resort. Now he owned it and over one hundred hotels, resorts, and conference centers spanning the globe.

He headed out at a fast trot, dodging deep puddles, as furious wind and rain slapped him around. Trees had fallen and branches hurled around like javelins. He finally reached the car and cautiously approached the driver's side window.

What he saw he never would have expected.

Chapter One

One day earlier…

"Mom, please! Stop fussing, would you?" Daryl Mason huffed in frustration. "I'm not a baby, you know."

Loretta Hill Mason sat down on the bed in her son's college dorm room and brushed her hand over an imaginary wrinkle in her neat, gray slacks. She was near tears, but she bit down on her bottom lip and held on. Indeed, her son wasn't a baby anymore. He was seventeen years old, soon-to-be eighteen, and starting college today. He was the last of the three children to leave home and the empty-nest syndrome was kicking her butt with full force.

Daryl put the last of his clothes in a drawer and turned to look at his mother. He wasn't angry with her. In fact, he loved her very much. All his life she was his cheerleader, support system, and confidant. His friends gravitated toward her, leaned on her when they had problems in their own households, and knew she would give them whatever moral support they needed. When he was younger, she was the first to volunteer to drive a carpool, organize a fund-raising event, or convince whatever power structure to support the children's efforts. What had always upset him, though, was she did so much for others and very little for herself.

"When do you have to go back to school?" he asked, observing his mother's pensive mood.

Loretta didn't lift her eyes as she ran a smoothing hand over her son's red, black, and green-colored, geometric-patterned comforter.

"The new term starts in another two or three weeks, I suppose," she said barely above a whisper.

"Another year, huh, Mom?" he asked quietly.

Loretta inhaled deeply, letting out her breath with her response. "Yes. Time does fly," she said, her voice trailing off.

"You became Head Mistress of Columbia Academy the year I started. Now I'm all grown up. You can retire, can't you, Mom?"

Loretta bent from her sitting position, lifted one of Daryl's duffle bags from the floor, and began to fold it.

She chuckled mirthlessly. "I'm not old enough, but I suppose I can."

Daryl took the bag from her hands and hung it in his closet. "Maybe you ought to do that then. Randy, Libby, and I are out of the house and on our own. You should take a vacation. Take some time for yourself. Maybe travel around the world or something." He closed the closet door and turned to look out the window, digging his hands in his pockets.

"No, I don't think so. Your father has work to do and he's—"

Daryl turned abruptly toward his mother, listening to her go on and on about his father's needs and wants, but not her own. With her head hung low, sitting primly on the edge of his bed with her knees together and legs properly crossed at the ankles, he could see a few individual gray strands in her otherwise thick, lustrous reddish-brown mane. Soft as velvet to the touch, he wondered why she wore it in such a severe and unbecoming ball at the nape of her neck. Hair like hers should be let loose, much like the woman herself. She should be free to enjoy her life now he and his older brother and sister were adults. Of course, she wouldn't think of herself as free. She never had. For that, he was grateful to her, yet annoyed. She was a wonderful mother and friend. He loved her dearly and hated to see what the years were doing to her. Maybe now she would find a new life of her own. He truly hoped so.

"Awwww, Mom, don't wait for Dad," he interrupted. "Why don't you and some of your friends just go? You know, maybe Ms. Olivia or Ms. Sylvia?"

Loretta tried to smile. It would be nice to travel with some of her dear friends, but she let the thought pass. "They've got responsibilities, too, Daryl. Husbands, families, and careers. They can't just pick up and go at the drop of a hat." Actually, they could, but they never would. They both had wonderful husbands they would want as traveling companions. She did not.

"I'll bet if you asked them they would go with you. Ms. Olivia probably would like a break from her grandkids and Ms. Sylvia, she—"

Loretta cut her eyes at Daryl for the slight English *faux pas* and he noticed.

"I mean, Ms. Sylvia's youngest, Aretha, is at Harvard this year."

Before she had an opportunity to discuss her future further, they heard familiar, heavy footsteps approaching the door. Loretta tensed. Randolph Mason, Senior's tall, hulking frame filled the doorway.

"I guess this is the last of it," he said, handing another duffle bag to Daryl.

"Thanks, Dad." Daryl took the bag from his father. "It should be. It's my football exercise gear."

"Well, now, you got everything?" Randolph asked, patting his son on the back. "Money in your bank account, meal card, books, and supplies?"

"Yes, sir, Mom took care of all of it for me." Daryl cut his eyes to his mother.

"Good!" Randolph said to Daryl, and then turned to his wife. "Well, then, c'mon, Retta, let's get on the road before it gets late. I don't want to get stuck in this Atlanta traffic during rush hour and a storm is brewing I hear." Then turning again to his son, Randolph grinned. "Bet you got some campus honey dipping to do."

Daryl took a deep breath and shook his head. "Naw, Dad. Coach says we've got a team meeting tonight. Then a bed check at ten. Football practice starts tomorrow bright and early."

"Well, my boy, in my day, we used to mix touch downs with a few—"

"Uh, yeah, Dad, I know," he interrupted. "You've told me already. I'll be fine."

"Still mooning over young, phine Miss Aretha Alexander, are you? Fine young woman she is, too. Takes after her mother, Sylvia. I declare that woman looks the spitting image of the songstress Phyllis Hyman. Sings as good as her, too. Yes, indeed, a fine piece if I ever saw one." Randolph winked. "Don't be shy about tapping some of the young, phine, little hunnies I've seen walking 'round this campus over the past few days. Remember, there are a lot of other college campuses here in Atlanta," he gushed. "Sure didn't build them honey dips like this when I was at Maryland University!"

"Yeah, Dad, I know," Daryl said, still eyeing his mother. "Mom, you gonna be all right?"

Loretta inhaled a ragged breath. Remorse, from leaving her youngest son at college and her husband's callousness, gripped her and tossed her into an emotional vortex. She involuntarily balled her fists and briefly closed her eyes. After nearly twenty years of marriage, she should be used to her husband's callous behavior. She wondered why Randolph wouldn't stop pushing Daryl. He was a good son and conscientious student. He had a crush on Aretha Alexander and wanted to hold on to the relationship, but no, Randolph wanted someone to follow in his lustful footsteps.

She had to get a grip and shake off the ire building within her. She wanted to scream and cry, to beat her fists against Randolph's callousness, but no, she couldn't do that either. She was a Hill, after all, and the Hills of Columbia County, South Carolina, didn't make a scene. Hill women were dutiful wives who supported their husbands no matter what and always observed proper decorum…well, at least most of them did. Everyone except her sister, Kayla.

Older than Loretta by four years, Kayla cut her own path. Loretta thought, not for the first time, how much she wanted to be more like Kayla, but, of course, that was impossible. Kayla Hill was a single woman whose career took her all over the world. As an agent for the U.S. State Department, Kayla opted for life on the fast track, while Loretta opted to walk two paces behind her husband and be a mother to their children. Although she often regretted the marriage to Randolph, she never regretted being a mother and homemaker.

"Yes, honey, I'll be fine." She tried to smile at her son, though she felt like her heart was breaking apart.

"C'mon, Retta," Randolph again prodded, now annoyed and touching her elbow.

Loretta moved away from her husband's touch and looked up into her son's handsome face. Daryl instinctively came to her and engulfed her in his massive embrace. *When had he gotten so tall and muscular?* she wondered. She was tall, too, but her head just met his chin. It seemed like it was only yesterday he was taking his first steps.

"Remember what I said, Mom," he whispered. "It's your turn. Randy, Libby, and I are all grown up now. We love you. Do something for yourself."

Loretta almost lost her composure as she embraced her son a little tighter, her face buried in his chest. *Where had the years gone?*

With his arm comfortingly around his mother's shoulders, Daryl walked with her and his father to their SUV. He gave her a kiss on her temple and another squeeze before he opened the car door and helped her inside. His father gave him a tip-of-the-hat salute before ducking into the driver's seat.

Loretta fastened her seat belt and waved to her son, as her husband pulled away from the curb. They rode in silence for a while in the building traffic and rain that started to fall around Atlanta, Georgia. Randolph was listening to a gut-belly Blues station booming lost-love songs on the XM Radio as he piloted the big, black Escalade SUV from Atlanta, Georgia, toward their home in Columbia County, South Carolina. Loretta looked through the raindrops out her side-view window and fell deep into thought. Her spirits bordering on depression were low as the soot-gray clouds, and she knew it. She would have to find a way to regroup before the fall term began.

It wouldn't have been so hard if her life was on track, but it wasn't. Somewhere in her existence, she had lost herself and disappeared into a parody of a matronly woman. This was not where she was supposed to be at this point in her life or in her heart.

Such high hopes and great dreams she had for herself when she graduated a year early from Howard University so many years ago. Always a good student, graduating before she was twenty-one, she won Ms. Palmetto State and could still remember the song she sang to clinch the title… *And I'm telling you, I'm not going…* She hummed it now in her thoughts. She brought the audience to its collective feet that night. Offers came her way to sing professionally, but her parents would not permit it and then, of course, Randolph Mason had her heart in those days.

She and Randolph had known each other since they crawled out of the cradle and their parents were still the best of friends.

Having graduated from Maryland University ahead of her, and drafted by a professional team, Randolph played in the National Football League. They were so much in love, she thought, until two weeks after their wedding and honeymoon when he presented her with his three-year-old son from a liaison he apparently had in college while they were dating. After the shock, she took the toddler in, cared for Randolph Junior as if he were her own, and loved him dearly, but she almost left her husband when he brought Elizabeth home a year later. She was still a baby, barely eight months old. Randolph pleaded with her, said it wouldn't happen again. He loved her, despite his affairs outside of their marriage. She couldn't leave, even though she wanted to, because she was pregnant with Daryl. Her family, even in light of Randolph's infidelities, wouldn't give her their moral support to leave him.

Her mother, aunts, and mother-in-law convinced her Randolph was just sowing wild oats, as most men in professional sports were used to doing. They argued that Randolph provided a good home for her and the children, and since he didn't physically abuse her, she should stay in her marriage because no matter what, a good Catholic wife never left her husband.

Her older sisters, Andrea, Evelyn, Denise, and Adrienne, agreed with their mother and aunts, even suggesting maybe it was her fault Randolph sought his pleasures outside their marriage. Maybe she was not submitting to him as often as she should. They never looked beyond the millions Randolph made playing professional sports.

Only her sister, Kayla, stood by her, insisting Randolph's behavior was unforgivable, regardless of his bank account and she should leave him. In the final stages of her pregnancy, Loretta bent to her mother's admonitions and stayed with Randolph. Her wedding vows still meant something to her, even if they didn't to Randolph. She took care of the children, while Randolph moved from team to team, but the fantasy of an idyllic married life died. Nearly twenty years of marriage. Where had the time gone?

"Retta, we have to talk," Randolph said, as he turned down the car radio. "I've come to a decision."

"About what?" Loretta asked, still mindlessly starring out her window at the passing countryside.

"I'm getting a divorce."

Chapter Two

"Good morning, Mr. McCoy," said Sissy, one of his secretaries, who set off a chain reaction from the ten or so assistants and other staff who lined the wide, lush corridor leading to his suite of executive offices.

Justin nodded, but kept up his brisk, long-legged, ground-eating pace to reach the glass doors encasing his executive assistant's, Marilyn Allen's, office.

"Good morning, Mr. McCoy," Ms. Allen said, as she gathered her iPad and followed him into his inner chamber. Without missing a beat, she began to brief him on his scheduled workday. "You have a video-conference call with the Delaware Group at nine-fifteen and then with Richardson Investigations and Security at ten o'clock. Mr. Westman asked if he could have a few minutes at ten-thirty. He said he would only need ten minutes, so I penciled him in. You have Duggans at ten-forty-five. He's bringing the Harris Group in for a conference and—"

"Bernie Harris?" Justin interrupted, while taking off his suit jacket and hanging it in the closet.

"Yes, sir. They've rethought their proposal for the South African Hotel chains. They want the contract to refurbish the hotels in Johannesburg."

"They're the ones with the child labor law violations?"

She nodded in the affirmative.

"Not interested," he said, moving toward his desk.

"Sir, they haven't been convicted—"

Justin raised only his obsidian eyes to Marilyn. She crossed the names off the schedule and continued rattling off his meeting-filled day.

"…Ms. Anderson wants to go to dinner at six. You have theater tickets for the eight o'clock show. Mrs. McCoy called again, third time this week, and wants you to call her—"

Again, Justin raised only his eyes. Marilyn moved on. "As requested, your Adventurer Executive Air flight will be ready late tonight. I've confirmed your flight plan and arranged for a car to pick you up at the airport and drive you to the Inn. I should mention, however, there are weather warnings out. A hurricane is approaching the coast, but is expected to stay out to sea or at least that's what they think now."

"Is that all, Ms. Allen?" he asked, reading over the reports on his desk from various departments making notations as he worked.

"No, sir. Mr. Mason, from Mason Liberty Mutual, Life and Casualty, called again. He wants to arrange a meeting with you to discuss several insurance plans for McCoy Enterprises and coverage for the properties in the hotel and restaurant divisions."

"Mason? Mason?" His brow beetled as he tried to recall the name.

"Uh, he's a friend of Ms. Anderson's," Marilyn offered.

"Ah, yes, now I remember. Former football linebacker. The sports media called him The Bull. Get Tucker with Richardson Investigations on it. Complete profile and dossier. Have Michael handle the preliminary contact and review the proposal."

"Yes, sir," she intoned efficiently. The telephone buzzed and Marilyn reached over Justin's large mahogany desk and answered it. "Mr. McCoy's office."

It was Erin in Reception. "Ms. Allen, Mrs. McCoy is in Reception and she's demanding to see Mr. McCoy. She's making a terrible scene down here. What should I do?" she nervously asked.

Marilyn glimpsed Justin's demeanor and said quietly, "Call security and have her escorted out of the—"

Justin heard the word "security" and looked up. "Carla?"

Marilyn nodded. "Yes, sir. She's in Reception."

Justin grabbed the back of his neck and blew out a frustrated breath. After a long, thought-filled moment, Justin said, "Admit her. How much time do I have?"

Marilyn looked at her watch. "Fifteen minutes before your first meeting."

Justin nodded and Marilyn relayed the message, giving further instructions to the receptionist. Then Marilyn continued outlining Justin's schedule and taking notes on his instructions.

Shortly, two uniformed security guards escorted the former Mrs. Justin W. McCoy into the office.

"Justin, darling," she cooed. "Is this really necessary?"

Carla Hamilton McCoy Greer Byrd was still a stunningly attractive woman who had celebrated the third anniversary of her thirty-ninth birthday. Tall, leggy, with a model's body, and an aristocratic carriage, she sauntered up to Marilyn and devilishly grinned.

"The ever-faithful, extremely efficient, and long-suffering *Ms.* Allen," Carla intoned derisively. "I'll bet these brutes are your idea."

"Ms. Hamilton," Marilyn acknowledged, using Carla's maiden name, not at all shaken by the woman's behavior.

Carla hauntingly raised her patrician head and shook back her beautiful waterfall of thick brown hair. "That's *Mrs.* McCoy to you, *Ms.* Allen, and do not forget it again," Carla demonstratively said. "You're dismissed and take your attack dogs with you."

Justin was holding his temper, but Carla was about to pluck his last nerve. "That's enough, Carla!" Justin said in a deadly, quiet, controlled tone.

"Mr. McCoy?" Marilyn asked in a non-verbal request to leave his office.

Justin nodded handing the signed reports and correspondence to her. "Thank you, Ms. Allen, we'll keep to the schedule as planned and please keep up with the weather reports."

"Yes, sir," Marilyn said, taking the work from her boss and rolling her eyes at Carla.

Once the heavy, oak doors closed behind his staff, Justin's eyes bored into Carla.

She was visibly affected by the power he exuded, but that's what had drawn her to him more than twenty-two years ago.

They met in college, he at Georgetown and she at Wellesley. He was on the debate team that came to a competition at Wellesley. Green from the South with hayseed still in his hair, Carla had seemed like a goddess to him then. Wealthy, from old New England money, her widowed father, John Harvey Hamilton, spoiled her rotten. He was a successful executive, who hired Justin straight out of graduate school, and gave him a mid-level position in his textile business. Years later, John Harvey suffered a stroke and Justin's business acumen saved Hamilton Textile Industries from ruin. Now, Hamilton Textile was a division of McCoy Enterprises International, but Carla never let Justin forget it was her father who gave him his first professional job. As if he would want to forget. He held his former boss, father-in-law, and mentor in high esteem and kept him in the business for that very reason.

"Going somewhere, darling?" Carla purred. "If so, I can make myself available to accompany you. I dearly need a vacation to some tropical—"

"How much?" Justin asked, reading the reason for Carla's frequent calls and now her impromptu visit.

"Justin, darling," she said, seductively rounding his desk. "No hello? No how are you, Carla?"

"How much?" he repeated, ignoring her offer and her advances.

Carla slid up to him, rubbing her perfectly manicured fingernails up the front of his crisp, white, monogrammed shirt, over his impressive pecs. She leaned in to kiss his lips, but he turned away from her, removing her hands from his body. "I won't ask you again," he said with quiet vehemence.

Carla huffed, but obviously knew she had reached the outer limits of Justin's patience. "One hundred thousand," she said with her nose in the air, looking away from him.

Justin reached for one of the many buttons on his desk's telephone console.

"Bennett," a voice answered, "Accounting."

"Rob, this is Justin McCoy. Please transfer one-hundred thousand from my personal account to the Carla Hamilton account."

"Uh, yes, sir. Code please."

Justin keyed in the security code.

"The usual restraints, sir?"

"Yes," Justin said, as he released the button.

"Really, Justin, you treat me like a child! Doling out money a month at a time. I'm your wife for Pete's sake and the mother of your child!"

"Wife? Here's a newsflash to help you with your short-term, memory-loss problem. We're divorced, Carla, and you've been married and divorced two times since then. Sound familiar? As for our daughter, you've never been a mother to her. Jessica isn't even permitted to call you mother in public!" Justin fumed, but he quickly reined in his ire. There was no need to rehash that chapter of his life. Thank goodness it was over ten years ago.

The vestiges lingered, however. Married and divorced twice since their divorce, Carla still insisted on calling herself Mrs. McCoy whenever expedient, and harassing him for money. She took the liberty to stay in any McCoy Hotel or Resort anywhere in the world free of charge with any number of her jet-set cronies occupying penthouse and prime accommodations. Most of the year, she lived in his London McCoy Grand Hotel on the penthouse level.

The two losers she married bilked her for every dime they could get their hands on before leaving her high and dry. Carla knew he would never turn his back on her because of his friendship with her father and his love for their daughter, but he was reaching his wit's end. She had lawyers who could have made contact with his lawyers, as was the usual practice, but she was pestering him for almost a year to rekindle their relationship. For him, that was out of the question. She, however, never took *no* for an answer.

"I read in the society columns you've been seeing the harlot, Daf-phony Anderson. A little young, wouldn't you say, darling? Is she even legal?"

"She's over the age of consent so I wouldn't say anything, Carla, were I you," he said with a directed stare. "That third husband of yours was young enough to still suffer from diaper rash. I wouldn't start slinging rocks at Ms. Anderson. She works for a living and she's a potential headliner for my US-based hotel conference centers and clubs. She's far from being 'phony," as you put it. Now you have what you came for. Good day."

"*Ha!*" she spat ignoring his dismissal as she paced his office annoyed. "That wench has her eyes on you, Justin! Conference center and clubs my Aunt Sadie Hawkins! She's trying to sleep her way to the top and you're just foolish enough to think she's some type of replacement for the country bumpkin that got away from you—"

"Enough!" Justin said through clinched teeth.

On cue, Marilyn knocked lightly and entered. "Mr. McCoy, your directors and managers are assembled and awaiting your arrival in Video-Conference Room A."

Justin inhaled deeply. "Thank you, Ms. Allen. *Ms.* Hamilton is leaving now. Please have security escort her to her limousine." He went to the closet and retrieved his jacket. Once he straightened his tie in the full-length closet mirror, he turned and waited.

Carla got the message. Her time with him was at an end, but she wasn't finished with him yet. Not by a long shot. She had a great deal of money riding on her ability to manipulate Justin.

Justin entered the Conference Room, as the sixteen department heads began to stand and usher forth greetings. The ones, via videoconferencing, located in areas around the globe came to attention. Marilyn was close on Justin's heels and took her usual seat to his right. Michael Rodgers, his senior Vice President, friend, and most trusted executive, sat to his left.

"Keep your seats, ladies and gentlemen," Justin said, seating himself at the center of the huge, round, hand-hewn conference table. The room was modern with a full row of ceiling to floor windows emitting the bright sunlight. A panoramic view of Washington lay beyond. Marilyn keyed in the telephone number and the videoconference screen on the back wall digitized.

"Good morning, McCoy," said Francesco "Frank" Vizzini Delaware, peering over his horn-rimmed glasses. A beautiful shock of thick, silver-white hair waved down his head.

"Mr. Delaware," Justin acknowledged. "It is my understanding you want to change the terms and conditions of our agreement. Am I correctly informed?"

"Justin, my friend. Always straight to the issue—" he began affably.

Justin cut him off. "No deal," he said, confident in his position. "I've made a *bona fide* offer to you for your hotels, resorts, and conference centers and you have accepted. Half a billion was the agreed upon price. However, if you feel these properties can be sold at a better price to another entity, I'll release you from our previous agreement. Perhaps we can work together on some future venture," he said comfortably from his executive chair. It was unlikely he would want to deal with Delaware on any basis in the future. If it were not for his keen interest in acquiring the hotel chain, he wouldn't have considered doing business with the man at all. He knew the tactics employed by some businessmen when they thought he was vulnerable, but he learned his lessons well with years of negotiating deals that rocked the financial markets to their Wall Street foundations. He was no pushover.

His vice presidents and directors uncomfortably shifted in their seats. Everyone, except Michael Rodgers. The man may look like he was a sweetheart, but ice water coursed through his veins. He was Justin's right hand and was as steady as a rock.

The Delaware Group's chain of hotels was the biggest acquisition McCoy Enterprises had gone after. Although the hotels were in need of serious revitalization, Justin hadn't gotten the industry nickname *The Rejuvenator* for nothing. He had a reputation for turning around some big, white elephants and making them profitable—very profitable. The Delaware Group was looking for a way to stay in the mix with a minority interest, but Justin wanted them out. All the way out. He wouldn't partner with Frank Delaware if his life depended on it, and still, he was concerned enough to think maybe it did. Delaware was "connected" and Justin wanted no further association with him or his "family" of mobsters.

"Now, Justin, my boy, don't be rash. This is a very interesting venture you're planning—"

Boy? That cut it! "Mr. Delaware, my original offer stands until close of business today. Tomorrow, the offer goes down to four hundred million and each day thereafter by one hundred million. By the week's end, the offer is withdrawn."

"Look here, McCoy!" Frank sputtered. "I can buy ten of you—"

"My best to your family, Mr. Delaware," Justin said.

"You've just made a grave error, McCoy. I assure you of that!"

Justin switched off the videoconference screen in mid-Delaware vitriol. The threat was not lost on him. He took it seriously. This was not the common gangster era anymore. Delaware would come after him if permitted to do so by higher ups in his criminal organization. It would be a subtle approach. Something very obscure. Justin knew he would have to be on his guard until the deal was done, and it would be done. Of that, he was also sure.

"Next order of business," Justin said, without missing a beat. Checking his watch, he noted he was ahead of schedule.

His senior staff let out audible gasps and glimpsed each other in amazement...and concern.

Justin had a late afternoon lunch at his desk, still working when Michael Rodgers, his Senior Vice President for Major Projects, knocked on the open door and entered the office.

"Got a minute, JW?"

"Only just." Justin sat back in his Italian leather executive chair. His tie was undone, shirt opened at the collar, and French cuffs rolled up to his elbows. "What's up?"

"I've reviewed Richardson's investigative reports on the Oceans Inn Resort. Looks like you were right. The management team was padding the books. Costly repairs they claimed were performed weren't. Your decision to fire the lot of them was very timely and they have no recourse. I've turned the matter over to the local LEOs, the FBI, and the US Attorney's office. Why don't you go the whole nine yards on this one and unload the property or shut it down and demolish it? It has never been self-sufficient or self-supporting, not to mention profitable. Now it is mired in red ink. It would take a massive infusion of capital to get the place back on its feet, in its current condition, and for what? It doesn't have the level of sophisticated clientele any of the other McCoy Resort Hotels have. It's more a place for losers and *it's* a real loser. The beachfront land is valuable though. Demolish the resort and build something new and modern."

"You never forget your first, Michael." Justin shifted in his chair and continued to read reports. "Historically, it was the only beach in South Carolina where people of color could go to swim in the ocean. It was also the first place I bought when I decided to go into the hotel business. I have a history there for many generations. Growing up in the area, I used to work in the kitchen and as a waiter every year while I was in college and grad school. It was my forty acres and a mule when I was making enough money to invest," he said, amused. "I've had it closed down for the season. I'm going to South Carolina tonight to take a look at the place. I've arranged for the Engineering and Construction Divisions to prepare a prospectus on the renovations needed and for the Financial Division to work up cost estimates. I should know something more by tomorrow when I return to the office."

"You still can't give up on any lost cause," Michael said, amused. "Just like when we were on the debate team as adversaries. You'd argue the most indefensible positions—and, unfortunately, it gained you more points than you deserved."

"Yeah," Justin said, grinning, "I enjoyed keeping you off balance."

Michael chuckled. "You still do. That's why I accepted your offer to work for you eleven years ago."

"Maybe you want to put a little wager on this one?" Justin speculatively asked.

Michael shook his head. "I've learned never to bet against you. It's like betting against the house. It would be a fool's wager."

"Good move," Justin said still working. "Hold off on any action on the Oceans Inn Resort. I'll give you a decision about what I want to do in a few days."

Just then, Marilyn entered and offered an apology for the interruption.

"Mr. McCoy, heavy weather seems to be moving in on the coastline. Perhaps you should reschedule your flight for later in the week. Should I make arrangements—"

"What is my window of opportunity?"

"If you mean today, perhaps four or five hours."

"Fine, that should be enough time. Call the airport and have my flight ready for departure within the hour. Then call Carlos, have him pack an overnight bag for me, casual clothes, and bring the car to the underground garage door entrance." He rose from his seat. "Reschedule the rest of my afternoon and evening appointments."

"Yes, sir, and Ms. Anderson?" she asked with a raised eyebrow.

"Oh, yes, Daphne." He paused, his brow beetled. Then he turned to his friend. "Uh, Michael, would you do a favor for me and take Daphne Anderson to dinner and to The Kennedy Center tonight?" Justin moved swiftly to shovel reports into his briefcase.

"Sure, JW." He grinned. "Sounds like she's yesterday's news, though."

Justin didn't answer, but, as usual, Michael's instincts were very much on target.

Later, after his arrival in South Carolina, Justin made his on-site assessment of Oceans Inn Resort before the storm, and then met with the remaining loyal employees over dinner to assure them their jobs with McCoy Enterprises were secure. Most of them worked at the Oceans Inn Resort for many years; nearly all of their adult lives. They were all much older now and so was the antebellum Inn with its Old World Southern charm. Situated on the South Carolina Grand Strand coastline overlooking the Atlantic Ocean, the Inn had weathered many storms. The one approaching the shore now might be the very one to render it to shambles, but eleven employees worked diligently and tirelessly to close all of the hurricane shutters in the empty resort and stow the deck and lawn furniture. Justin rolled up his shirtsleeves and worked shoulder-to-shoulder with his faithful employees, many of whom lived in cottages on the forty-acre, golf course, and resort grounds.

The storm Marilyn mentioned was in full sway when Justin was informed a car was sitting for some time in front of the Oceans Inn Resort gate with its lights on. He could see a silhouette, which appeared to be motionless in the late model Escalade SUV. Concerned someone might be ill, Justin sprinted out into the driving rain and wind, approached the vehicle, and tapped on the driver's window.

"Are you in need of assistance?" he shouted over the howling wind.

The motionless form didn't answer, but the person's blank expression concerned him. Justin opened the driver's door and tried again to rouse the woman who sat gripping the steering wheel. He immediately sensed the woman was in severe distress or shock, fear or a catatonic state and in need of help.

Chapter Three

Loretta turned in the warm, Downy-fresh-smelling bed and raked her fingers up into her hair. She could feel the vehemence of the storm raging outside and the creaks of the house bending and holding against the strong, whistling, and moaning wind. Rain beat against the exterior of the building and the churn of the ocean loudly crashed against the shore.

Her eyes still closed, she thought, *Wait a minute! Creaks? Ocean? Why does the house sound like that? Why was there a smell of salt water in the air?* After all, the Mason Mansion was built of cement, brick, and block, not wood and shingles, and situated on five acres of land on the outskirts of Columbia, South Carolina, not an ocean to be found in a hundred miles. Her eyes drifted open and adjusted to the dimness in the room. *Where am I?* She looked around, moving only her eyes. This was not her bedroom or her bed and worst still, someone was in the room with her. She heard the person's breathing. It was decidedly a masculine sound. Certainly not Randolph's loud snore, she knew. Although they no longer shared a bedroom, she could still hear his cow calling down the hall from his room.

Justin felt, more than heard, the quiet fear from his guest. He opened his eyes and, for a fleeting moment, the beautiful, wide, light brownish-green irises that stared back at him during lightning strikes captivated him. Confusion evident on her gamine, honey-toned face, he didn't move from his restful position on the chaise lounge across the room. He anticipated the questions that must have been streaking across her mind as she stared at him. At least she seemed to be more alert than she was earlier that night, when she seemed almost catatonic and gripped in despair.

When she was still in the car, he noted her foot was pressing the accelerator although the car was out of gas. The motor had stopped, but the battery still held the headlights on. Noting no hazard signals were flashing, he properly surmised his unexpected guest was unaware of her situation or surroundings. He guided her into the Inn where two of his female employees helped her out of her wet clothing and put her to bed. After sending his weary employees back to bed, he opted to stay in the same room to await her awakening and reassure her of her safety.

"You're all right, Mrs. Mason," he said calmly. "You're at the Oceans Inn Resort. Your car ran out of gas in front of the entrance and Mrs. Williams and Ms.—"

"Out of gas?" she asked quietly. "I was in a car, you say?" Her eyes narrowed, showing her confusion. She gingerly pressed her temples.

"Yes," he answered, not wanting to throw too much at her at once.

Loretta eyed the even, olive brown-skinned man as her eyes skittered in her head, searching for memory of what had happened to bring her to this place. Why was she here? Why was she in a car? The last thing she remembered was getting out of the car in the circular driveway in front of her home, looking up at the massive structure and then… What? What had she done then?

Her eyes went back to the suavely handsome man reclining on the chaise, whose facial features resembled the actor Morris Chestnut before he started sporting a shaved head. His upper body was covered with a white T-shirt of no great distinction, but the subtle, finely defined, muscular torso gave life to the garment as he moved slowly to put his feet on the floor.

"Where are you going?" she asked, instantly alarmed.

Justin turned to meet her questioning gaze. "If you're up to it, I thought you might like something to eat. The electricity is off and we're operating on a back-up generator, but I have some sandwiches. The gas is still turned on and I can make tea and soup for you."

The thunder clapped and Loretta tensed. She hated storms. She had since she was a little girl.

"You're frightened," Justin said calmly, watching Loretta clutch at the bed coverings with a near death grip. He moved to her luggage on the other side of the bedroom and picked up a robe that lay across it. Then he moved toward her and laid the robe on the bed. As he turned his back, he heard her climb from beneath the covers, gather the robe, and pushed her feet into her slippers. "Ready?" he, asked, not turning to look at her.

"Yes," she said just above a whisper.

Justin moved out of the bedroom suite and entered the hallway that led to the lobby of the Inn. Only the emergency lights were on, casting a dim, golden haze along the corridor. Another clap of thunder and he felt Loretta skitter up close to him, nervously clutching his elbow. They crossed the beautifully appointed, but empty lobby and headed into an equally fine dining room.

"Wait here and I'll bring—" Another clap of thunder sent Loretta visibly shaking into his arms. "It's okay," he soothingly whispered, holding her loosely against his body.

Loretta's fear eased somewhat with the soft timbre of this stranger's voice. Mellow and low, it comforted her even in the midst of the storm that raged outside the walls.

They moved into the antiquated, but homey, kitchen overstocked with huge pots and pans, many of which hung on hooks from a pot rack attached to the ceiling.

The kitchen was her favorite room in her home. Somehow, this one, although not nearly as upgraded as hers, made her feel warm and secure. The man sat her at a butcher-block table and lit a candle, further illuminating the gathering darkness. She clutched her flannel robe together with both hands, assuring no portion of her skin was exposed. Proper decorum dictated such behavior in the company of a stranger, but no woman of decent upbringing would find herself in this predicament. Certainly, no Hill woman would allow a man who was not her husband to see her dressed in nightclothes.

She sat in a chair, board-stiff, with feet and knees together, watching the stranger move around the darkened kitchen preparing the meal. He seemed comfortable there, somehow capable. She would have moved to prepare the meal herself as she had done over the nearly twenty years of her marriage, if these were ordinary circumstances or if this were her kitchen. Of course, these were not ordinary circumstances and she no longer had a home. What would her husband and...

Suddenly, it came to her. Husband. Randolph would not be her husband soon. He was filing for divorce out of state, he told her. Some place where a divorce took only a few weeks to become final. He was seeing someone else—another woman—a younger woman, and he was going to marry her as soon as the divorce became final.

The children were grown now, he had reasoned. There would be no question of child support. The children's college careers were fully funded. He was selling the house they called home and lived in for the last part of their married life, and would give her a small, one-time settlement, he had said. She was employed—gainfully—and his attorney said he would not have to pay her alimony. She could keep the vehicle—the Escalade SUV—he bought for her last birthday. It was paid for, and, of course, any of the furniture she wanted. She would have to be packed and ready to move her things to wherever she was going to live within a few weeks. In the interim, he was going on vacation with his new woman and he expected her to be gone before he returned.

His words hit her at the speed of an automatic weapon, wounding her deeply with how easily he erased her from his life. After a lifetime of knowing him and nearly twenty years of marriage, it all came down to a vehicle, used furniture, and a small settlement. *How sad*, she thought.

"Do you take lemon or cream with your tea?" a comforting voice interjected into her maelstrom of thoughts.

Loretta turned with a jerk, suddenly back in the kitchen of this Inn with a stranger offering tea—and sympathy for a stranded wayfarer.

"Lemon," she said, still clutching her robe. *I must look a hot mess*, she thought, as she raked her hand through her untamed hair. Graying strands clung to her wedding rings. She studied them for a moment and then brushed them away.

"Careful, this is very hot," Justin said, pouring the hot water into a teapot to let it steep.

Loretta involuntarily shivered and balled herself up even more tightly.

He noticed her movement. "Are you cold?"

"A little," she said, not looking up into his face.

"I'll get a blanket for you, if you don't mind me leaving you here for a few minutes."

"No, please, don't leave," she said in a rush. "I'll be fine. The tea will help."

"I'll just turn on one of the ovens. That should knock the chill off the room."

Justin put the tray of tuna sandwiches and cups of hot tomato soup down on the table between them before he started an oven. He retrieved the small luncheon plates, some potato chips, and pickles before he sat down across from her. He crossed himself, saying a silent prayer and ended it with another crossing of his body. Loretta noticed the familiar gesture.

"You're Catholic, aren't you?"

"At one time, perhaps. I'm probably more than half lapsed now," he said. "That's an interesting question to ask a complete stranger." He smiled, encouraging her subtly to participate in a conversation. "Why don't we start with my name, Mrs..."

"Loretta. My name is Loretta." There seems to be no need for formality. She no longer wanted to have people know her as the wife of... She dropped the thought. "And you are?"

"Why don't you call me Willis?" he said, for some reason not wanting to associate with his business personae. After all, he was better known here as Willis since the days he came to work there as a kitchen helper and waiter. He extended his hand across the table to her.

"Willis," she repeated, giving his hand a single brief shake.

"Your tea and soup are getting cold," he said, reaching for one of the sandwich halves he prepared earlier while she slept.

"This is a hotel?"

"Of sorts. It's an Inn at a golf course resort."

"We seem to be the only people around. Where are the other guests?"

"The season's pretty much over so the Inn is closed for renovations. We don't get the large crowds at the seashore after Labor Day, especially not during the hurricane season. People tend to go further south to the Florida Keys or the islands."

"Oh, I see. Are you the only one who works here?"

"Uh, no, but they'll be back. Mrs. Williams and Ms. Nettie Baker are asleep upstairs. They plan to head out on vacation early in the morning. Since the Inn is closed, most of the employees are going away for a while to visit family and friends. There are only about a dozen workers on the property right now."

"And you, of course."

"Uh, yes," he answered. Obviously, his appearance led her to believe he was an employee, not the owner of this establishment or any other, he guessed. The anonymity felt strangely invigorating. "The owner may be preparing to sell or demolish the Inn."

"Oh, no! Sell it? Why would the owner want to do anything to such a beautiful resort as this?"

"Well, I guess because it's not very modern or up-to-date."

"From the little that I could see in the suite, the lobby, and dining room, it's utterly charming. You can't find places like this anymore. It's got style and class. Granted, it does need a little sprucing up, maybe a new coat of paint, strip down and re-stain the woodwork, and the hardwood floors, but it would be a mistake to change it very much. With a little entertainment, it could be a world-class resort."

Justin grinned. "You really think so?"

"Definitely. There is so much a place like this has to offer in every season. My room is very large with a nice fireplace and four-poster bed, nice sitting room, and the bathroom is—" Loretta stopped talking when she noticed Justin grinning at her. "I guess I do go on, don't I?" She slightly smiled while shaking her head. "I'm not telling you something you don't already know. After all, you do work here."

"That's okay. It's nice to know someone else sees this Inn the way I do. It's also interesting you noticed so much in such a short period of time."

Loretta looked away. He was making fun of her. Teasing her, but her decorator's eye noticed so much as they worked their way to the kitchen. She knew class when she saw it. After all, she was a Hill, the upper crust of society and the Head Mistress of the Columbia Academy, an exclusive boarding and day school. She personally decorated the common areas of the main house and the dormitories and received critical acclaim for her efforts. Her twin degrees in interior design and interior decorating, with a minor in education, helped her career and helped create a beautiful setting for a loving home.

Over the years, she obtained a master's in education and some credits toward a doctorate. She could teach almost anywhere when Randolph was playing professional football. Not that she really needed to work, but teaching gave her such joy in those early days of their marriage. Raising children, taking care of her home and her family, trying to love a man whose career always seemed to come before her and the children was the lot of a Hill woman; an old-fashioned, southern woman.

Still the dutiful daughter, she did as her mother instructed. She held on to her family toward a day when she and Randolph would settle into middle age together and look forward to their grandchildren. She would spoil them, love them, and help raise them. The happy thought falling away, replaced by the stark reality that, after all the years, all the sacrifices, all the love she offered in their beautifully decorated showcase home and award-winning garden, she would be cast aside and alone.

Although he talked, Justin could sense his companion was not listening. He saw the play of emotions crossing her face, deposited in her eyes that seemed near tears. A hollowness in her cheeks, a drawn, shallowness in her eyes, and his heart galvanized, but he kept talking, hoping she would come back from the despair he saw in her demeanor.

". . . but some people still like Inns that aren't too showy, too pretentious," Justin was saying, as they continued their conversation.

"I hope you'll tell the owners you're not the only one who thinks this place is a hidden treasure. From what I could see in the wide hallway, large tastefully decorated lobby/lounge and spacious dining room, this place has a lot of charm to offer."

She was back! Justin smiled. "I'll be sure to mention it."

As the storm raged outside, Willis and Loretta sat over the dim, flickering candlelight quietly talking. Neither invaded the other's privacy nor asked questions that would elicit personal information. Later, as the candlelight died a natural death, Justin escorted Loretta back to her room, using a hurricane lamp to help light their way. Once settled in the oversized bed again, Loretta laid her head against the cool, soft, fragrant sheets. Justin agreed to stay in the room and sleep on the chaise until morning. With a polite "thank you" and "good night," Loretta closed her eyes.

During the night, sobs coming from the direction of the bed awakened Justin. In the darkness, he padded barefoot across the room and watched Loretta's fitful rest for a moment. *So much pain, anguish, and sadness*, he thought, as he noticed a tear streaming down her soft, supple-looking cheek. He was not sure what to do to ease her malaise. Finally, he sat propped up against the headboard and held her in his arms until she rested more quietly. She never woke, but nestled herself closer to him. He closed his eyes and slept.

Chapter Four

Morning came and Loretta rose to wakefulness to the sound of squawking sea gulls and much calmer surf lapping against the shore. Strange, unfamiliar warmth surrounded and comforted her as she attempted to break the bonds of sleep. A thumping rhythm vibrated against her cheek. A soft and quiet breathing reached her unshielded ear, while an intoxicating myrrh tantalized her nose.

Suddenly, her eyes shuttered open and all of her senses went on alert. Her eyes caught the sight of the white T-shirt and dark blue jeans. Then the toes that peeked out from beneath the edge of the jeans. Finally, it registered. Willis was in the bed with her! His arm wrapped around her and she lay against his muscular chest. Yet, she was under the covers, while he lay on top of them. Her flannel nightgown was still in place, covering her from her throat down to her toes. Moving only her eyes, she looked the length of him, confusion gripping her for what may have happened during the night. She recalled the horror of the dreams that riveted her, but not in great detail, and then the calming influence that stilled her fretfulness throughout the night.

With great care, if not stealth, Loretta extricated herself from Willis' embrace. Standing on the floor, looking down at him through the dimness of early morning, she noticed the sparkle of gray in his otherwise thick, black, wavy hair. *Oddly handsome,* she thought. His relaxed features separately not of any particular significance, but together, with the dark eyebrows, thick lashes, and overnight growth on the hard lines of his stubble jaw, an interesting array of features.

Loretta silently moved toward the bathroom and attended to her needs. Reentering the bedroom, she went toward the sound of the surf outside the shuttered French doors. As she opened them and the hurricane shutters, the brilliant sunshine broke through, causing her to arc her hand to shade her eyes. The sun played peek-a-boo with the dancing clouds over the vast, untamed ocean that stretched out before her as far as the eye could see. The sight was humbling and simultaneously invigorating. She deeply inhaled the salt sea air and watched as the ocean's awesome power rose and fell. The brisk sea breezes brushed and lifted her hair away from her face. The crystal sand stung her cheeks and she clutched her hand to the neck of her robe as the wind whipped around her.

Closing her eyes, she lifted her face to bathe in the warm sunlight. It was breathtaking, she thought, as she padded barefooted beyond the stone veranda, the demarcation between the Inn and the warm, damp, sandy beach.

She looked out over the ocean. *What now?* Why had her life turned upside down in the matter of a few moments? Twenty years of marriage had slipped away. She knew nothing else. She married Randolph two days after she graduated from college and lived with him as his wife, raising their family. After his professional football career ended, she helped him build his insurance business. Was it ten, no twelve years ago? Yes, it was twelve years because he played for three different teams over the eight-year span of his NFL career. When they moved back home to Columbia, South Carolina, after he retired from professional sports, she worked as a teacher during the day and as his assistant after school to help him with the details of starting his business. She decorated his office and their home. Because he was so frugal and didn't want to hire an assistant, she typed mountains of contracts, arranged for repairs and maintenance for both their home and his business office. She hired staff and worked out schedules while continuing to grade papers, give homework assignments, cook meals, do laundry, buy groceries, shop for school clothes, chauffeur children to sports events, school plays, dental and doctor appointments, attend meetings...the list was endless. Now he was very successful and a pillar of their community. Their life together was fraught with infidelity problems, but they made an unspoken peace with their circumstances. They lived separate lives in private, but in public, they were the model couple, so her friends told her. She kept up the façade, for the sake of the children, and buried her own needs and desires to assure the stable growth and development of an emotionally healthy family. Now the children were grown and would soon leave the beautifully furnished, decorated, and landscaped nest—but so would Randolph.

Justin stood in the doorway and watched Loretta standing at the edge of the ocean. She stood almost statue still, while the sea breeze whipped her robe and nightgown up around her impressive, shapely legs. Her long, thick, reddish-brown mane flew in all directions, but she did not move to still her crowning glory. *Something is strangely familiar about her,* he thought. Then, he brushed the thought away. Nonetheless, he wondered who Loretta Mason was and how she came to be in such deep despair. She seemed such a lost, lonely soul adrift on a sea of emotions while fragile and in need of comfort—even protection from whatever set her adrift. Yet, even in her needfulness, a glimmer of strength seemed to burn deep within. An inner light shone and her hidden beauty glowed as they sat and talked by candlelight the night before. Her honey-bronze skin and youthful features belied the strands of gray in her hair. Worn, he thought. Worn and harried. Years of despair. Much like his Inn, she was in need of rejuvenation. Not a major overhaul, but careful and skillful attention to details were in order.

"It's chilly out here," Justin said, wrapping a warm blanket around Loretta's shoulders.

She slightly jolted at his voice. "Is it? I didn't really notice. It's so beautiful." She breathed deeply. "So peaceful and calming to the spirit."

"It's one of my favorite places," he said, perusing the vast untamed ocean that spread out in front of them still in the grip of the hurricane that skirted the coastline, but was now farther north and out to sea. "It seems to have a life of its own, always changing and going somewhere."

"There is comfort and safety in staying unchanged," she said wistfully, cryptically.

"Is that where you were going when you got caught in the storm? Somewhere safe and comfortable?"

A single tear rolled down Loretta's cheek. Justin wished with all his might he had not asked the question; not caused her the distress he now saw on her angelic face. He wanted to envelop her in his arms and assure her no matter what was troubling her, all would be well; she would be safe and protected in his care; and her life would take on new meaning.

"Is there someone you want to call?"

Loretta turned only her head toward him. Her brownish-green, doe-like eyes sad.

"No, no one," she said barely above a whisper.

Later that morning, Loretta placed a tablecloth on the small butcher-block table in the kitchen, smoothing the folds to the edges. She moved to set the emblem-crested, bone-china plates, silverware, and crystal stemware in their proper place. It seemed so natural and familiar to be dressing the table for breakfast. Like the loving tasks she performed every day for twenty years before the house emptied and everyone left on their daily-appointed rounds. The sugar bowl and creamer, then salt and pepper in place, she moved on to the stove to stir the heaping pot of hominy grits. A tune came to mind and she hummed it from the inner recesses of her soul to her throat as she worked. It gave her joy to be doing something so necessary and familiar. Cooking for her family was never a chore. Rather, each meal was a confirmation of her level of deep caring. Besides, she loved this quaint kitchen with its old, oak cabinets slightly askew on their hinges, the worn tile floor that had seen better days and the huge utensils hand-made by old artisans.

She looked over her shoulder at the table. It needed something. Candles and flowers, she thought. Quickly, she grabbed a pair of shears and went through the kitchen door to a garden, cut a bunch of fresh, brightly colored, fall flowers and prepared them in an artistic arrangement. She set them on the table between two candles that were already there, then stepped back, cocking her head to one side and then the other to assure the table now looked properly balanced and inviting. She skillfully folded two napkins until they resembled birds ready to take flight.

With the tune she hummed still wafting in the kitchen air, she moved to complete the breakfast preparations. Salmon cakes and eggs scrambled with onion and green and red pepper. Buttermilk biscuits made from scratch with jam were her family's favorites and, as she sniffed the air, she knew they were almost ready. Her fingers were quick and efficient as she cut up fresh fruit for compote.

In an instant, he knew why she seemed familiar. He had seen her years ago on stage during the Miss Palmetto beauty and talent pageant. Justin stood motionless in the doorway, listening to the dulcet tones reaching his ears. The enticing aromas emanating from the kitchen teased his hunger, but nothing was as strong in his mind and body as the vision of Loretta moving gracefully about the room. Her figure was that of a woman, not the anorexic girls with whom he had liaisons in loveless sex. Rather, where they seemed aerobicized into hard angular muscle, Loretta seemed soft, warm, and pliable. It stirred something inside him with escalating speed. Watching the gabardine slacks mold to her rounded hips when she bent to check whatever was in the oven spoke to something primal in him. He wished her black, knit, sweater top didn't define her full breasts with such precision. Her carriage was innocently erotic, he noted, as her flat, black shoes soundlessly moved around the kitchen. He wanted to unleash her thick mane now tamed into a matronly ball at the back of her head and run his fingers through it…

Stop right there! he cautioned himself. Loretta was a married woman, evidenced by the diamond ring and wedding band on her finger. Lusting after another man's wife was never Justin's forte. Women of easy virtue were his staple, though he longed for someone to shower with the unrequited love that resided within him. He snapped his thoughts back to the present and the hauntingly beautiful tune Loretta hummed so skillfully.

"The telephone lines are still down and my cell phone is not working," he said, moving into Loretta's line of sight as though he had just returned to the kitchen. "Mmmm, something smells great! What's for breakfast? I'm starving," he said with a smile.

Loretta smiled at the arrival of her breakfast partner as she continued to work.

"Not so fast, Willis. Did you wash your hands?" she asked, with a tilt of her head and a teasing smile edging her mouth.

"Uh, I'll take care of that right now." he smiled contritely, moving toward the kitchen sink.

"Not in my sink, you won't. I'm sure you can find somewhere else to wash that car grime off your hands."

"Uh, yes, Ma'am," he playfully intoned.

A few minutes later, Justin returned and displayed his hands for Loretta's inspection. She took them and flipped them over, inspecting for the slightest speck of grease or grime. What she found was electricity that shocked her as she held his hands in hers. Strong, soft, and warm hands they were, she noted. Nails clean and, apparently, well-manicured. Strange for a worker who had been rooting around in a gardener's shed looking for a can of gasoline to restore her car to life.

Then she made the error of her life. She looked up into his obsidian eyes and read something that chilled—and thrilled—her. Something she had not seen glow in Randolph's eyes when he occasionally visited her in her bedroom. She never denied Randolph access to her body, but then she couldn't. She was his wife and he was entitled to take his pleasure at his discretion. Though she never enjoyed his lovemaking, she dutifully submitted. That was her responsibility to service her husband's needs. Willis, on the other hand, stirred something she never felt before. She released his hands and turned back to the stove to attend to their meal.

Justin stood rooted to the spot so close to Loretta her body brushed his when she turned away. It took all the strength within him not to turn her into his arms and take full possession of her intoxicating-looking mouth. While she held his hands in hers, he thought his heart would beat through his chest. Hot blood coursing through his body sent a signal to his now responsive phallus, blotting out the signals of reason and restraint that went to his head. For a very uncomfortable moment, Justin couldn't or wouldn't move.

"Have a seat, Willis. Breakfast is ready," Loretta said.

Justin snapped out of his fixation. "Is there something I can do to help?"

"Uh, no, it's all done."

"May I say, Loretta, very beautifully done." He perused the charmingly dressed table. Many days in his youth, he sat at that same table while working his way through college and grad school on a combination kitchen helper's and waiter's salary, surviving on tips and bonuses during summer breaks and other holidays. Long, arduous hours he worked doing any task that would give him enough money to continue his education. Never before had that table looked so beautiful, he thought. In fact, he sat at tables in the finest restaurants all over the world, even some he owned, and never felt loving hands dressed them with such care just for him. Even in his own home, when he was still married to Carla, the housekeeper, cook, or maid took care of that chore.

Willis' nearness made Loretta's heart pound erratically. He had a quiet power that made her want to do things she had never dreamed of doing before. He radiated a manliness that sent unchecked chills up her spine and raised goose bumps on her arms. As she watched him go through the familiar prayer before eating, she knew she would need to go to confession for her thoughts. Catholic school all of her life taught her about the cardinal sins and she wanted to break all of the rules. *Silly*, she thought. She didn't even know this man, yet he exuded such an impact on her that she had to rein in her emotions. They ate in near silence.

Justin sat back in his seat sated after the scrumptious meal. His eyes smiled his delight.

"Thank you, Loretta. You've made my day."

Loretta beamed under her honey-toned skin. No one said how much they appreciated the extra care she gave to preparing meals. Randolph rarely made it home for dinner anymore and the children were often too busy with their friends or other activities to have dinner at home. *Home,* she thought. *She didn't have a home anymore. What was she going to do?*

Justin saw the shadow of remorse edging its way back across Loretta's face. He wanted to reach out, touch her, and wipe away the despair from her heart. She was trying so hard to be brave, but for what? Who had wounded her so deeply?

"I, uh, I heard you humming earlier. You have a very nice voice. Are you a singer?"

Loretta snapped out of her malaise at the sound of Willis' voice. "A singer? Uh, no, not really." She laughed self-deprecatingly. "I sing in the choir, but nothing professional."

"You should. You've got talent. Where is the church?"

"Church? Oh, you mean where I sing?" Loretta chuckled. "Columbia, South Carolina."

"You're a long way from home. Where were you headed?"

"I don't know, I mean, no place in particular. I just started driving." She shrugged.

"Well, now that the storm has passed, I'm sure your family will be wondering about you and your safety. I think I'll continue to scout around for some gasoline for your car. Maybe the telephone lines will be back in operation soon and you can continue your trip."

Chapter Five

While Loretta repacked her bag and then wandered aimlessly through the lobby of the Inn, waiting for him to return, Justin found a secluded spot and pulled his cell phone from his briefcase.

"McCoy Enterprises. How may I direct your call please?" Erin greeted cheerfully.

"Erin, this is Justin McCoy. Put me through to Michael Rodgers."

"Yes, sir, Mr. McCoy," she said and made the connection.

"JW, where are you? You've had everyone worried. What happened?"

"I'm still in South Carolina at the shore. You must have heard a hurricane passed through here last night. Fortunately, we only received a glancing blow, not a full-blown event, but that's not why I called. I want you to get a dossier together on a Loretta—"

Michael chuckled. "I knew it had to be about a woman."

"Uh, not this time." Justin laughed. "However, I do want the background check done."

"Will do. When will you be arriving? You've got several hot items on the agenda this week."

"Handle them for me, Michael. You know my routine. Anything you don't feel comfortable with put it on hold until next week."

"Next week? This must really be some woman." Michael chuckled again. "You usually don't let anyone make your decisions for you."

"Stop speculating and get the information for me."

"All right, JW, am I looking for something specific?"

"Check South Carolina for a missing person's report on a Loretta Mason."

"Missing person? JW, what's—"

"Thanks, Michael," Justin said, cutting him off. He wasn't ready to deal with the surgical questions he knew Michael would ask. "Oh, and don't call me. I will call the office later today. Also, send some clothes to me, preferably casual—and arrange for delivery of some gasoline—"

"Wait a minute, JW. This is beginning to sound—"

"I'm not going into any details, Michael. Just do it," he said, as he continued with other detailed requests and instructions.

Loretta was sitting at the front desk in the lobby when a young couple came in. She looked up and noticed the smiles on their glowing faces. Newlyweds, she guessed. It had been a long time since she was a new bride and the glow lasted only a few weeks for her. *It's over*, she thought, as she noticed the couple looking around for assistance.

"Excuse me, miss," the young man said. "We'd like a room."

Loretta stood behind the desk. "A room? Uh, well I don't know…" She looked around for Willis, but he was nowhere in sight. He must be in the office, she surmised.

"We can pay, ma'am. I mean, we don't have a lot of money. We just got married, but we'd like to spend at least one night here. The storm, you see. A lot of hotels and motels were full up or closed. So, we just kept driving. We're tired and we have a long way to go to get to Florida. I'm in the military, stationed…I mean, I don't expect anything just because…but anyway, Lottie and I saw this place from the road and she thought…well, we both think it's beautiful."

"Yes, it's such a beautiful Inn," the young bride said, her pretty, blue eyes shining.

"It is, isn't it?" Loretta asked absently, marveling at the old, lush decor, the smell of aged mahogany walls and furniture. "But, I'm not sure you can be accommodated here. You see, the Inn is—"

"Undergoing some renovations," Willis interrupted, suddenly beside Loretta, "but if you don't mind that, I'm sure we can make room for you." The young couple beamed and Willis found their delight enchanting. He grabbed a key with a big, round emblem disk from a cubby and handed it to the young man. "The bridal suite is upstairs, center. Nice balcony and view of the ocean," he said, smiling. The young couple's excitement warmed Willis.

When the newlyweds disappeared up the staircase, Loretta turned to Willis. "I thought you said the Inn was closed. How are you going to be able to provide service with no employees? Also, why didn't you make them register or give some type of payment?"

Willis shrugged. "I don't know. Seemed like the right thing to do at the time."

Loretta smiled and shook her head. "They did seem pretty happy, didn't they? Nice to be at the beginning of something. Just starting a new life together," she said almost wistfully.

Willis noticed the melancholia returning. He moved quickly to change the subject. "Well, how about giving me a hand? You know, spending a few days here helping them with the start of their lives together. My cooks are away for a week or two on vacation with their families. I could pay you for cooking meals, not that I think the young couple has food on their minds, but if breakfast was any indication, it would at least give them a start."

Taken aback, Loretta pondered the thought. Actually, she had no place to go. Nothing to do. School would not be starting for another couple weeks. Certainly, Randolph wouldn't miss her since he was away with his new woman, and the children, well, they had their own lives away at school. Why the heck not take a few days to get her bearings, figure out what she was going to do with the rest of her life?

"Well, someone has to keep you from losing your job."

Willis smiled curiously. "Losing my job?"

"Yes, when the owners of this beautiful old Inn find out you're giving away rooms without payment, you could get fired."

"Oh, uh, yes, you're right. Thanks, Loretta, I'll have to remember that."

Willis and Loretta spruced up the dining room in the Inn, dusting and vacuuming, before Loretta made lunch. When the young, newlywed couple didn't come out of their room, Loretta and Willis tapped on the door and left their lunch outside the bridal suite then ate together, having an easy conversation. Later in the afternoon, Loretta took a long walk on the beach, while Willis and some of his employees began to clear away the debris left by the storm. When Loretta returned from her walk, she wandered into the dining room and noticed the covered baby grand piano. She pushed the cover back and lifted the lid over the keys. With skillful fingers, she ran the scales, noting the instrument was perfectly tuned. As she sat down on the bench and ran her fingers over the ivory keys, a tune came to mind, then another, and another. So engrossed in the music, she didn't notice for quite a while she had an audience.

Willis sat in awe as he watched Loretta play the piano and hum to the music she created. He noticed a wide range of emotions play across her face, sadness being the most prevalent. He didn't understand why such a beautiful and talented woman should be sad. Even more appalling was the fact no one was looking for her. Michael confirmed no one filed a missing person's report. Loretta had no credit in her own name and the car she drove was paid for in cash. She was someone's wife. He was sure of that. She had the grace and charm of a hostess of great skill and ability. Creative, too. The table she dressed for lunch was even more beautiful than the one she dressed for breakfast. Lunch was spectacular and the dinner cooking in the kitchen smelled sumptuous.

The applause emanating from behind him, as Loretta finished playing another piece, startled him, and drew him out of his thoughts. He joined the young couple and some of his employees in adoration of Loretta's skill, applauding even more loudly.

Loretta smiled when she heard the applause. "Thank you. I'm a little rusty."

"That was wonderful," the young bride enthused. "Are you a famous performer?"

"No." Loretta smiled, with embarrassment. "I just like the music. It's a kind of hobby of mine. Now, how about some dinner?"

"Would you play for us again?" the young groom asked.

"Sure she will," Willis interjected. "And I'll be your waiter for the evening."

Later that night, when telephone service was restored, Loretta called her sister in Washington, DC.

"Kayla, it's Retta."

"Mouse, where are you? I hear water, like the ocean or something."

"I'm at the shore. I'm standing outside on a patio."

"Sounds pretty romantic. Don't tell me Randolph finally took you on a well-deserved vacation. It's about time that old ass—"

"Kayla, Randolph isn't with me. He's—" She choked.

"Retta," Kayla said with concern. "What is it? Don't cover up for that bastard! What has he done now?!"

Loretta took a deep breath before answering, tears welling in her eyes. "He's divorcing me."

There was a momentary silence.

"*Hallelujah!*" Kayla exclaimed excitedly. "There is a God! This is the best news I've had since Neiman Marcus had a sale on shoes!"

"Kayla, I know you never liked Randolph, but he is my husband."

" 'Liked him?' Little sister, I hate the bastard! Now I could kiss him! It's no secret, Mouse, I resent the way he treats you by having affairs and how he talked to you, like you were some child or piece of furniture. Always going on and on about *his* glory days in the NFL, *his* perfect children and *his* big successes in business—as if you didn't play a major role in helping him get to where he is today! Geeze-o-flip, Retta, the man was a dog from the get go! The damn cock hound with an ego the size of Alaska! I'll be glad for you to see the back of him!"

"Kayla, you don't understand," she pleaded. "My marriage is crumbling and I can't do anything to hold it together. My life is—" She broke down sobbing.

"Your life is just beginning, little sister!" Kayla said irreverently. "Look, I know I'm being insensitive, but you deserve better than Mr. Randolph Asshole Mason!"

"We're Catholic, remember? I vowed to love, honor, and obey, for better or worse. What am I going to do with the rest of my life, Kayla? How will I explain this to our parents, our children or be able to hold up my head in public?" Loretta asked between sobs. "I feel like such a failure."

"*That's bull!* They ought to call you Saint Loretta or the Mason Madonna right up there with Saint Mary! As for what to do with the rest of your life—hell, live it! It's time to go for the gusto!"

"Easy for you to say. You've never wanted to be married nor have children. I've committed my life—"

"Yes, you have, and got damn little in return. That's the reason I never married. You give and give and give and what do you get? Axed! That's what!"

"I didn't get married to get something in return. I did it because that's what was expected of me. I wanted what our parents had, a good stable home with someone who loved me."

"Humph, you ought to ask Mama what she goes through with our father sometime. To say Papa is a rolling stone is putting it diplomatically. Papa is a boulder rolling down Mama Mount Saint Helen! You've always worn rose-colored glasses, little sister. None of the rest of our brood did." She softened her tone, as she heard her youngest sister sniffling. "Look, hon, I won't be a hypocrite and say I'm sorry you and Randolph have split up, but I do care that you're hurting over this. I want to be there for you. Why don't you come to DC for a while?"

"No." She sniffled. "I saw you on television with the Canadian Prime Minister. You've probably got more foreign dignitaries to chaperone or something and I really need to be by myself to get a grip on what I'm going to do."

"Well, I could come to you for a few days, if you'd like. The State Department does have me scheduled for some diplomatic missions, but I can alter my itinerary. Maybe I can arrange it so one of my staff people will take my place."

"I'll call you if I need you to come or I'll come to Washington. Don't change your schedule for me."

"All right, hon, but be sure you call no matter what time of day or night, you hear me?"

"Yes, I hear you," Loretta said quietly.

"I love you, hon, and it's going to be all right. I promise."

They hung up and Loretta wrapped her arms around herself, fighting back the pain. It wasn't all right. It would never be all right. Not ever. She went back inside and crawled into the comforting bed.

When had it ever been all right? Certainly not when she was a child. Her mother, Helen Kingman Hill, said she was the ugly duckling of her five sisters, and she would have to work harder to get a man. Daniel Hill, her father, said she was just a late bloomer and her gangly legs and pencil-straight body would fill out some day. Well, Daddy was right. She did fill out and won the Ms. Palmetto State Contest. Mama said it was not because of her looks, but because of her voice that she won. Nevertheless, it was a hollow victory. Her voice never took her anywhere. She kept her body toned with a personal trainer four out of seven days a week. Mama said exercising was necessary to keep her husband taking care of her. Mama had a great influence on her and prodded her to marry Randolph Mason, a local boy in their social circle who made it big in the sports industry. The Hills and Masons were the cream of Columbia County society and lifelong friends.

Singing in church was her only solace, fed on a steady diet of the woes of sin and forbidden lust. Women, Mama said, weren't supposed to enjoy sex. They were just supposed to submit to it in order to have babies and lots of them to tie the man to the home. "Cook a good meal, set a good table, and feed the male beast" was what she heard all of her life and she was compliant. Not her sisters though. They escaped Mama's mantra because they were beautiful and polished. Their husbands worshipped them and, as a result, life treated them more kindly than her. She kept to the old ways and tolerated whatever burden Randolph handed to her to carry. Now he was leaving her, with nearly nothing, for another, younger woman. Mama would blame her for that, too. She knew she would, and maybe it was her fault after all.

Loretta buried her face in her pillow and wept.

Chapter Six

"Well, that's it, JW," Michael said after briefing Justin in detail on the day's events. "Delaware tried to find out where you were or how to get in touch with you. He was sweating bullets. Made the trip to DC to try to see you to convince you to rethink your decision. When he was satisfied you couldn't be reached and it would make no difference if he could talk with you, he signed the preliminary contracts before close of business today."

"Saved us one hundred million on the deal. Somehow, I thought he'd hold out longer."

"Somehow, I thought he would, too, but I should have known he couldn't stand it. According to Richardson Investigations' report, he needs the capital you're offering him. However, I'd look out for him down the road. The investigator confirmed your suspicion Delaware is a very dangerous character. He may try something later."

"That's his MO all right. I'm not sure he needs the capital as much as he's desperate to find a way to launder money."

"You thinking what I'm thinking?"

"Hostile takeover. Yes, perhaps. He'll try something because he thinks McCoy Enterprises is cash poor now and couldn't mount a defense or instigate a poison pill."

"JW, he's right. You're spread awfully thin with the hotels you've acquired, the record company, and entertainment division, the food service division for the hotel and transportation industries, the travel agency, the research and development division, and holding on to the textile division. You really don't have to make the fabrics and furnishings for the hotel properties, you know? Old man Hamilton has seen his better days and—"

"End of conversation, Michael. As long as John Harvey wants to run the textile division, he can. I don't care how much it costs. I won't shut it down or sell it."

"What about his daughter? The ever-present Carla Hamilton?"

"I don't have to justify my actions to you, Michael. Suffice it to say Carla is Jessica's mother. She'll never go wanting if I have a dime in my pocket."

"Carla knows it, too, JW. You've been more than generous with her. She'll keep up this emotional blackmail just because she knows she can."

Justin was becoming tired of the same argument. He and Michael had been friends for a very long time. In fact, since grad school. Otherwise, he would not have tolerated the intrusion into his private affairs. He decided to change the subject to avoid an argument.

"How were dinner and the show?" he asked.

"Humph! I don't know how you do it, man!"

"Do what?" Justin laughed.

"Keep all these women at arm's length, that's what. Needless-to-say, Ms. Daphne Anderson was pissed off when I showed up instead of you. She swore you were with another woman. I tried to explain to her you were called away suddenly on business and her remark was, and I quote, 'Funny business'. Apparently, Carla cornered her some time yesterday at a spa and told her to back off of you. Also told Ms. Anderson you gave her a hundred K as walk around money."

Justin laughed. "Did she now? Well, Carla got the amount right, but I suspect she wanted the money to pay her gambling debts. It's actually an advance on her allowance for next month. I just gave it to her early."

"Carla is going to put you in the poor house and Ms. Anderson is going to put you in the dog house if you don't get back here soon. What about this Loretta?"

"Don't start, Michael. It's not what you think."

"You must be looking for a challenge or something."

"No, I just want to help a person out of a bad place," he said, focusing on the woman sleeping down the hall from his room. The music she played so beautifully and skillfully during dinner lifted everyone's spirits. The food, starting with tomato bisque and field greens salad, then the main course: Cornish hens, wild rice, and steamed broccoli followed by a crème boule, white wine, coffee, and an after-dinner aperitif were top notch and the atmosphere charming. He, the young couple, and some of his employees sat for hours just listening and relaxing. He was enjoying the slower pace his life had never been before he took this unscheduled hiatus.

Loretta was intoxicating, but still deep within herself. The music seemed to lift her spirits as it had everyone who heard her play. Even the other few remaining employees who came to work after the storm were enchanted. No one wanted her to stop playing, but the hour had gotten late.

"Justin, are you still there?"

"Uh, yes. Sorry. I've got a few things on my mind."

"All of them about this Loretta, no doubt," Michael said just above a whisper.

"I heard that, Michael," he cautioned. "I told you, it's—"

"Not what I think. I know."

"Have a good night, Michael."

He chuckled. "Yeah, you too, buddy."

Justin hung up the phone and through off the burden Justin McCoy was required to carry and slipped easily back into the Willis personae. He sat thinking for few moments. Then he heard soft sobs. It couldn't be coming from the bridal suite, he knew. That young couple made a lot of noise when they made love. This sound had to be coming from Loretta's room. He heard her crying before. It was such a painfully pitiful sound. Almost inhuman. He wanted to go to her, but he paced the floor helplessly, waiting for her to trust him enough to confide in him. He couldn't and wouldn't intrude on her privacy. He had already done more of that than he should have by having background information developed on her. He did not read the report though. He simply assured himself she was not the subject of an all-points bulletin or missing person's search. The rest he would wait for her to tell him in her own time and in her own way. Until then, he would make her as comfortable as he could and keep her as active and busy as possible. Maybe then she would develop some sense of how truly special she was and what great talents she possessed.

As Loretta's sobs subsided, Justin padded barefooted across his bedroom floor and opened a door that led to the beach. He leaned against the doorjamb, as the ocean's breeze blew across his bare chest. Arms folded and legs crossed at the ankle, he looked out into the darkened waters. It was quiet and peaceful. Much as he had remembered in his youth.

Ah, youth, he thought. In those days, he was full of vim, vigor, and vitality. His passions ruled him during the summer nights after work was finished for the day. Young women of all types and descriptions flocked to the seashore in droves. He seduced more than his share from the beach bunnies who pranced across the golden sands of the Grand Strand or hung out in the clubs at night. *Those were the days*, he thought, but as intriguing as they were, he didn't want to go back to that time. Then he had nothing to offer any woman in terms of a future. Now he had everything to offer and no woman with whom to share it. Then, he spent his life between bedrooms. Now, he spent his life between boardrooms. Both held certain excitements, but neither filled his life. He had one failed marriage and a wonderful daughter to show for his time on earth.

What a dichotomy, he thought. Out of something as burdensome as his marriage to Carla had come someone as beautiful as his Jessica. She had her mother's good looks, but, fortunately, not her mother's disposition. Jessica had the soul of an angel.

Thinking of his daughter reminded him he hadn't spoken with her in a while. Not since she said she was going to Nice in France for a few weeks with school friends before heading back to the campus in Switzerland. He wondered whether she enjoyed the French Riviera and then thought, *Is she parading across the beach in front of some lecherous young men?* Naw, he groused, and then thought, *Not my angel. Not my Jessica.* After all, she was only seventeen. He glimpsed his watch. It was too late to call her tonight, but he'd make a point to call her tomorrow. Maybe it was time he had a talk with her—about boys.

Two weeks passed so swiftly Loretta had not even noticed. She was so busy with supervising and preparing meals, arranging dinner parties, and performing on the piano she hadn't observed the time slip away. Willis was busy, too. He permitted more people to come to the Inn, but this time he was charging them—at least the off-season rate—and supervising the Inn's renovations. The small staff of employees grew in number and was busy, but not too busy to invite their friends and family members to the evening cocktail hours and dinner buffet.

It was Friday night and, if the number of people waiting for a table were any indication, it would be a packed house.

Loretta stood at the podium assigning tables to the guests. Two elderly women came in together, chatting excitedly, and approached the podium. One of the women looked vaguely familiar.

"Well, hello, dear." One woman smiled up at Loretta.

"Hello," she said while trying to place the woman's face among those she had known. "Welcome to Oceans Inn Club...I apologize for being presumptuous, but your face is familiar. Have we met before?"

"We have, yes, years ago. My name is Hanna Ivy Benson. I'm Sylvia Benson Alexander's grand aunt."

"Of course, now I remember. That would make you Aretha Alexander's great grand aunt," Loretta said, pleased to have made the connection to people she knew and respected.

"That's correct. Your son, Daryl, was dating my great grandniece, Aretha. You were the chorale director for the youth who were in the inaugural presidential parade. You were wonderful."

"Thank you, Ms. Benson."

"You are welcome. This is my friend, Alma Lewis. She moved here from Washington, DC, last year."

"Hello, Mrs. Lewis," Loretta said, smiling at the other stately elderly woman, and noting the wedding band on her finger. "I'm Loretta. Welcome to South Carolina."

"Thank you, Loretta. I must say I'm enjoying being here at the shore. I really like driving a golf cart everywhere."

"You live here in Atlantic Beach?" asked Loretta with surprise.

"We do, yes, about a half mile south of the resort. The head chef here at the resort, Nettie Baker, is a distant relative. She invited us to come tonight. So we cranked up the golf cart and here we are," Ms. Benson said, with a big, warm smile.

"Since you're Ms. Nettie's guests, I'll have your hostess tell her you've arrived. You'll have VIP seating." Loretta turned to Bonnie Shay and instructed her where to seat them. "Enjoy your evening."

Loretta decided she would add a few of Ms. Benson's niece's top selling selections to her repertoire tonight. The famous singer and actress, known worldwide as The French Mariah, was Ms. Benson's grandniece. What a small world. Mariah Benson had long been one of her lifelong idols. Though she had known the Alexanders of Goodwill, Summer County, South Carolina, for many years, she had not made the connection between Sylvia Benson Alexander and Mariah Benson. They were sisters and although Sylvia possessed a good singing voice, her daughter, Aretha Grace Alexander's voice and musical talent were phenomenal. She would have to mention the connection to Daryl when next they spoke.

Yes, indeed, a really small world, she mused and then turned to the next person in line.

A tall, handsome, urbane-looking man sidled up to where she was standing and eyed her in a manner that was odd and somewhat disconcerting. She had not seen him before, she assured herself. He was so handsome she would have remembered if they had ever met and it was strange that someone like him was alone. Well-built and extremely polished, his designer suit spoke to a level of sophistication she saw when Randolph hosted receptions for his most important or potential clients. She wondered whether the man was lost, but he seemed to know exactly where he was and what he wanted to do at any time.

"Welcome to the Oceans Inn Club," she said and smiled. "How many in your party tonight, sir?"

"My party? Oh, uh, I'm looking for the owner. My name is Michael—"

"Uh, I'll handle this, Loretta," Willis said, suddenly at her side. "This way, sir."

Loretta was surprised at Willis' abrupt intrusion, but there were too many people standing in line waiting to be seated to pay further attention to him. She watched the two men walk away, but quickly turned to the next person in line.

"What the hell are you doing here, Michael?" Justin raged behind the closed office door.

"I should be asking you the same question, JW. You originally planned a one-day trip to assess this place. You've been gone for damn near two weeks and no one knows what's going on or why. Now be pissed with me if you want to, but I need some answers— and I intend to get them!"

"You're not entitled to any explanations! You just do what I tell you—" Justin closed his eyes and bit back the anger. "Michael, I apologize," he said sincerely. "You didn't deserve that."

Justin grabbed the back of his neck and slowly paced the floor. He knew Michael's eyes were on him, awaiting an answer for his uncharacteristic behavior, but Justin had no answers to give. That is, none that would probably make any sense to his Vice President of Major Operations. "I needed a break, Michael," was all he could offer.

Michael nodded in understanding. "Yes, I can believe that. You haven't had a real vacation in years, but here? Why here? You've got properties all over the world. You've also got the Research and Development Division scouting new locations where you might have joined the search to make this a working holiday. Moreover, if this is a vacation, why are you wound as tight as a spring in a new bed? The reports I'm getting from our Construction Division indicate you're pouring more money into this place than it deserves. I understand the Inn holds memories—" Something came to Michael as he observed Justin. "She doesn't know who you are, does she?"

Justin looked away. "She who?"

"Don't give me that bull. You know exactly whom I'm talking about. Ms. Palmetto State out there. Richardson ran the background check on her, remember? She's the one, isn't she? The one you told me about who sang that night at the beauty pageant. That's it, isn't it?"

Justin exhaled sharply. "How are things in the office?" he asked, changing the subject.

"You know as well as I do how things are. Marilyn Allen gives detailed reports to you and implements your directives as if you were there. So don't try to change the subject on me, old buddy. It won't fly."

"If I order you to go back to Washington?"

Michael took off his suit jacket, loosened his expensive, silk, Hermes tie, undid the top button of his monogramed shirt, and rolled up the sleeves on his billion-count, shirt before taking a seat in one of two high-back chairs. He drew a solid-gold, cigar case from his pocket, lit up, and leaned back in the comfortable chair crossing his right ankle over his left knee. "Remy Martin," he said, eyeing Justin, "neat."

Justin knew his long-time friend wasn't about to budge. He went to the wet bar and poured two drinks with no ice. He passed one to Michael, sat in the opposite matching chair, and leaned forward with his elbows on his knees.

"I don't have any answers, Michael, so don't ask, unless you want me to start lying. No, she doesn't know who I am. She hasn't even asked my last name. All she knows or wants to know is a person called Willis who befriended her on what must have been the worst night of her life. She doesn't talk about herself or anyone else. She's just Loretta. No past, no present, and no particular future. She needs time to get over whatever it was that happened to her.

"The last time I saw her before this was nearly twenty-three years ago on stage singing so effortlessly she made it seem easier than breathing. She didn't know me from Adam's house cat. We were never introduced, but she was so beautiful I couldn't get her image out of my mind. Now she seems to have lost the spirit, the sparkle that won the title for her. She gave so much of herself when she sang; I just want to help her get something in return." Justin swallowed the liquor in one gulp and grimaced at its sharpness.

Michael sat forward in the same manner as Justin, with his elbows resting on his knees reverently. "Damn, I'm glad I didn't see her twenty-odd years ago because she's stunning now." He grinned. "No wonder you're wound as tight as a spring, you need some bed action."

Justin cocked his head to the side and looked at his friend. Michael's grin grew into a broad smile. Justin just shook his head.

"I should have known you wouldn't understand."

"Oh, I understand, all right. The moment I laid eyes on that hidden beauty, I knew what time it was. I believe you want to help her because that's your MO. The Rejuvenator is at it again. Only this time it's not a hotel, it's a—"

Justin raised a hand, silencing his friend. Michael swallowed his drink and passed the empty glass to Justin.

"Three fingers this time, buddy, while I decide what I want from you to keep silent."

Justin got up and gave an ungentlemanly snort. "There isn't anything I've got you don't already have many times over. You've got more than Donald Trump."

"Don't go into that poor-boy-from-the-country bull, either. Yeah, my family has money, but I made it the hard way just like you did. Now, about your yacht…"

Loretta arranged to seat the last guest and surveyed the audience. Everyone seemed to be having a great time. Complete strangers were socializing and chatting up each other at shared tables. Singles were making hookups in clusters of mingling men or women. Laughter, fun, and frivolity emanated from throughout the densely packed room. Waiters and servers were busy delivering drinks to guests and assuring the buffet tables were replenished.

She turned and looked toward the office door, where Willis and the Michael person disappeared almost an hour earlier. She wondered what was going on inside that office. Michael whoever had asked for the owner. *Clearly, that isn't Willis*, she thought, *but perhaps it has something to do with the Inn.* It seemed an odd time of the night to be conducting business, but then Randolph was often late coming home, claiming some business meeting or other delayed him. She ignored the lipstick traces and smell of perfume on Randolph's clothes and, as Mama cautioned, she never complained. What if she had? Would it have changed his behavior? She doubted it. It hadn't stopped him in his years as a football star and she stopped asking for any explanation many years ago.

Funny, she thought. She had not thought of Randolph for nearly a week, but she would have to face the music sometime. School would be opening on Monday and she would have to return to Columbia. Her mental-health vacation was ending sooner than she wanted. Only a few more days and she would make the drive back to Columbia, South Carolina, and resume her position as Head Mistress of Columbia Academy.

While her life was spiraling out of control, the private boarding and day school and her children held her together for so many years. She had committee meetings for an inordinate number of charities and sorority events to host. There was more than enough to take up her spare time, but now she would be solo without an escort at upcoming events. Would Randolph continue to be out and about in their circle of friends with his new, younger woman on his arm? A fresh pain gripped her at the thought. She could not go out by herself, because she would be the center of pity. It just wasn't done. Her mother would be mortified. What would happen now?

"Miss Loretta?" Bonnie Shay, one of the servers broke her train of thought. "Would you play for us now?"

Loretta snapped back to the present. She smiled at Bonnie and nodded. It gave her great pleasure to play the piano. She moved through the densely packed tables and milling crowd toward the baby grand and stepped up on the stage. She heard the applause that began to mount as the piped-in, house music faded. She admitted to herself it thrilled her that people actually wanted to listen to her improvisations on the keyboard. People quickly got to their seats or stood around the walls and quieted, while she began with a few up-tempo tunes and then settled into one of her favorites. "Evergreen." As she went into the chorus, she heard a voice from the back of the club—a falsetto strong and true, begging for her contralto to join in harmony.

"Go on, girl! Let her rip!" Kayla Hill called out and then sang in synchronization with the music Loretta continued to play.

The audience applauded her sister and encouraged Loretta to sing. She begged off as she continued to accompany her sister on the piano, but Kayla wouldn't back off as she weaved her way through the audience toward the stage, singing and encouraging the audience to demand Loretta participate. Kayla won and Loretta reached and captured a high note, settling the audience into an awesome silence. The sound felt so good the hair stood on the back of Loretta's neck and a delightful chill danced up her spine and arms. Her body got into it as she played and swayed, smiled at her sister, and sang a duet with her like she hadn't sung in too many years. Her fingers flew over the piano keys and she and Kayla were in perfect harmony, as they were as children singing to each other in private, away from their parents' ears.

Loretta felt so light and airy she could have floated off the piano bench. One song led into another and before she knew it, she was singing alone. Kayla stood by smiling and occasionally adding backup, but, for the most part, it was only her voice floating in the room.

Willis stood in rapturous attention as he listened to Loretta's strong, sure, and skillful voice. Her range was incredible—as low as Nina Simone, as raspy as Macy Gray, and as high as Minnie

Riperton. Her voice could be as strong as Patti LaBelle or as soft as Janet Jackson. She had a natural voice control like the late Whitney Houston and her cousins, Leontyne Price and Dionne Warwick. Loretta had it all and the feeling for each note and each sound showed in her sparkling eyes. She was breathtaking even with the streaks of gray hair pulled back in an unflattering style and the dress that reminded him of his first grade teacher who was an old maid. No makeup to speak of, just a little lip-gloss. Yet there was so much untapped beauty going wanting for a little attention.

Loretta's voice didn't pale by comparison to the woman who initiated the duets. Both women had excellent voices, but Loretta had greater range and more control. Justin figured they must be related based on the pronounced resemblance between the two women. She had flowing hair, too, but hers was cut in a very attractive style. Her amber makeup enhanced her striking features and her hourglass shape turned more than a few heads. Whoever she was, she knew *who* she was. Still, if Michael's fixed stare was any indication, others wanted to know her, too.

Loretta rose from the piano and walked into Kayla's open arms. The audience was on its collective feet, clapping, stomping, and whistling, while they hugged and long after they broke to acknowledge the applause and adoration.

"My sister, ladies and gentlemen, Kayla Hill," Loretta announced into the microphone and then beamed, making the introduction.

"My sister, ladies and gentlemen, Loretta Hill," Kayla responded to even greater applause.

The house music came on again, while the sisters acknowledged the warmth with smiles and hugs for each other and then made their way through the still standing crowd, shaking hands and issuing "thank you" along the way. Once in the kitchen, they giggled at each other and then sobered. They walked into each other's arms, rocking gently and kissing each other on the cheek.

"How you doin', Mouse?" Kayla asked, still hugging her younger sister.

"I don't know, Kayla," Loretta answered honestly. "I really don't know."

Kayla leaned back from Loretta to search her eyes. "Well, you look like hell." Kayla smiled, appraising her sister and placing an errant tendril back in place. "You look old as Methuselah, girl. I'd be ashamed to tell anyone you're my younger sister. You look older than Mama."

Loretta pursed her lips. "Everyone can't be a glamour girl, Kayla, and you and the rest of our sisters have the position all sewed up."

"That's true," she boasted with no amount of chagrin. "We are beautiful women, but there's room for you." She turned Loretta around. "And what's with this hair?" she said, releasing the bun. She fluffed out Loretta's hair that fell down between her shoulder blades and noticed the sad expression on her face. A tear started to fall and Kayla gathered Loretta in her arms again. "None of that, Mouse," she said, calling her sister by her pet childhood nickname. "You've cried enough. Now is the time for happy tears, not sadness."

Loretta choked back her tears. "How did you find me? I didn't tell you where I was."

Kayla laughed. "Kid, I work for the U.S. State Department, remember? I took your number from my caller ID and made a few phone calls and, *voila*, here I am. Not a minute too soon, I might add. We've got to get you back in the land of the living if you're finally going to do something with that great talent of yours."

Loretta slowly shook her head. "No, it was just something to do for a few weeks while I got my bearings. I'm headed home—I mean to Columbia on Sunday. School starts Monday. I suppose I'll have to find a place to stay during the school year. I can stay in the Mother House for a while."

"School? You mean you're thinking of going back to that boring job? Hon, did you hear that applause out there? You haven't lost your touch. Your voice is still as good as it ever was, if not better. Time for you to do something with it and I mean now."

"You must not have heard me. I have a job to go to. How else do you expect me to take care of myself now that Randolph has left me? I've got to work and try to start rebuilding my life."

"*Job?* Mouse, you can make *a career* for yourself on the stage. I'll support you until you make it big. That won't be too far in the future, I can tell and I can afford it."

"Are you going to sing with me every night, too?" Loretta asked, smiling sadly. "That applause was for you, too, you know. I wasn't the only one out there on stage tonight. If it hadn't been for you, I would have just played a few pieces and called it a night."

"Uh uh uh, still the mousey little girl who never thought she could make it in the real world. Mama did a real job on your self-esteem. I love her, too, but believe me when I say she can be a real tool. So, little sister, I'm telling you that you *can*—and *will*— make it. Mouse, you're going to roar! I'll just talk to the management of this place and see how many weeks they want to book you. I'll—"

"That won't be necessary," a deep, male voice said from behind them.

Loretta and Kayla both turned to see Willis smiling at them.

"Oh, Willis," Loretta said, surprised at his sudden appearance, "this is my sister, Kayla Hill. Kayla, this is Willis…"

"Just call me Willis, Ms. Hill," he said, shaking her hand. "You have a very good voice. I enjoyed your duets with Loretta."

"Well, thank you...uh, Willis, is it?" she crooned, holding on to his hand a second longer than necessary. "It's certainly a distinct pleasure to meet you," she said, her eyes rolling over him like a waterfall. "You work here?"

"Uh, yes, you could say that."

"Kayla, Willis is the manager."

"Oh, really? Imagine that," Kayla crooned. "Well, you're just the man I wanted to see—uh, for a number of reasons—particularly about my sister's contract to perform in this establishment. Excuse us, Mouse," she said, taking his arm, guiding Willis to the table in the corner of the kitchen, and sat.

Kayla Hill is a knock out, Willis thought. Smooth as satin and just as shiny. He dated women like her before—confident and critical. Her eyes slid over him like he was gravy ready to be sopped up with a biscuit. He was sure she had the skill to lick every drop. Under other circumstances, he would have volunteered to ooze all over her, but she wasn't his mission, Loretta was.

"One of the owner's executives is here tonight. He liked what he saw and heard, and he wants Loretta to perform here for an indefinite period. He's waiting outside in the hall, if you want to talk with him," Willis said, nodding toward the door.

Kayla confidently grinned. "Be back in a moment, hon," she said over her shoulder to Loretta, not taking her eyes off Willis.

"Kayla!" Loretta's sharply intruded. "You know I can't—"

"Keep her busy, uh, Willis," she said, drawing out his name with a slow, sexy grin.

"Sure." He smiled. "Whatever you say."

"Hmmm, I'll bet," she intoned, as she rose from the table and left the kitchen.

Loretta stood, fuming, and Willis noticed.

"Sisters, huh?" He stood and nodded toward the exiting Kayla.

"Well, maybe," Loretta huffed. "Sometimes I wonder whether one of us was switched at birth."

Willis smiled. "She's some piece of work, huh?"

"Truly," Loretta said, still fuming. "And then some."

Kayla sidled up to the tall, dark, and very handsome Michael Rodgers, placed her hands on her impressive hips, and shifted her weight to one side. Her eyes climbed Michael as if he were Mount Everest—slowly, carefully, and with purpose. She thoughtfully ran her tongue over her pouty lips and then tilted her head up, signaling the end of her mental deliberations.

"So, tell me, Mr. Rodgers, what's one of the most eligible bachelors in the United States doing playing Inn keeper in this neighborhood?"

"Why, Ms. Hill, it's been a long time. I should ask you what one of the most sought after beauties is doing in this little seaside town. I didn't think you'd remember me among those who have worshiped at your feet."

"Cozumel, a little villa by the sea, five nights, six days, a few eons ago. How could I forget?"

"It was six glorious nights and seven exciting days, Ms. Hill, six months ago. You were on a State Department trade delegation mission to Mexico. Yellow bikini, when you chose to wear anything at all to go swimming, sea-green cover that didn't hide the rosy birthmark on your—"

"I stand corrected, Mr. Rodgers. Still do that thing with your —"

"All night long. I've perfected the practice since last we met. Care to have a demonstration of the new and improved version?" He grinned, eyeing her from the bottom up.

She grinned back. "What room?"

"Bridal suite. Upper level." He nodded, lasciviously perusing her body.

"Midnight?"

"Uh, uh, eleven. I can't wait the extra hour."

"I'll be there at ten-fifty-five. You needn't dress for the occasion. I want you naked and my hands on you. Now that we've dispensed with the important issues, Mr. Rodgers, let's move on while you tell me about your neighborhood and especially about why *the* Justin Willis McCoy of McCoy Enterprises International is here."

Loretta's ire at her sister's behavior began to dissipate when she noticed Willis' directed gaze. She nearly sizzled when she caught him looking at her that way. She even tingled a bit.

"What?" she asked when she could no longer stand it.

"You're fantastic, you know that?" Loretta bashfully smiled and looked away. He turned her face back to his with a finger to her chin. "You have a very beautiful voice, but, of course, you already know that, too."

As she stood before him, Loretta's feelings were beginning to stir from his touch, his caress of her face, but she dare not let them loose or show her feelings. She feared what would happen if she ever did. Singing lusty songs, like Chaka Chan's "Tell Me Something Good," full out in public with the decadently sexy, breathy sounds in the lyrics, gave her a high she had only felt in private when she sang to keep from crying. Singing with her sister in front of an audience of over a hundred people threatened the neatly packaged beliefs she held of right and wrong. Besides, what she felt when she sang had to be wrong. Her parents and grandparents, particularly her mother, laid her foundation early, and she lived within the box they built around her all her life. A boxed life securely sheltered from the outside world. Now, standing before Willis' admiring gaze, she felt she could do almost anything—but certainly not everything she wanted to do.

"Thank you," she said quietly. "My sister is much better at singing and a lot of other things than I am, but, of course, you heard how good she is."

Willis nodded. "Yes, she has a very good sound, but you— well, suffice it to say she's not in your league," he said and reached out to finger the tips of her long, lustrous, curly hair.

Their eyes met and held a gaze for a few uncomfortable moments. Then Kayla came back into the kitchen. She stopped short and raised a perfectly arched eyebrow when she noticed Justin caressing Loretta's face and hair. Then he removed his hand as she approached them and they both turned toward her.

"Well, little sister, I believe I've struck a deal that should make you very happy."

"You didn't!" Loretta fussed. "Are you losing it, Kayla? You know that I have responsibilities…"

"I'll handle them. You're going on sabbatical for a year. Just enough time for you to get your bearings and then—"

"Kayla! You're not listening to me! Read my lips! I've got a hus—" she started and the word caught in her throat. Anger mixed with pain as Loretta huffed and stormed out of the kitchen leaving Willis and Kayla in her wake.

Willis turned his attention to Kayla who also swung her gaze toward him.

"The real McCoy," Kayla said with purpose.

Justin got her meaning. "It's not what you think, Ms. Hill."

"Tell me, Mr. McCoy, what should I be thinking? My sister has twenty-twenty vision, but she can't see the handwriting on the wall. I, on the other hand, can read the bottom of the eye chart perfectly."

"What do you see, Ms. Hill?" he asked with feet apart and arms folded across his broad chest.

"I see one of the most powerful, influential, and charming men in the states trying to lead my little, unsuspecting and completely vulnerable sister down the primrose path wearing rose-colored glasses."

"You've completely misjudged the situation."

"Perhaps, but let me make myself crystal clear, Mr. McCoy," she said, leaning dangerously toward him. "If my sister sheds one tear as a result of her relationship with you, you can kiss McCoy International goodbye." She held his gaze.

"Your sister is a grown woman. She can think for herself."

"So were they all, were they not? Your reputation for leaving a string of broken hearts in your wake never, to the best of my knowledge, included women under the age of consent. Supposedly, they were capable of thinking for themselves, too. Women of some experience with the opposite sex seem to fare no better. Apparently, they were as unprepared as Loretta to deal with the *real* McCoy."

"You give me more credit than I am due on that score," he said, leaning to meet her challenging stance. "I've never lied to any woman and I don't intend to start now."

"Oh, so my sister knows who you are? You've introduced yourself to her as Justin McCoy, have you, *Willis*?"

She had him there. "Willis is my legal middle name. However, Ms. Hill, I don't like to be threatened—by anyone," he growled through gritted teeth.

"Oh, that wasn't a threat, Mr. McCoy, that was a promise and I keep my promises," she flung back.

Chapter Seven

Loretta awoke and rolled in the king-sized bed. The sun shone through the cream-colored sheers and bathed the room in a soft light. Her eyes went around the nicely appointed room and then narrowed. *Where is Kayla?* She looked at the empty space next to her. It was clear Kayla did not sleep there last night. If not there, then where was she?

Kayla sucked in a ragged breath, biting her lower lip and shutting her eyes tightly against the exquisite pain of another orgasmic reaction. This man had more stamina than any man she had ever known intimately, of which there was quite an impressive list. She rolled her head against the Downy-soft sheets on the oversized bed, arching her back as Michael roused her to even greater heights in her euphoria than she had ever experienced.

"God, woman! You drive me crazy!" he growled, lifting her body to straddle him. He settled her on his engorged phallus and they both shuttered at the joining.

"Insanity is a state of mind," she panted, as her mouth closed on his, "it's what you do to my body that sends me into orbit."

"That, too." He breathed. "You've ravaged me all night and I still can't get enough of you. Are you going to torture me for another lifetime and walk out of my life again? You know I still want you in my life, Kayla."

"Ask me no questions and I'll tell you no lies, lover." She breathed heavily as she rode him.

"Lie to me, baby," he gritted out. "Tell me you've forgotten what we mean to each other. What we do for and to each other. Marry me, Kayla. I'm in love with you."

Kayla pumped him harder and more erotically. "Men say anything in the heat of passion."

Michael's body stiffened as he grabbed her by her arms and forced her to look at him. "I've told you I love you when we weren't making love. I have asked you to marry me when we were close, and when we have been far apart on opposite sides of the globe. That time in London, in Geneva, in Toronto, in Texas. When will you get it through your beautiful head I mean what I say? You are a beautiful, dynamic, intoxicating, and thoroughly enchanting woman, Kayla Hill. Why shouldn't I be in love with you, damn it? Why can't you fall in love with me?"

Kayla eased out of his grip, quickly losing the rapture she felt. Her hooded eyes somber, but steely, rose to meet his gaze. She saw the passion there, but knew it would be fleeting. Men didn't stick around long with any one woman—not even a good woman like Loretta could hold a man forever and always.

She wordlessly uncoupled herself from him and started to rise from the bed. Michael stopped her and laid her back against the damp sheets that evidenced their night of heated passion.

"Needing you and wanting you are two different things, Kayla," he said passionately. She remained passive like steel in a silken glove. "Damn it! I need you, Kayla," he said as he took her mouth again and then her body.

Loretta emerged from the bathroom, towel drying her hair, as Kayla entered the bedroom.

"Just where have you been, Ms. Hill?" Loretta flashed.

"Surfing," Kayla quipped as she tossed her overnight bag on a nearby chair.

"Surfing?" Loretta asked in complete confusion. "I didn't know you surfed."

"Neither did he," she said beneath her breath.

"What was that?"

"Never mind. Now. Take off that old robe, turn around, and let me look at you."

"Naked?" she screeched, her brows beetled.

"Don't worry, Mouse. I may be a little perverse at times, but I'm not into incest. Just take it all off."

Loretta did as her sister asked, feeling foolish and modest. Kayla walked around her, studying her from different posed positions, tapping one of her long, neatly manicured fingernails against her teeth.

"You'll do, I suppose," she finally said, finishing her appraisal.

"I'll do what—exactly?" Loretta asked not sure, but suspicious of the meaning of her sister's cryptic remark.

"Just hurry and get dressed. We have a lot to do before tonight's performance."

"Huh?"

"Man, you look beat!" Justin chuckled, as Michael dragged himself into the empty dining room.

He turned a chair backward and sat down with a thud. Balancing his elbow on the back of the chair, he rubbed his eyes with the heels of his hands. Then he exhaled in frustration.

"Yeah, I am."

"I don't mean to be getting up in your business, but—"

Michael raised his hand and shook his head. "Don't ask or I'll have to lie to you."

Justin didn't. He turned his attention to the reports he was reading. He lifted his coffee mug to his face and peered at Michael over the rim. Replacing his cup on the table, he swung his long legs off the chair beside him, planted them on the floor, and transferred the stack of reports from his lap onto the table.

"Coffee?" he asked.

"Yeah. That sounds like something I can handle."

Justin rarely, if ever, knew of anything Michael Rodgers couldn't handle. They often played chess together. The man was a monument to deft strategic moves and business negotiations. Keen insight and practiced diplomacy marked Michael as a titan in a world filled with gutsy business wizards. Feared and revered by those known as high rollers in the mine fields of corporate America, the man who sat opposite him now looked as if he had just caused Wall Street to crash and burn…again.

Justin and Michael had known and respected each other for far too many years for Justin to intrude on Michael's privacy. Whatever it was, if Michael wanted to talk about it, he would come to him as they had done for each other many times in the past. Justin was a patient man to a fault. For that matter, so was Michael. They were alike in so many ways.

"Kenneth Alexander was in town and stopped by the office last week," said Michael. "He's agreed to have CompuCorrect

International install new computer equipment, software and hardware throughout the hotel, resort, and conference centers and he'll hyper network the systems together on a closed, intranet connection and cloud. The security aspects were phenomenal and virtually incorruptible. He agreed to a fair price for the project."

"Yeah, I expected as much. Kenneth is a good brother. One of a kind. I like the way he does business. No hidden agendas. A real straight shooter," Justin agreed.

"When we first discussed upgrading the computer systems, I didn't understand why you didn't want to put the contract out for competitive bids and directed me to go after an agreement with Alexander's company. I did a complete dossier on him and I'm impressed with what I found. Now I understand."

"Good. I'm concerned our current system is too easily hacked. It'll be a nice change working with someone I can trust."

"Speaking of working, when are you coming back?"

"Don't know yet," Justin said, sipping his coffee while continuing to read reports. "Don't you like running the company?"

"It passes the time," Michael said, sipping the black, hot brew. "Mmmm, this is good. Did we change coffee distributors?"

"Uh, no, we didn't. Loretta made coffee before she and her sister left."

"So she's gone again?" Michael said more as a mournful statement than a question.

"Hey, buddy, it's not that bad. I think they went shopping or something. Loretta didn't look too happy about the outing. I believe they'll be back fairly soon."

"Then I'm outta here," Michael said, swallowing the last of his coffee and swinging up from his chair. "You finished signing those contracts?"

"Chill, my brother," Justin said, watching Michael swiftly rise. "You look like someone peed in your corn flakes."

"Yeah, someone did," he said cryptically.

"Male or female?"

"What do you think?" Michael asked with a raised eyebrow.

"*No mas*, my brother, but tell me, how does Kayla Hill know who I am?"

Michael derisively laughed and sat again. "Ms. Hill is a high-level operative in the U.S. State Department; attached to the Secretary of State's office. She has the best Rolodex in DC. Woodward and Bernstein would call *her* to see who and what they should know."

"I see," Justin said absently.

"I doubt it," Michael intoned with an edge.

"Unfinished business, I gather."

"According to her, it is finished now, but the jury's still out on that question."

"A man needs to know his limitations." Justin smiled.

"I'm not even pushing the envelope just yet." Michael grinned.

Justin smiled with an acknowledging nod of his head. The Michael Rodgers he knew was back—with a vengeance.

"If you *think* I'm going to wear that whisper of a dress—if you could call that dental floss a dress!" Loretta huffed. "You have lost your ever-loving mind, Kayla Hill! I let you talk me into coloring and trimming my hair; smothering me with all this glop on my face, having my eyebrows ripped off, and hair removed from my private parts, having these designs put on my nails, and buying all of these lacy, skimpy, little under things, and a year's paycheck worth of new clothes and shoes, but if you *think* for one moment I'm going to spend good, American money, even if it's your money, on something where half the material stays in the store—well, sister, you got another *think* coming!"

"Way to go, Retta!" Kayla laughed, thoroughly enjoying herself and her younger sister's tirade. "That's the kind of fire I like to see in your eyes. Get mad! Really mad! Then get into this dress, while I look for some more dresses and some shoes to match."

"You think this is some kind of joke, don't you?" Loretta flashed. "Well, yes, I'm mad. Mad as the Hatter for letting you push and poke at me for nearly a whole day!"

"Yeah, that's it! Keep going," Kayla said, holding out the barely there frock with one confident finger. "Tell me about myself while you slip into this."

"*This?*" Loretta fumed. "You can't wear *this* with anything, but perfume and body hair! Of course, you've seen to it that I don't have body hair anymore!" She snatched the frock from Kayla.

Kayla grinned and pointed an arrow straight finger toward the dressing room. Loretta turned on her heels, huffed in frustration, and marched away. While Loretta was dressing, Kayla made a few telephone calls. When she finished she noticed Loretta peeking out from behind the dressing room curtains.

"Is the coast clear?" Loretta asked.

"It's only me and a camera crew from *Vogue*." Kayla grinned. "Show us what you're working with, little sister."

Loretta blew out a hard breath and tentatively stepped out from behind the curtain, looking around to assure no one else was in the vicinity.

A slow grin curved Kayla's mouth. "Forty sure as hell ain't fatal! It's fierce!" Kayla said with emotion, perusing the garment and her sister in it.

"Kayla, I'm not forty yet, but I'd drop dead of embarrassment if I wore something like this in public."

"You'll live, but every man in the joint is going to get a hard on and every woman is going to want to scratch your eyes out! Look at you! You're drop-dead gorgeous and stacked, girl!"

Chapter Eight

"Bonnie, where is Loretta?" Justin asked, as the room filled to capacity. "Who hired those musicians?"

"I guess Ms. Kayla did, Mr. Willis." Bonnie shrugged, as she continued to look over the seating chart. "Ms. Kayla said Ms. Loretta needed to make an entrance and not be bothered by welcoming the guests. She told me to handle it."

"She did, did she? Well, I'll see about that. Where is *Ms.* Kayla Hill?"

"Back stage with Ms. Loretta, I guess," she said, checking her watch. "Ms. Kayla said for me to have everyone seated before the eight o'clock show or she'd have my hide and it's almost that time now."

"The only hide that's going to get gotten is—"

"Ladies and Gentlemen," a disembodied female voice said over the improved sound system, as the lights lowered, the audience silenced, and a spotlight shined center of a newly decorated stage. "Oceans Inn Resort proudly welcomes you and provides for your listening pleasure...*Loretta!*"

The combo began with a flourish and went into the opening intro of "I'm Every Woman," with a slow, melodic beat. Behind the backlit curtains, a voice began and crescendo, then the combo began to rock and the curtains opened. The light cast behind the perfect figure of a woman who Justin thought must be Kayla, because the voice was so lusty and sensual. As the figure moved forward with the erotic sway of hips, Justin caught his breath. *Damn, Kayla had some moves on her,* he thought, but wondered where Loretta was. Then the spotlights flashed, strobes flickering and distorting the woman's features. Then suddenly, *POW!* The woman burst forth with a vengeance and Justin froze.

Loretta moved sensuously across the stage. Justin stood stone still. Audible gasps could be heard throughout the audience and men leapt to their feet in frantic applause. *"Damn!"* Justin inhaled a ragged breath through gritted teeth. Loretta was a vision, a marvelously mature Beyoncé. Her hair was full with deep, reddish-brown curls flowing madly over her shoulders, nowhere near the white glittering sheath that hugged her body as if it had been painted on. Her breasts, full and high, made Justin want to be the fabric that caressed her nipples protruding under the deep plunging *décolletage* to her navel. The dress clung to Loretta's rounded hips and Justin clung with sheer will power to his fleeting control. Two long slits from ankle to thigh played peek-a-boo with her long, shapely legs in shimmering pantyhose. Diamond-studded ankle strapped shoes continued the thousand points of light shimmering in the white gown. Loretta tossed her head and diamond earrings continuously caught the light from the flashing strobes.

Everything around Justin ceased to exist for him. He only saw Loretta and the shining gleam in her eyes. Her voice caressed and enlivened him, bringing every hair on his body to full attention. Her fingers wrapped around the microphone and he saw diamonds glittering on the nails of her ring fingers. His body began to tingle as he stood in rapt awe.

"*Wow*, huh?" a voice said beside him, as Loretta hit a high difficult note with force and confidence and held it until the audience leapt to its collective feet again.

Justin didn't realize he had forgotten to breathe until Loretta finished. He never took his eyes off her. As the song implied, she was, indeed, every woman.

"I want to put her under contract and bring her into the studio for a demo. I think we can—"

"No," Justin said.

"JW, do you hear what I hear?" Michael asked. "She's better than anyone I've heard. Better than anyone we've currently got under contract."

"I know," he said quietly. "She's sensational. She's megastar quality."

"Yeah, so what..." Michael looked sideways at Justin. "Uh huh," he intoned. "Well, my brother, you can't keep her all to yourself. Her kind of talent belongs to the world."

"I know that, too," he said, still mesmerized by the shining vision before him across the darkened room.

Loretta was feeling a force she never felt before. It was as if she were another person all together. Someone or something possessed her body and took it soaring on a supersonic jet ride. The music was in her and she was in her music. The combo hit every cue perfectly as if they had been performing together for years. She sang with a robust abandon that belied her age and her background. Energy poured from every molecule of her body. She was petrified before the curtain opened. Kayla rehearsed with her and the band at an off-site location for more than three hours on the moves, the stage presence, and the inflections, but she moved on from there, letting the music inspire her, and inspire her it did. It thrilled her and her voice exploded with each note she sang. She was in a zone outside of time and space.

Michael was right, Justin mused. He couldn't stay at Oceans Inn forever and neither could Loretta. He had a business to run and Loretta's talent deserved to be shared. Justin turned to Michael and nodded. "Set it up. No connection to McCoy Enterprises. Create a label if you have to for her and her alone."

"That's going to take a while, JW. At least four to six weeks."

"Just do it, Michael. Make it work in less time than that," he said, as he walked away.

Michael watched Justin go slowly through the lobby with his head bent and hands dug deep in his pockets. He shook his head in understanding. Another Hill woman was getting under a man's skin and burrowing into his heart.

"I know how you feel, my friend," Michael said to the air. He turned back to see Loretta accepting a well-deserved show of appreciation from her audience. "I know just how you feel."

When Loretta finished the ten o'clock show, it was after midnight. She was exhilarated and still on an emotional high. After signing so many autographs and the playbill, her fingers were nearly numb. A smile was still plastered on her face though. She couldn't believe the evening she had. Two shows and she was just as energetic for the second show as she was for the first. Nervous energy still coursed through her body after Kayla profusely praised her for her performances. Everyone told her in glowing terms how well she performed. Everyone, that is, except Willis.

She had not seen him since early that morning over coffee in the kitchen. Just the two of them sat there talking and even laughing a bit. It was so nice and comforting to be with him—easy and lighthearted talking with him. He was a good listener who didn't pry, but didn't reveal much about himself. She wanted to ask—to know more about him. He was a good friend when she needed one the most. Always subtle and confidently encouraging her. He made her feel special and feminine. He made her feel. Period. His deep, melodic voice caressed her and she talked with him about things she never told another human being, not even Kayla, but where was he now? Now that she was feeling on top of the world.

Loretta twirled into her bedroom suite and twirled around again. She un-strapped the high heels and stepped out of them. At the French doors, she flung them open, wrapping her arms around her body in delight. Her eyes opened and she looked toward the moonlit night, star-studded sky, and shining sea. A smile crossed her lips and she shuddered in her excitement. Kayla was right. She did need a change of pace. Her son, Daryl, was right, too.

It was her turn.

Now was the time for *her* to stretch *her* wings and fly, she thought, as she flung her arms up and open wide. She found her niche. She could go on singing at the Oceans Inn Resort forever!

Loretta's eyes fixed on a form standing at the water's edge. Feet apart, hands in pockets and staring out across the dark ocean. She padded barefoot toward the form.

"Willis?" She gingerly approached. "Is that you? I've been looking for you. Where have you been?"

He didn't turn at her approach. His thoughts were on her and suddenly there she was as if he had conjured her up in a dream. It was an erotic dream of them together entwined in a lifelong embrace as ageless as forever.

"Willis, is something wrong?" She touched his arms.

"No, there's nothing wrong. I couldn't sleep yet."

"Me either. I felt like I was waking from a long sleep." She threaded her arm through his. "Tonight was like a fairytale, a dream come true."

"You were sensational. You have incredible talent. You're going to be something beyond belief."

"Thanks, Willis." She smiled, resting her head against his shoulder and taking in the view of the ocean as he did. "I wanted you to be proud of me. You've helped me so much over the past few weeks. You've become a very good friend. It matters to me what you think. I don't know how I'm ever going to thank you, but as for stardom, well, I'm not planning to go anywhere. As my sister suggested, I am going to take a year's sabbatical and stay here."

Willis turned and looked into Loretta's dazzling eyes. "You're welcome to stay. Nothing would make me happier. You're, uh, you're good for business." He knew he was in trouble when Loretta smiled up at him. Her eyes danced with light that made his stomach do a slow dive off a high perch. *She is so beautiful,* he thought, as he caressed her face.

Before he knew what his head told him not to do, his lips touched down on hers. He held her in a loose embrace. Her sweet mouth spun him into orbit, but he had to let her go. She was, after all, another man's wife.

He remembered the pain that racked him when he discovered Carla in their bed with another man, giving her body to him in a complete lack of restraint.

He had come home early from a business trip to find Carla so deep in the throes of passion she never noticed he was there. He knew that feeling of loss and deep hurt. He didn't want to be the cause of another man's pain and he would have been if he didn't release Loretta at that moment.

Willis stepped away from her and looked into her eyes. "I apologize. I should not have done that," he said softly. He walked away, leaving her standing on the beach, and headed for his room.

Kayla packed the last of her clothes and noticed Loretta had been silently sitting in the same spot on her bed with fingers to her lips for nearly half an hour.

"Mouse, cat got your tongue or something?" Kayla teased. "You've been in a trance all morning."

Vaguely, Loretta heard her sister's question, but didn't answer. She hardly slept a wink, thinking about the mind-numbing kiss Willis planted on her last night. Nothing had ever felt as warm and wonderful as his mouth on hers and the feel of his strong, muscular body pressed against her. Just that simple act sent electricity shooting through her system with lightning speed. It was a slow, soft, mouth-watering kiss surprisingly she didn't want to end, but it did almost as abruptly as it began.

"Mouse?" Kayla touched her shoulder.

"Huh? Oh, yes," she fumbled, drawing back from the dream that had gripped her. "What were you saying?"

"I asked whether something was wrong. You're not upset because I have to leave and go back to Washington, are you?"

"No, no," she answered quickly, then, "Kayla, do men apologize after they kiss you?"

Kayla drew back in surprise. "No, not unless they do it wrong," she quipped. "Is this just idle curiosity or did something happen I don't know about?"

"How do you feel after they kiss you? I mean, do you feel like you've been hit by a Mack truck? Or do you just tingle all over?"

Kayla cocked her head to the side in confusion. "I've been known to experience both sensations simultaneously a time or two—quite recently in fact—but what—"

"Do you want to sing and cry all at the same time? Does your head spin and you want to melt into his—"

"Loretta Louise Hill, what's gotten into you? There is definitely something going on here! You're glowing like a neon light!"

Loretta rose from the bed and kissed her sister briefly on the forehead. "That's what I thought." She smiled as she dashed into the bathroom.

Kayla was struck dumb, which, for her, was something she rarely felt. She had never seen Loretta like that, but she had a feeling she knew what, and particularly *whom*, had put the stars in her younger sister's eyes. She grabbed her packed bag and headed for the lobby.

"Yes, I kissed her, if it's any of your damn business!" Justin railed. "I didn't sleep with her and I won't! Give me some credit, would you?"

"I'm warning you, McCoy, don't mess with her mind! She's had enough heartache to last a lifetime! You hurt her and you'll have me to deal with!"

Justin turned in fury and stalked up to Kayla. "Deal with your own devastation, *Ms*. Hill," he growled lowly, his jaws tight.

Kayla drew back. "What does that mean?" she snapped.

"Michael Rodgers is not only my right hand, but also a very good friend of mine. I don't like it when people try to play him! In fact, I can be downright deadly when a friend of mine is hurting!"

Kayla blinked at the force and power Justin exuded. She heard he was cunning in his business dealings. A tiger shark was tame compared to him, she had been told, and now she was witnessing firsthand what appeared to be the tip of the iceberg. His cold, calculating stare infuriated her and warned her to tread lightly, but she refused to heed the warning signals.

"Stay out of my affairs, McCoy!" she growled back through gritted teeth.

"You do the same, Ms. Hill!"

"Oh, there you are, Kayla," Loretta said, unexpectedly entering the parlor.

Both combatants relaxed their stances, but not before Loretta noticed electric sparks shooting off around them. She was not sure what was going on, but they regarded each other malevolently. Immediately, it came to her. Kayla inspired men to do a number of uncharacteristic things—fall in love with her was one of them and hate her was another. Sometimes simultaneously. She wondered whether Willis had succumbed to Kayla's many charms. Quickly, she recalled Kayla had not slept in their room, again. A chill danced up her spine. Had she slept with Willis? *Oh, my God*, she shuddered, *that must be it!* Kayla seduced Willis and now he didn't want to let her go. They must have been arguing about it when she walked in. She steeled her stance and veiled her emotions.

"Kayla, the Inn's courtesy van is ready to take you to the airport," Loretta said, devoid of outward emotion, while her heart disintegrated.

"Thanks, Mouse," she intoned, still staring down Willis.

Loretta could not take it any longer. She turned and walked from the energy-charged room to give them privacy. Once out of sight and earshot, she slumped against the wall. Why should she care what Willis did or with whom—even with her sister? At the same time, she felt rejected and empty, just as Randolph made her feel for so many years. Tears, again, edged her eyes as an emotional fog began to cloud her brain. Who did she think she was? Here she was a mother of three young adults and nearly forty years old, mooning like a schoolgirl over a man she barely knew. A man who likely now knew her sister in more than a biblical sense. She couldn't compete with Kayla's prowess with a man. Most of them were putty in Kayla's hand or grist for her mill. Why shouldn't Willis find Kayla alluring? He was a man, after all, not an immortal, but strong and virile. *The perfect match for Kayla*, she thought.

"I've got to go, hon," Kayla said, turning Loretta into her arms.

Loretta saw Willis' dark and angry demeanor over Kayla's shoulder. The tears broke from the rims of Loretta's eyes as she kissed Kayla on both cheeks.

"None of that, Mouse." Kayla softly kissed Loretta's tear-stained face. "Only happy tears from now on, okay?"

"Okay." Loretta nodded and tried to find a smile, but the tears welled up again as she saw Willis turn, dig his hands in his pockets, hang his head, and walk away.

Chapter Nine

Each night of the week, Loretta performed except Sunday and Monday, and twice on Friday and Saturday nights, gaining more confidence with each show. Weeks passed since that first night when she broke out of the box where she was stored most of her life. Costumes, more daring and provocative than those she had ever worn before, were arriving almost weekly sent by Kayla from exotic places all over the world. It never ceased to amaze Loretta how Kayla could carry on such a hectic, high-profile schedule and lifestyle and remain so energetic, attractive, and enchanting.

Yet, it bothered her that Willis busied himself, personally supervising more of the renovations to the Inn, barely spending a moment with her since Kayla left. She felt he was still brooding over her sister's departure, though Willis never asked about Kayla over the many intervening weeks. She never intruded on his privacy either. Kayla was her sister, but what was between Kayla and Willis was their business. She steeled herself against the jealousy she felt about them. It was totally out of place for her to pry, although she had a growing respect for Willis. Kayla dismissed many good men from her life, but Willis was no ordinary man. Where Willis was concerned, Loretta felt Kayla was making a grave error by leaving him, but she would not interfere.

Every day after she and her band practiced, she concentrated on her music and helping with different table arrangements. Randolph wasn't on her mind nearly at all these days. Her life had changed substantially and she wondered whether she would ever be able to return to the private school and a mundane existence as its Head Mistress once her yearlong sabbatical was over. *What would I do then?*

Justin grabbed the back of his neck and stalked back and forth across his room like a caged animal. He had just seen Loretta's performance and his body was still reeling from the experience. She wore a little, red, postage stamp of a number and every red-blooded man in the joint nearly came unglued. *Beyoncé who?* He was rattled, too, and he knew it all too painfully. She wasn't a single lady, but he wanted to put more than just a ring on it! He was in deep trouble with no relief in sight. The thought, of what was going through the minds of the other men when Loretta moved so sensuously across the stage with her gorgeous, long legs and toned thighs on display, nearly drove him over the edge. Although they acted respectfully, he knew what they were thinking. Hell, he was thinking the same thing! Her maturely, voluptuous, womanly body was awesome. He was wearing a hole in the carpet each night, trying to control his raging hormones like some randy teenager until he could sleep, but tonight, like too many others, sleep was as elusive as the Fountain of Youth. If only he could convince his body he was not a young man again.

Justin had enough of his restlessness. It was late and the Inn seemed to have quieted for the night. He stripped, put on a short robe, threw a towel around his neck, and headed for the indoor swimming pool. He didn't turn on the overhead lights and swam using just the low ambient pool lighting. A few laps and maybe he could expend enough of his pent-up energy to rest. The heated pool was warm, and Justin stroked up and back along the Olympic-sized area so many times, he lost count. Finally, he pushed himself up against the wall on the deep end, breathing hard, but that wasn't the only thing that was hard.

Why couldn't he just walk away from her? Loretta was healing. She didn't need him anymore to give her moral support. She found an inner strength that pulled her through her malaise. Emotionally, she seemed to be on her feet again, so why couldn't he let go? Go back to his life as President and CEO of McCoy Enterprises. He was never away from the office for more than a few days. Now, his escape was approaching two months. He didn't need to be at the Oceans Inn Resort. He promoted some of his faithful, long-term employees and hired a new management team. His Construction Division was more than capable of handling the remaining renovations. Hell, they could have handled the whole thing without him. More importantly, why couldn't he tell Loretta who he was?

Justin buried his face in his hands and wiped away the chlorinated water. He wanted her. That's why he couldn't leave. He wanted Loretta in ways he never wanted any other woman before. Not only was it the transformation she made, changing from a near-matronly-looking woman into the vision he saw many years ago on stage, singing her soulful tune, but now he cursed the fact he ever met her. He would never have her and he knew it.

Loretta padded silently to the kitchen to warm some water for tea. The fall ocean-side air chilled her room. Although she lay under a heavy comforter and a fire blazed in the hearth, she could not sleep. The swathing silkiness of her nightgown teased her skin. Her sister's taste in intimate apparel ran to the exotic, Loretta thought, as she ran her hands down the garment. She had to admit, though, she liked the feel of the silk and satin fabrics better than the cotton and flannel she used to wear. These things made her feel feminine, if not completely warm. She thought a cup of chamomile tea might help her quiet her restlessness and warm her body. Thinking about Willis was driving her to distraction.

Loretta's head came up and she listened to a distant sound in the silent Inn. *Must be the ocean*, she thought, but the ocean sounds were different from what she was hearing. As she put the kettle on to heat, she walked silently toward the sound. Finally, she stopped by the glass partition that lined the indoor swimming pool. There, in the water, was a man swimming. His brown bottom was bare as he stroked the water, cutting through it with prowess and agility. Willis. She would know that finely chiseled torso anywhere. She continued to watch from her protected position, as he hoisted himself out of the water to the edge of the pool. She gasped audibly and cupped her hand over her mouth. Powerfully built, far beyond what she would have expected a man of his stature to be, He had a firm, flat, six-pack, and muscular legs. His thick torso finely sculptured, not like a boy or younger man, but a manly, mature physique. He was breathtaking! Not even Randolph's athletic body had so intoxicated her, as did the sight of Willis in the buff. She wondered, for more than a few moments, what it would feel like to be loved by him. If she didn't think the question to be so odd coming from her, she would have asked her sister. Certainly, Kayla would know. What difference would it make if she did know what transpired between Kayla and Willis? She would never have the opportunity to sample his wares. She, with all of her vast experience with one man, her husband, Randolph, she self-deprecatingly thought.

When Willis stood to put on his robe, Loretta took a long, needful look and then silently, but quickly, went back to her room. She had just closed her bedroom door when she remembered the kettle on the stove. Biting her bottom lip, she feared a fire might start if she didn't get back to the kitchen in time to turn off the flame. She listened at the door, hoping to hear Willis go back to his room down the hall from hers so she could slip back to the kitchen. Slowly, she opened the door and looked carefully in both directions. Not hearing Willis, she stole stealthily back down the corridor through the lobby and dining room. She rushed into the kitchen, looking over her shoulder, and slammed into a hard, immovable object. Willis.

"Uh, oh, I'm sorry," she stuttered. "I was going to make some tea and I..." her words caught in her throat, her fingers meshed in the soft, tangled hairs of Willis' warm, wet chest. His arms were loosely around her, keeping her from tumbling over in her haste.

They stared into each other's eyes. Loretta inhaled the scent of chlorine water on Willis' skin; some moisture still clung to him.

"I heard the kettle whistling and...Guess I'm not the only one having a hard time getting to sleep," he said, looking down at her. The feel and sight of the deep maroon, silk negligee against her honey-toned skin felt so soft beneath his fingertips and looked so good that Willis could barely focus on what he was saying or doing. Loretta had bolted into him as if something was after her and he had to brace himself for the impact of her body slamming against his. Her fingers sprayed across his chest and clutched at his flesh to cushion her potential fall. He would never let her fall though, he thought, as he held her against his throbbing body. That is, unless she was tumbling on top of him onto his bed.

No!

He could not think like that, he cautioned himself. She was no one-night-stand. Not someone who he wanted, just for the moment. She was another man's wife! He set her away from him and then closed his robe as she removed her hands. "Did you make enough for two?" he asked into the yawning silence.

"Huh?" she asked, still a bit dazed.

"The tea? Did you brew enough for two cups?"

"Oh, uh, yes. I think so."

"Good. Would you make a cup for me? I'll be back in a moment."

Before she could answer, Willis disappeared through the kitchen door. Loretta sighed in relief. Being so close to him, with nothing, but the thin fabric between them, was more than she could bear. She wiped the slight sheen of perspiration from her brow and cupped her face in her hands. She suddenly felt flushed and hot. Early onset menopause, she tried to convince herself, but something inside her screamed *Willis*. Lately, every time she was around him, she felt warmth growing inside of her. It was a devil of a feeling and she would hear her mother's warnings about lusting after a man. Loretta heeded those warnings and never let her true sexuality loose, even with Randolph. How could she have when she didn't trust him? Besides the fear of the venereal diseases Randolph may have subjected her to, his foreplay in lovemaking was nearly nonexistent. From the first night he touched her on their wedding night, he was an insensitive and impatient lover.

Never once had she felt an orgasmic reaction. Of course, she read about it in books and magazines. She even heard about them from her sisters and friends or acquaintances and even from her stepdaughter, Elizabeth, who confided everything to her.

Yet, nothing between her and Randolph ever remotely approached what she had learned. When Randolph touched her, she always felt he wasn't actually touching *her*; rather he was just using her because one of his usual lovers was unavailable. As a result, she never felt responsive to his needs, but submitted out of a sense of duty to her wedding vows. She wondered if that was it. Had Randolph known she never truly gave herself to him after she found out about Randy and then Elizabeth? Is that why he sought comfort in the arms of other women? She always submitted to him whenever he wanted, but it was such a hollow and unfulfilling experience, she never participated fully in their lovemaking. She certainly never initiated it.

What did she know of such things? No one ever schooled her on how to love a man. Undoubtedly, her mother never had and she was too embarrassed to ask her sisters. They seemed to have adjusted. Without doubt, Kayla had. She doubted their mother told Kayla or her other sisters anything more than she told her, but somehow her sisters seemed to have very fulfilling sexual relations with their husbands, although all of them were married except Kayla.

Kayla opted for a career rather than a marriage, much to their mother's dismay. Woman's role was to procreate, raise children, and take care of her man's home. Well, she did as her mother instructed and look what it had gotten her...*a divorce.*

Willis furiously searched for the bottoms that went with the short robe he wore. *Damn it, it must be here somewhere,* he fussed to himself. Truth be told, he never wore anything to sleep in. He hadn't even mentioned it to Michael, but Michael had Carlos send clothes at his request. The sleeping apparel had not seen any use since it arrived, until that night.

Finally, he found the bottom and slipped into it. It was more or less just a pair of loose-fitting shorts, but his engorged phallus strained against the fabric for release. That's why he bolted from the kitchen leaving Loretta in his wake. Having her warm, voluptuous body against his was mind numbing, but that's all that had been numbed. He took several calming breaths. It had been a long time since he slept with a woman and that fact was creating havoc with his psyche. He was a half-lapsed Catholic, but far from being celibate. His paramour of the month, Daphne Anderson, had just about run her course with him, before he came to Oceans Inn, but he would have to see her or someone else as soon as he got back into his old life. For now, he would dismiss all thoughts of sex from his mind.

Willis found a small pot of hot, steaming tea sitting on a lit cradle waiting for his return. As usual, Loretta made it special with a tablecloth, flowers, and candles. She pensively sat with the cup to her lips when he sat down across from her.

"What's this?" He smiled, seeing her special cinnamon buns, cheese wedges, and plump, fresh strawberries on a plate between them and a glass of orange juice nearby.

"You obviously went swimming. I thought you might like a snack."

"Thanks. You're right, I am a little hungry." He took a bite of the bun. "Mmmm, that's good. You heated it."

Loretta smiled. "Yes, when my sisters and I were little, we used to help my mother make these sweet buns with raisins, nuts, and bits of dried pineapple. It was usually our dessert and we used to heat it up. The aroma of the hot buns used to fill the house."

"You're a very good cook, Loretta. Did your mother teach you?"

"Yes. She taught us all how to prepare meals, clean a house, and to shop for good, quality food. My father is a salesman and he often has dinner parties for his clients. Everything had to be perfect, so we all lent a hand. Mama is the best cook in the county, so my father always asks her to cater his business dinners. She is such a grand hostess. She made pocket money catering events."

"You learned very well. We've had quite a few compliments about the food and the decor."

"Thank you, but it's just something I do for my family..." Her words hung in the air.

Willis noticed the catch in her voice. Her family was very important to her. That was obvious. "You have children, I suppose," he said to remove the uncomfortable silence and finally ready to ask questions that had long weighed on his mind.

"Yes, three, well, I mean, Daryl is the only child I had, but my husband," another catch, "I mean, Randolph has two other children who came to live with us when they were very young."

"I see. Where are they now? Your children, I mean."

"Randolph Junior, we call him Randy, is in medical school. Elizabeth, we call Libby, is in law school, and this is Daryl's first year in college."

"Your husband?"

"Randolph is...well, I..."

Willis reached across the table and placed his hand on hers. The pain in her eyes was too much. She was having difficulty and he didn't want to cause her any more stress.

"Tell me, do you have children?" she asked, removing her hand from his and brushing a tear from her face.

Willis brightened and a smile grew on his face. "Yes, but only one. Her name is Jessica. She's away at school. I call her Jesse."

It had not dawned on Loretta how little she knew about the man who sat across from her. The man who had befriended her.

"Your wife?"

"Uh, divorced many years ago."

"Oh, I'm sorry," she said warmly.

"I'm not," he said under his breath, remembering the pain mixed with relief he felt when he received the final divorce decree.

"What was that?" Loretta asked, not hearing his last comment.

"Oh, nothing," Willis said, turning his attention again to the wonderful woman across from him. "Tell me about you and your sisters. There must be a million stories with six girls."

"Two million," she said, as she began to talk about Andrea, Evelyn, Adrienne, Denise, and Kayla.

An hour later, Loretta and Willis were hysterically laughing and Loretta was wiping tears of joy from her face. She had shared many funny stories with Willis about her and her sisters as the night wore on. Willis was enjoying each story and the beautiful woman who told them with accompanying animation. He loved to see her smile and laugh as much as he loved to hear her sing.

"...and then my father said, '*Young man, I think you have the wrong house!*' and slammed the door right in his face," Loretta said dramatically and laughed out loud, with Willis following suit. "He wouldn't let any of us out of the house for a month," she said and laughed again. "We could have been stars in a modern-day version of Louisa May Alcott's *Little Women* and its sequel, *Good Wives*. Kayla would have been a perfect Jo March. She's not the oldest, but she's the most uninhibited. Our parents made sure all of us made the right match and married well."

"Sounds a lot like what I would say to some scruffy-looking character who came calling on Jessica." Willis smirked. "I guess fathers are all alike."

"Not all of them," Loretta said under her breath. She remembered the occasions when Randolph would parade Elizabeth around in front of his clients, as if she were part of his bargain. She brushed the thought aside. Libby was fine now that she was away from her father.

So was Randy who his father pushed to date 'all the right young women' to further his father's public and private needs. When Randy found out his father was sleeping with a young woman he was seriously dating, he was crushed. That incident caused a deep rift between father and son that still had not healed.

Her family had been torn asunder and now the final blow—a divorce. She felt the urge to cry, but fought it. She rose from the table and washed the few dishes. Willis dried them and put them away.

"I should go to bed now," she said, pulling the silky robe close at the neck and waist.

Willis was not ready to let her go. All night, he watched her smiling face and just as suddenly, something unpleasant put a pall on her otherwise lovely demeanor. The way the lace of her nightgown caressed her breasts had him enthralled, but he knew where these thoughts would lead so he pushed them out of his mind.

"Yes, it's very late. Maybe we can both sleep now."

They silently and slowly walked down the hallway, stopping in front of Loretta's bedroom door.

"Well, goodnight, Willis," she said softly, as she turned and looked up into his mesmerizing, obsidian eyes. She had an overwhelming urge to kiss him and she did as she tiptoed and planted a soft chaste kiss to the right of his mouth.

That was the straw that broke the camel's back, so to speak. Willis took the opportunity to turn into the kiss and gathered Loretta into his embrace. It was something he ached to do for far too long since the last time he kissed her on the beach. A needful murmur escaped Loretta's throat that caused Willis to deepen his assault on her mouth. When he felt her arms slowly and tentatively circle his neck, he parted her lips with his tongue and feasted on her sweetness. She tasted of all that was woman, sacred and loving. He wanted her right then and there in the darkened hallway. He wanted to take her hard and fast, but somehow knew that would not be the way to love her. His mind fought with his heart and his body, but his emotions were winning the war. His passions won and he opened her bedroom door behind her, lifted her, and carried her across the threshold without breaking the hold they had on each other. Once inside, he kicked the door closed and moved slowly toward the bed.

Loretta knew she had surely lost her mind. She wanted this man. She wanted to give herself to him and that fact alone should have frightened her, but it didn't. When he took possession of her mouth, something in her soul followed. Soon her body was inflamed with a passion she had never known before. The feel of his muscles as he engulfed her, his natural, manly scent mixed with a hint of chlorine, and the intensity and power of his presence combined to render her senseless. Something akin to madness must have seized her body and her mind because she felt out of control. Her breaths came in short pants when he lifted her in his arms, but now she was breathless.

"Loretta," Willis said, lying atop her on her bed. "I want to make love with you, but I didn't plan this. I'm not prepared and I would want to protect you."

Something snapped inside of her and her sanity returned. Her body went ridged and Willis must have felt the change.

What am I doing? her brain screamed. She was a married woman! This was a man who slept with her sister! *Oh God*, she lamented silently, her mother was right after all. Lusting after a man would result in pain and not pleasure. She came to the edge and now backed away from her blatant desire.

"I can't do this. I owe my husband and only him my..."

"*Your husband?*" Willis asked in annoyed disbelief. "Where the hell is the son-of-a-bitch now? Where has he been for damn near two months when you've needed him the most?" Loretta began to cry silently, but Willis refused to be moved by her tears. "Go back to him then! Take him in your arms and love him!" It was hurt and anger speaking and Willis' rage would not be quelled causing him to storm out of the bedroom suite, slamming the door behind him. Immediately, his eyes slammed shut. Loretta was right. He had no right to demand intimacy from her. His hurt pride ruled his behavior. Going back into the room and apologizing would have been the right thing to do, but he heard Loretta's mournful cries and went to his own room instead. Once there, he picked up the telephone and dialed.

"This better be good," Michael's near breathless voice on the other end answered.

"What's holding up the arrangement?" Willis stormed.

"Uh, JW, it's nearly three in the morning and you want to talk business?"

"I asked you a simple question and I want an answer now!"

Silence hung in the air for a pregnant moment. "It's done," Michael said, none too politely. "Someone will approach her in a few days and..."

"I don't want to know the details! You handle it personally. It's time for me to end this! I'm coming back to the office!" he said, as he slammed down the telephone.

Chapter Ten

Loretta sat in a stupor nearly all the morning long. Nettie Baker, one of the chief cooks, brought breakfast to her room and suggested she didn't look well enough to practice today. Loretta barely said a word, while Nettie made small talk and forced her to eat.

Now Loretta sat alone, trying to fathom what was going on in her life. She needed to get control of what she was doing. Finally, she showered and dressed. She had to see Willis to tell him she was sorry for the way she acted.

Three telephone calls later, she felt she was ready. Now she had to face her life if she were ever to be a whole person again. Not finding Willis anywhere, Loretta went to bed early. The next morning she got into her Escalade and began the drive to her home. She had delayed this confrontation long enough. Now she was ready to handle her business.

"Ahhh," Randolph Mason heaved, as his heavy body released. "Damn, you're good, baby!" He laughed.

"There's a lot more where that came from, Big Daddy," the woman said, giggling.

"Uh, let a man catch his breath," he said, rolling off her and reaching for the pack of cigars on an end table. He lit up and blew out a long puff of smoke. The woman curled into his arms. "Thought you said this man was a friend of yours?"

"He is, Big Daddy, but he's been away. Some business trip or something. I've seen his wife around town lately, so he'll be back. That wench watches him like a hawk!"

Randolph slapped his companion on her naked butt. "You better not be giving him what you're giving me. I don't take to being second. You just keep him interested. The man would be crazy to stay away from you too long," he chuckled, "but you get me in to see him, ya' hear?"

"Yes, Big Daddy," she cooed, as she began to fondle him.

"You little devil," he growled, as his nature began to rise again. "Come here and show Big Daddy how much you love me."

"Mr. McCoy?" Erin asked, surprised to see him come in. "Uh, I mean, good morning, Mr. McCoy."

Justin didn't acknowledge any of the barrages of greetings with more than a nod as he stalked toward his office. Marilyn looked up from her desk, but hid her surprise. She gathered her iPad and followed him into his office.

"You have nothing scheduled for today, Mr. McCoy, but Mr. Hamilton wanted to see you whenever you returned. He didn't indicate a topic so—"

"Schedule it," Justin snapped, moving to sit at his desk.

"Yes, sir. There are a number of requests for conferences and business meetings. First, Mr—"

"Just schedule them all, Ms. Allen. You've worked for me long enough to know how to handle it. Now, if you'll excuse me."

"Yes, sir," she said, as she started to leave. Then she turned and walked back to his desk. "Justin," she said quietly. "You know, if there's anything I can do."

Justin looked up at his executive assistant's warm, caring face. He rose from his desk, rounded it to hug her. "Thanks for putting up with me," he said. "I'm sorry if I've been—"

"Don't you dare apologize," she chastised. "Now, get to work," she scolded gently.

"Yes, ma'am." He smiled.

Marilyn left the office and Justin tried to get back into his routine, but Loretta was ever present on his mind. By late afternoon, he had worked himself into a mild state of exhaustion. Back-to-back meetings were his routine before he went on hiatus at the Oceans Inn Resort, but now after only one day, he yearned to be back at the water's edge, listening to Loretta's beautiful voice. The telephone interrupted his wool gathering and Justin answered sharply.

"Yes," he said after punching the button.

"Mr. Hamilton is here to see you, Mr. McCoy. Shall I send him in?"

"Yes, have him come in," Justin said, as he rose from his chair and crossed the wide expanse of his office to the double mahogany doors. He opened them, extended his hand, and smiled. "John Harvey, this must be important for you to fly down here from Connecticut today."

"Justin, my son, it's always a pleasure to see you." the older man smiled, giving Justin a firm two-handed shake.

"Come in and have a seat." he motioned the stately looking man to a deep, leather sofa before a glass and Italian marble cocktail table and high-back matching chairs. "Can I get anything for you?"

"Just a little something to cut the cold," John Harvey said.

"Sure." Justin moved to the closeted bar. "Stolichnaya, neat, right?"

"You never forget. You're a good son, you know that, Justin?"

"Thanks, John Harvey. You've been more than a man could want in a father-in-law."

"Shame my silly daughter didn't understand what she had when you two were together."

"Is that why you're here?" Justin handed a drink to John Harvey.

"Uh, you're not joining me?" he asked before Justin sat.

"No, it's a little early in the day for me."

"Son, it's after five. I think you're going to need a little something to take the edge off what I'm here to discuss."

Justin furrowed his brow and John Harvey noticed. "Trust me, son."

Justin went back to the bar and poured a short drink for himself. He had hours more work to complete, but he needed to be clear headed before his day ended. Then he sat down across from his friend and mentor.

"To family," John Harvey toasted and then downed his drink in one gulp.

Justin seriously regarded his former father-in-law before he followed suit. He set his empty glass on the cocktail table between them, still eyeing the older man, sat forward in his chair, and clasped his hands together, resting his elbows on his knees.

"John Harvey, you're not ill or anything, are you?" Justin asked with grave concern.

"Me? No, son, I'm fine. I've recovered pretty well from my stroke. I get plenty of exercise and I eat right, thanks to you."

"You gave me my start in business. I owe everything to you."

John Harvey held up his hand to silence him. Justin saved his business and kept him on, paying him far more than he felt he was worth. He knew his news would rock Justin and he wanted to be there to cushion the blow.

"Justin, we know who's done what for whom around here. You tolerated my poor business practices until you were forced to take over to save my company. Then you tolerated my daughter's deceit and infidelities. I hope your level of tolerance for family matters hasn't diminished."

"It's Carla, isn't it? I'm sorry, John Harvey. I've been away for a couple of months. I should have, at least, called you. I know what a handful Carla can be, but I'm back now." Justin exhaled in frustration. "What has she done now?"

"You've been more than generous with my daughter, Justin. I know you paid dearly to keep her indiscretions out of the press and news media and you've paid her gambling debts when I couldn't afford to do it. After you divorced her you even paid off those two losers she married after you. I spoiled her and...well, that's another topic. This time it's not about Carla."

"That's a relief. So, what is it, John Harvey?"

"It's Jessica, Justin. She's pregnant."

The bolt of lightning that struck nearly knocked Justin off his chair. His little girl was pregnant? It couldn't be true! She was entirely too young! She shouldn't know anything about sex at her tender age!

John Harvey got up quickly and poured another drink for Justin. He could see Justin's reaction and knew he needed something. He looked as if the wind had been knocked out of him.

"Pregnant?" Justin repeated almost in a stupor. Then his anger rose. "I'll kill the bastard who touched—"

"Hold on, Justin. There's more."

"More? Damn it! What more could there be? You tell me that my daughter, your granddaughter, is pregnant and you expect me not to want to ring the bastard's neck who did this to her? You're crazy, John Harvey! I'll crucify him!"

"They say they're in love, Justin. They want to get married with your blessings."

"Married? The hell you say!"

"Justin, calm yourself. This news is disconcerting, I'll admit, but I've never seen you this angry before. You'll never be able to handle the rest of this in your current state of mind."

"The rest?" Justin huffed.

"Yes, Jesse asked me to come here, but she and her young man are waiting in your outer office." Justin's rage propelled him toward the door, but his former father-in-law nimbly stepped in front of him, blocking his way. "Don't make a mistake and lose Jesse in the process. Remember, she's your daughter, she admires and loves you, and most of all, she wants your forgiveness and your blessing. She hasn't had much of a loving family life just as you didn't, Justin, but she's still family. Try to remember that."

Justin's shoulders slumped. He closed his eyes, shook his head, digging the heels of his hands into his eyes. Slowly, he began to gain control of his emotions. John Harvey was right. He was much to blame for this predicament. He allowed Carla to ship Jessica off to private schools most of her life, thinking it was better for her than living at home with the animosity that existed between him and Carla. He thought she would be safe at the exclusive, private, boarding school in Switzerland. It had an impeccable reputation and many wealthy families sent their children there.

It was a far cry from his meager beginnings. His mother died when he was young and his father relentlessly chased women. His two older brothers were as distant from him as the sun was from the next galaxy. He wanted desperately to have a good marriage and a house full of love and children, but Carla was not the one he should have married for that. Someone like Loretta would have been the wife he needed. Certainly, he would never have betrayed her faith and confidence in him the way her husband obviously had. Odd that he should think of Loretta at a time like this. He cleared her from his mind.

"All right, John Harvey. I'll try to handle this more thoughtfully." He went to his desk and punched a button. "Ms. Allen, please send in my daughter."

"Yes, sir."

When the doors opened, a timid, teary-eyed Jessica McCoy entered. She looked from her grandfather to her father and then walked slowly across the room to stand in front of her father. Justin's heart was thundering in his chest, as she approached. Her fair, almond-colored skin, beautiful features, and slim physique made her look more like thirteen than seventeen. Reed thin with a youthful, rounded body, he tried not to think of the many times he had taken some father's daughter not much older than Jessica to his bed, but never a teenager. His Jessica was beautiful, sweet, and innocent. Their eyes met and held. Slowly, he took his hands from his pockets and she walked into his open embrace.

"Hi, Daddy," she said, as a flood of tears dampened Justin's crisp white shirt.

"Hi, baby." He squeezed her tightly while he kissed the top of her head.

"Please say you don't hate me," she cried, looking up into his eyes.

"Of course, I don't hate you," he said, setting her back from him and caressing her face with both hands. "I love you, pumpkin. I could never hate you."

"Carla said that...that..." she started, but fresh tears stopped her in mid-thought.

"Shhh." he calmed her worried brow and wiped away her tears with his thumbs. "Your mother and I don't see eye-to-eye on everything. You know that."

"She's very angry with me, Daddy. She refuses to accept David and...oh, I almost forgot." She turned and smiled at the two men standing in the office. "Daddy, this is David Vito Delaware and his father, Frank. David, this is my father, Justin Willis McCoy."

Justin's demeanor turned to stone as he regarded the two men—father and son—standing in his office. His head was throbbing, heart pounding like a jackhammer in his chest; he gritted his teeth and balled his fists. John Harvey's gentle touch on Justin's sleeve stopped the rage that was building toward overflowing inside him.

"Ah, Justin, my *boy*. Seems we will be connected again," the elder Delaware said, grinning. "Our families will be linked in holy matrimony. Now perhaps we can also do some business after the wedding of my son to your daughter."

Jessica turned from Frank Delaware to her father in surprise and confusion. "You two know each other? Daddy, isn't this a wonderful coincidence?"

Justin's eyes bore into the elder Delaware. He suspected this man would find a way to get back at him. A way into his business, but he hadn't contemplated it would be through his daughter or any member of his family. She was his Achilles Heel and Delaware knew it. He regarded the younger Delaware's smug smile. He was clearly over thirty years old. The Delawares used his daughter to get to him—and it was working. Jessica was precious to him, but he'd give his entire wealth to charity before he'd let Jessica be caught up in his business and hurt because of it. She had unwittingly already been used in the most heinous way and he would not make her pain worse by telling her who she had fallen in love with. Nor would he stand by and see her marry into a family whose nefarious dealings Richardson Investigations reported were the subject of more than one DEA and FBI investigation.

"Yes, baby, I'm acquainted with Mr. Delaware," he said tightly. Then he softened his tone and looked down into his daughter's doe-like eyes. He forced a smile. "Honey, why don't you and David wait in the outer office while I speak with David's father?"

"Sure, Daddy, but what—"

"Come along, sweetheart," John Harvey interjected, guiding his granddaughter out of Justin's office along with the younger Delaware.

Once only Justin and Frank Delaware stood face-to-face in the spacious office, the tension mounted between them.

"What do you want, Delaware?" Justin's jaw was ridged.

Delaware sauntered around Justin's office, assessing some of the priceless art on display.

"You have very good taste, my *boy*, in women as well as art. You see, I have often met your wife. Since she is barred from your casinos, she gambles habitually at my resorts. She does not frequently win, but," he lifted his shoulders on a windy sigh, "she is lovely to look at and so…adventurous…shall we say in bed?"

"I'm not *your boy*!" Justin said, barely controlling his anger. "Carla is a grown woman. She can sleep with whomever she wants." He would not permit Delaware to see that mentioning Carla would get a rise out of him, particularly for John Harvey's sake, but Jessica was a different story altogether. Controlling his rage took herculean effort. "I asked you what you want to get your bastard son out of my daughter's life. I also want Carla's access to your resorts cut off."

Delaware's brow knitted. "I offer my son to your daughter for marriage in friendship. Do you treat that offer as a privilege many have sought to gain my favor? No, you do not. Yet you think your daughter, she's too good for him, don't you? Mr. High and Mighty Wheeler Dealer! Your father and brothers sell cheap shoes on that Internet. You come from nothing! Still, I offer you everything! How dare you treat me like some common thug! You've caused me some degree of dishonor in my family. I deserve respect and so does my son! We will get it from you, *boy*!"

"You deserve *nothing* from me!" Justin raged. "Or her mother or from my daughter! I do not seek your favor and I do not ask to wed my daughter to your son. Now I'm asking you for the very last time. *What. Do. You. Want?*"

Delaware regarded the vehemence in Justin's demeanor. "Forty-nine percent of McCoy Enterprises and International," he said quickly.

"Done! Now keep that bastard away from my daughter, stop allowing Carla to gamble at your resorts, and get the hell out of my office!"

Delaware was clearly shocked. His eyes bucked, but he sensed properly he dared not press McCoy further. He could and would be dealt with later. Once he got what he wanted, McCoy was expendable. He would meet with some unfortunate accident. The Delaware family would have access to McCoy Industries through the daughter, the heir to the McCoy empire. She would be easily manipulated as his son's wife. After they were married, David would slap the McCoy heiress around as he did all of his women to bring her to heel. He turned and walked toward the door. With his hand on the knob, he turned and looked over his shoulder at Justin. "Humph, and I thought you were tough," he said, laughing derisively. Then he slid out of the door and was gone.

"I am, you bastard," Justin said after the door closed. "You'll see just how tough I am."

After Justin talked again with his daughter, arranging to have dinner with her and her grandfather that night at their home in the Maryland suburbs, outside of Washington, DC, he paced his office. He summoned Michael Rodgers and shortly his friend entered his office.

"We've got work to do," Justin said, without preamble as he paced. "I need for you to call in a few favors for me."

Michael drew an uneasy breath, dug his hand in his pocket for his cell phone, and dialed one number.

Loretta took Daryl's outstretched hand to climb out of the back seat of the Cadillac SUV. Elizabeth came around the car accompanied by Randolph Junior to stand by her side. She looked up at the mansion where she spent much of her married life. The "For Sale" sign swung gently in the fall breeze. Loretta looked around the neatly manicured and landscaped lawn and to the dying fall flowers. She planted every bush, every flower, and every tree with her own hands. This house was her life, her showcase. Now it looked like the monster that devoured her youth.

"Mama?" Daryl asked. "Are you sure you want to do this?"

New eyes looked at her youngest son and then to Elizabeth and Randolph Junior. "He's your father and he's been my husband for many years."

"Mama," Elizabeth said. "It's not necessary for you to put yourself through this."

"She's right," Randy agreed. "When you called and asked us to meet you, frankly we thought you were just coming back to pack your things."

Loretta smiled at the three she raised. "I'm through with running from my life. I want to do this, to bring proper closure to this segment of our family life, and I want to do it with all of you here with us."

"All right, if that's the way you want it," Daryl said.

They advanced from the circular driveway toward the front door. Randolph Junior opened it and stood back to let Loretta enter first. Immediately, they heard a woman's laughter and Randolph's deep, lust-filled voice. Undaunted, Loretta moved forward through the wide, black-and-white tile, two-story vestibule, large enough to be considered a room, toward the expansive living room.

"Baby, baby," Randolph growled from an unseen location. "You got some ass on you! Come on and give Big Daddy some of that...oooh, yeah, baby, suck that—"

"Excuse me," Loretta said, standing at the door to the living room. "Did we come at a bad time?"

Randolph's head popped up from one of the sofas followed by a redhead.

"Oh, I didn't know you were entertaining a guest," Loretta said and smiled sweetly; one hand on her hip, the other sprayed over her chest as if in surprise. "Well, hello, Maloney. How are you?"

"Retta? Is that you?" Randolph Senior asked, clearly not sure whether the vision of loveliness standing before him was his former wife. She was wearing a plum-colored suit with a short jacket and a short, hip caressing skirt. Her log, shapely legs looked like they went on forever in spiked high heels.

Then reality must have dawned as Maloney dove down deeper in the sofa beneath him. "What the hell!" Randolph began, still astonished to find Loretta standing at the entrance to the living room, looking like she stepped off the cover of a high-fashion magazine with their children at her sides.

"Hi, Dad," Elizabeth said and waved, moving to stand beside Loretta.

Each son greeted his father as well.

"What? What's going on here?" he demanded.

"I'm home, honey," Loretta said. "Don't let us disturb you and Maloney. Dinner will be ready in about an hour. You're welcome to stay, Maloney. In fact, why don't you call your husband and invite him to dinner, too...or if you're too busy, I'll call Roy for you. I'm sure I must still have his cell phone number or the number at his law offices. Oh, it is Sunday, isn't it? That means he's at the football game. He has season tickets, doesn't he, for the Atlanta team? They're doing well this season. I wouldn't want to disturb him just to fly back for Sunday dinner with us. Maybe he can join us another time for dessert."

With that, Loretta and the children turned on their heels and left the living room, closing the pocket doors behind them.

"Way to go, Mama," Daryl said quietly.

Loretta hugged him around his waist and smiled up into his handsome face so much like his father's. "Thanks, baby. Now, let's get these groceries sorted out and see what we're going to make for tonight's dinner."

"Mama, you sure have changed." Elizabeth commented, leaning against the kitchen sink, having a glass of wine as Loretta and Daryl continued to prepare a feast. "New hairstyle, makeup, clothes. You look *hot* and more like Aunt Kayla, but even better. What's gotten into you?"

"Life, baby. Your brother said something to me when your father and I were leaving him at college. He said, 'Mama, it's your turn.'"

"Your turn to do what?"

"Live, baby. Just live. I've lived such a little life, Libby. I've spent the better part of it trying to please everyone except myself. I didn't complain because I felt it was my responsibility, my duty to take care of everyone. I was the mother, the wife, the homemaker, the chauffer, the general dogsbody. I simply forgot I'm included in 'everyone.' So now, it's my turn to take care of me."

Sunday dinner was served using the best china, crystal, and silverware with a beautifully dressed table and appropriate music playing in the background, but the atmosphere was deadly silent. Maloney had opted not to stay, claiming she had to get home and plan dinner for her husband, Roy, when he got back from the game in Atlanta with their children. No one objected to her departure. Randolph Senior sequestered himself in the den until time for dinner. Daryl, Elizabeth, and Randolph Junior set about their appointed tasks assigned by Loretta and then helped with setting the twenty-seat dining room table for five.

After dinner, Loretta took picture albums from the library, went to her bedroom suite to relax and read the mail that accumulated in her absence, leaving the rest of her family to clear away the dinner dishes and tidy the kitchen.

When she read the divorce decree that was stacked with her other mail, she didn't shed a tear. She was a divorced woman now, but, surprisingly, she wasn't depressed. Rather, somehow she felt like a heavy weight had been lifted from her shoulders.

Later, Loretta sat looking through family picture albums and packing them away. She sorted through her other belongings, marking most as donations and then showered and prepared for bed. As she sat placing fragrant oil on her body, she thought of Willis. She did not have time to say goodbye to him before she left Oceans Inn that morning before dawn. She closed her eyes and thought of the second magical kiss they shared. Taking a deep, cleansing breath, she wondered where that night would have taken them were it not for…Someone knocked on her door, disturbing her train of thought.

"Yes?" she called out.

Randolph Senior looked in and his eyes widened. Loretta leaned back on the chaise lounge, propping her arms around the curved back. She raised one knee and then tossed her hair seductively. One strap of her scant negligee teasingly slid down her shoulder.

"Yes?" she asked again, smiling pleasantly. "Was there something you wanted?"

"Retta, I'm, uh…I uh, just thought we should, uh…" His eyes scanned her provocative pose, and he stammered fitfully, licking his lips. "Could we, uh, talk about…things? Maybe the divorce was premature. I mean, it's legal and final, but, I mean, I've never seen you look… You look, uh, delicious."

"Why, thank you, Randolph," she said, shifting her position to an even more provocative one and wetting her lips. "What did you want to talk about? I thought you said it all months ago in the car after we took Daryl to college. You were divorcing me for uh, who was it now? I don't remember names anymore. There have been so many. Did you and what's-her-name have a nice vacation?"

He came further into the room, his eyes riveted to her body. "Uh, Retta, now you know I've always had an eye for the ladies, but, baby, you never looked like *this* before. I mean, now that you're back, we can, uh, maybe we can pick up where we left off and try to make things work between us," he said, easing down beside her and stroking her leg to her thigh. "Ummm, you smell so good," he said as he leaned toward the base of her throat to sniff. "You know I've always come home to you, baby, no matter what."

"Have you?" she cooed, stroking his face.

"Yeah," he growled, as he took her in his arms. "Now maybe I won't have to leave home to find some pleasure."

Loretta simply smiled, as he tried to arouse her. Two months ago, if Randolph had come to her with even the slightest offer of reconciliation, she would have jumped at the chance to rebuild her marriage. Now, he didn't have a snowball's chance in hell of winning her back. She could feel his temperature rising and she was doing everything humanly possible to encourage it. He was hot as a firecracker when he parted her legs and began to take her.

"Randolph," she breathed into his ear. "Do you have a condom?"

Randolph leaned back and suspiciously peered at her. "A condom? Why would I need a condom? You're my wife, for Pete's sake."

"Your *former* wife, remember? We're divorced. For our mutual protection, of course, you should wear a condom," she said with a Mona Lisa smile on her lips. "I wouldn't want you to catch anything, darling," she cooed.

"Catch anything? What are you talking about, Retta?" he demanded. "Have you been screwing around on me?"

Loretta let her languid fingers glide down Randolph's chest to rest on his totally erect phallus. She eyed him seductively, her lips curved in a slow grin. She heard Randolph's moan catch in his throat, his eyes slammed shut, and he bared his teeth, savoring her seduction. Loretta leaned forward, licking his lips lightly with the tip of her tongue. The beads of perspiration shimmered on his face as his grip tightened on her forearms.

"Ask me no questions, Big Daddy, I'll tell you no lies," she cooed against his lips.

"Day-am!" he spat.

Loretta eased out of his grip, slid off the chaise lounge, and sauntered from the sitting area to her bedroom door. She opened the door, leaned back against it in a provocative pose, giving Randolph a full view of her scantily-clad body.

"Good night, darling," she cooed. "Sleep well."

Randolph painfully rose from the chaise and crossed to stand in front of her. "Loretta, I—"

Loretta kissed her index finger and pressed it to his lips. "Maybe next time you'll be better prepared, *Big Daddy*," she cooed.

Randolph's shoulders slumped as he shuffled his hulking frame out of the door and then turned to look at her, pleading with his eyes. She closed the door on his obvious, burning desire for her and locked it. Loretta leaned her back against the door and quietly wept.

The next morning after breakfast, Randolph disappeared, vowing to return very quickly. When he did, he carried a magnum of Champagne, two-dozen, long-stem, red roses, and a huge box of condoms. Loretta was waiting in the living room when Randolph came in. A broad grin sliced his still handsome face when he regarded her relaxed pose on the sofa.

"Where is everybody?" he asked.

Loretta rose from her seat, stuck her hands into the pockets of her slacks, and raised her chin. "That's not important. What is important is this: I'm leaving you. I should have done this years ago, but I tried to love you. I tried to be a good wife to you. I tried to keep your home a place where you wanted to be—and should have been. However, you chose otherwise. You have degraded our marriage time and time again and I permitted it to happen. You have humiliated me in front of our family and friends and you have disrespected our home.

"You tried to use Randy to pimp women for you. Then you slept with a young woman you knew our son was serious about. You tried to use Libby to lure reluctant clients, and you tried to make Daryl walk in your footsteps, but you forgot something, my dear *former* husband: You forgot I raised them to be better people than you or I. They're strong, resilient young adults now and able to stand on their own two feet without either one of us.

"Now you've gotten a divorce from the best person who ever cared about you," she shrugged, "well, so be it, Randolph, but I don't want anything else from you. I've taken enough. Keep the house, the furniture, and your money with best wishes from me for your future." She approached him, pulling something from her pocket. She placed it under his nose and smiled. "I wore these panties last night. Just a little somethin' somethin' to remember me by, *Big Daddy*," she said derisively, placing the panties in his jacket pocket where she often found other women's used garments. She walked away from him toward the front door of the house.

Randolph was struck dumb. He pulled the lacy panties from his pocket, still holding the Champagne, roses, and condoms.

Finally, he found his voice. "Where are you going, Loretta?" he stormed.

She didn't stop walking. "Surfing," she said around an unladylike snort, as she walked out of the front door and closed it behind her.

Her children stood in front of a rented van filled with the only personal possessions she wanted to keep. She handed the keys to her Escalade SUV to Daryl as a gift. They helped her inside and drove away. Loretta never looked back.

Chapter Eleven

"When will she be approached?" Justin asked, as he steepled his fingers before him, his forehead resting on them, eyes closed as if in prayer. He had to make sacrifices in his life before and this one, giving up the woman he loved, was by far the most difficult.

"Tonight should be her last performance at Oceans Inn Resort. As you requested, I'll handle it personally. Tomorrow she'll be offered a deal. The contracts have been prepared and reviewed. We're getting another act in starting tomorrow night through New Year's," Michael said, regarding Justin's bowed head with a look of concern. "Look, JW, why are you torturing yourself this way? It's obvious Loretta means something to you. I should know. Over the years, I've seen you go through women like they were water. You've treated all of them well, but Loretta you've placed on some type of pedestal."

"She's a rare commodity. She's a good woman. I haven't run into many like her before and, as you've said, I had more than my fair share."

"Then why are you letting her go? You're pushing her away from you. Tell her who you are and how you feel about her. Let her decide whether she wants to be with you or not."

"What have I got to offer her?" he asked rhetorically. "I've mislead her since the moment I met her. I was with her every day since she came to the resort. She thinks I'm a kindly man who happened to be there when she needed someone to lean on. It's too soon for her to make rational judgments. She was deeply hurt and distraught when I found her sitting in her car outside of the Inn. She's beginning to grow and I want her to have her dream come true. Whether that means returning to her husband and family or moving on with her life. That's more important to me than my needs. She's more important—" he cut off his thought, steeling his feelings.

"The first time I heard her sing years ago she had such a fire in her eyes and an obvious zest for life and loving. She held that audience in the palms of her hands and she served them something like they were her own family. Just as she gives so much of herself now. I want her to get something in return for a change. I only want to hear her sing one last time. Right now, I can't be close to her or let on she means anything to me or she could be in danger." Justin raised his head. "Have you taken care of the other plans?"

"Operation: Tiny State is in play. All factions strategically located, but I still think this is a very risky business, JW."

"It is, but Jesse is worth the risk. I won't have her in the middle of this. I know you had to call in some painful markers on this one, Michael. Kayla Hill is still a sore subject with you."

"She's an itch I can't scratch," Michael said, as he rose from his seat. "Yet, without doubt she's the right person to spearhead this operation."

"I hope you're right because I'm entrusting her with my life and the lives of my family."

"Have you seen Willis?" Loretta asked Nettie, one of the cooks, as she supervised the preparation of the dinner for that night.

"Uh, no, Loretta, I haven't seen him. Do you want the white or red wine served with the second course?"

"White wine with fish. Let's go with the Moscato," Loretta said absently, as she continued to work, but her thoughts were not on what she was supposed to be doing. She hadn't seen Willis before she left to bring closure to her marriage and she hadn't seen him since her return.

She was busy most of the day looking for a small house to rent in the area and a car to buy. That did not go very well because she didn't have credit in her own name. She had a bank account now with an ample amount of money in it, she was on sabbatical from her job, and taking on a risky career as an entertainer. Essentially, she was starting from scratch. Her practice time with her band did go very well though. She was going to use some new material and the combo sounded better than ever.

After rehearsal, she walked back and forth between the lobby, kitchen, and other areas of the Inn where Willis was known to frequent, but as yet, he had not appeared.

Loretta looked at her watch. She would have to go and dress soon for her eight o'clock show. *Where is Willis?*

"Awful fidgety today, Loretta," Nettie observed, as she julienned white potatoes for au gratin.

"Not really, Miss Nettie. I'm always this way before a performance. Comes with the territory."

"Humph, seems to me you been looking out for somebody. Thought you would have settled down after goin' home and all. Can't say as you seem to be more like a cat on a hot tin roof since you got back yesterday."

"It's just nerves. You sure you haven't seen Willis, Miss Nettie?"

"Man's been gone a while. He'll turn up when he's ready. Always has and always will."

Loretta sat down beside Nettie, propped her face on the palm of her hand, and watched Nettie's hands skillfully separate the potato skin from the meat.

"You've known Willis a while, haven't you, Miss Nettie?"

"A while, I'd say," she answered.

"Do you know much about him?"

"'Spect I know as much as the next one."

"So?"

Nettie cut Loretta a sideways look. "What you wanna know 'bout Willis, chile?" She smiled knowingly.

"Just curious. He doesn't talk about himself much."

"Man keeps his business, his business. That's what a man do."

"Yes, but—"

"Now, chile, you stop studdin' on Willis and his business. He want you to know somethin', he'll come and tell you."

"Miss Net-tie," Loretta prodded, whining.

Nettie chuckled. "Go on with yourself, chile, 'fo you ease up on somethin' you can't get around."

"What do you mean, Miss Nettie?"

"Well, chile, you still wearing them weddin' rings, ain't chu?" She nodded to Loretta's left hand. "Lessen you a widow woman, you got a man somewheres. Willis, he a proper kind of man. He don't cotton to other men's women. Now you ease up on him, wearin' them there rings on yo' finger, you libel to get yo'self in deep trouble with yo' man. Not to mention with Willis."

Loretta chucked. "I thought you said Willis was a proper gentleman who wouldn't mess with another man's woman. So how would I be getting myself in trouble with him?"

Nettie smiled knowingly. "Storm's a comin' tonight." She evaded Loretta's question, which only heightened Loretta's curiosity.

"Net-tie," she prodded. "Answer me."

Nettie smiled. "Chile, these ol" eyes been watchin' that boy Willis since he wore short pants. Mine ain't the onliest one sees what's goin' on. He been studdin' you mighty much since you come here during that hurricane. Ain't no tellin' what be on his mind most the time, but, mmm umph, I sure can tell you been on his mind. Now, I ain't one for gettin' in nobody else's business, but that man got some unfinished business with you. So, don't you be worrin' 'bout where Willis is. He'll be around shortly. Now you shoo and go get pretty so you can sing him a pretty song."

Loretta hugged Nettie around the shoulders. "Thanks, Miss Nettie."

"Go on with yo'self, chile." Nettie chuckled. "Mind yo'self now."

Loretta went to her room to shower and dress while turning over Nettie's comments in her head. She noticed Willis frequently looking at her when he thought she wasn't paying attention, but other than the mindboggling, aborted tryst they shared, which ended with him storming out of her bedroom, he hadn't said or done anything considered "out of the ordinary." Maybe the rings were a deterrent, she thought, as she looked at them on her hand. She twisted them nervously and they slipped from her finger with ease. It was kind of a shock to see her fingers naked. There wasn't even much of a shadow from where they had been for nearly twenty years. Funny how her hands didn't even seem to miss them, she thought, as she dropped the rings in a jewelry bag.

Willis walked into the Inn after the eight o'clock show started. The storm delayed his arrival and the rain was pouring in silver white sheets outside. He shook off his damp jacket and laid it on a chair near the entrance to the dining room that was being converted into a multi-tiered supper club. The combo was playing "Journey," something he had not heard them use before as an opening selection. Then as the composition ended, Loretta's voice came clear and hauntingly from off stage. Quietly, he slipped into the room and found a seat near the back in the dark.

The spotlight focused on Loretta who stood with a microphone in her hand. She slipped smoothly from one ballad to the next, swaying and swinging on time with the beat. Her tones played joyously with the rhythm scatting old style, much to the audience's delight. They constantly and vigorously applauded her. The spotlight narrowed and focused only on her face. Her beautiful, youthful, smooth face, Willis thought, as he leaned forward on the table. Her eyes were sparkling and bright as he heard the first strains of "It's My Turn." She embellished the opening chords, starting from a deep tone in her voice register and effortlessly climbed to the highs. She sang as if the words were her own story.

Something was different, Justin thought. Her stage presence was dynamic, as usual. He had listened to her riveting tones each night since she began singing, each set improving over perfection, but tonight she sang with a deeper passion for the lyrics. He was captivated and so was everyone else in the room. Not a whisper could be heard. Eyes closed, swaying to the melodic tempo, as she repeated the chorus: *It's my turn.* People mouthed the words and got deep into the rhythm and the pace. Justin looked up at Loretta and caught his breath. She was incomparable. Her talent unquestionable. She would go far and do extremely well.

The spontaneous applause jerked Justin out of his thought. The combo picked up with "The Heart Is a Lonely Hunter" to give Loretta a well-deserved respite, but then he noticed it was Loretta on the piano, energetically stroking the keys. The combo gave her the lead and she was off, mesmerizing the audience and him. She picked up the beat with "Stars In Your Eyes," this time with the guitar lead. She sang the lyrics: *You've got stars in your eyes.* She was playing with her audience and they were loving it. She moved off the piano bench and the piano player slipped right in on cue, as she started moving in step with the music repeating the familiar reframe. Then she launched into "Do What You Gotta Do" and Justin thought she was lamenting her relationship with her husband. The thought clawed at his gut, as her plaintive voice filled each note with pain and heartache. She moved on to "Disguises." Justin was fully enthralled in her treatment of the music throughout the entire evening.

Between the two shows, Justin called the pilot to determine whether he could fly back to Washington that night. The area was completely socked in with thick fog and heavy weather. He decided to wait until morning. During the second set, Loretta donned a black, glittery gown that nearly stopped Justin's heart. Her voluptuous curves gave him more to cope with than his body could take and he closed his eyes to avoid staring so intently at her.

Morning can't come too soon, he thought.

Loretta released a deep sigh. *No Willis*, she thought, as she prepared for bed. She hadn't seen him all night. She was on a temporary high, but Willis' absence was bothering her as much as the noisy storm outside. She quickly showered and used the fragrant oil on her skin Kayla sent to her. She wondered where he was. After she dressed for bed, she started down the hall to make tea. Then changed her mind. It wouldn't be the same without Willis there to share it with her. When she returned to her room, she found the door locked. She didn't have the key and everyone had left for the night. She ambled down the hallway, trying the other doors to see whether any were open. Surprisingly one was. Willis' door was unlocked. She crept in. The storm had just knocked out the electricity, again, so she felt her way to the bed and crawled in. Within minutes, she was sound asleep, thoughts of Willis still dancing in her head.

Willis washed the cup he used and put it away. He missed not having tea and a snack late at night with Loretta. It had become somewhat of a ritual with them since the first night she came to the Inn. He threw his damp towel over his shoulder. His swim relaxed his tired body and the tea soothed him. He yawned as he walked down the hall toward his room. He paused at Loretta's door and listened. The storm must not have been bothering her tonight, he thought. He headed for his room, still yawning as he went.

Silently, he entered his room, dropped the towel and his robe on the floor, and climbed into the bed. He found a comfortable spot and fell immediately into sleep. As had been his experience of late, Loretta was the first vision in his dreams. He expected it would happen. It always did when he relaxed, but his dreams had become more erotic and realistic of late. Turning fitfully in his bed, he could feel how her warm, pliant body felt the night they almost stepped over the threshold from friendship into lust. It was so tangible in his dream he could still taste her lips. Feel her body pressed against his. Touch the roundness of her breasts and feel the firmness of her thighs next to his. He was in heaven and in hell simultaneously. His body ached with desire for her and burned with need.

Loretta's mind opened to the dream she dared not even imagine before. Willis' arms engulfing her. His hot body next to hers. Her breasts being fondled lovingly, then her buttocks. She inhaled a ragged breath as she turned in her sleep and lips descended on hers in the most erotic kiss she had ever known. Her senses heightened, making her hot with unfulfilled desire. Like the sun's early light beginning to rise, her nature heated. She wanted more of the dream to enliven her. A needful murmur caught in her throat as she dreamed Willis' tongue stroked hers. Her arms felt heavy as she moved closer to the dream. A deep lusty groan was bringing her from the depth of her dream. She had been dreaming, she thought, and then her dream became a reality.

Justin's eyes shuttered open. Slowly, he began to focus as they met two eyes that were also as round as silver dollars with surprise. He leaped out of the bed and turned on a bedside lamp. Thankfully, the new backup generators were working.

"*What??* What are you doing in here?" he yelled, oblivious to his nude appearance. His aroused state not of consequence to him as his heart slammed against the wall of his chest.

"*Me?* What are you doing here?" she shouted, clutching the sheet up around her neck. "I got locked out of my room. I didn't know what else to do and your door was the only one open! I came in here to get some sleep because I thought you were away!"

He looked at her skeptically with furrowed brow. "You shouldn't do that to any man, Loretta! I could have…I almost…I mean…never mind what I almost did to you!"

"I didn't do it on purpose! Can I help it if you…I mean, ahh!" she fumed, cupping her face and rubbing her eyes. "You should have said something!"

"To whom? I thought I was dreaming about you! Now here you are…I mean, you should have stopped me!"

"Stopped you?" she shouted, throwing back the covers and scrambling out of bed. She bent from the waist trying to find her robe on the floor.

Justin's eyes focused on her rounded bottom. He grabbed the back of his neck and bit out an expletive, but Loretta heard him.

"I guess it doesn't matter who's in your bed! Obviously you behave the same way!"

Justin's eyes grew wide. "Oh, that's rich!" he yelled, throwing his arms up in the air in animated frustration. "I'm in *my* bed, minding *my* own business, and *you* blame *me* for what I'm dreaming when I'm asleep?" His hands landed on his hips and suddenly he realized he was not dressed for this conversation. His manhood was as excited as he was frustrated.

The vehemence of the moment did not distract Loretta enough not to notice the fine physique that paraded before her. Her eyes strayed from his face more than a few times before something dawned on her. "You were dreaming…about me?" she asked, unsure she had understood him correctly.

Justin felt as if hoist on his own petard…literally. Now it was his turn to look for cover. He quickly found his robe on the floor. When he stood and wrapped the garment around himself, his eyes locked with Loretta's. Slowly, their vehemence began to subside and their eyes began to water, trying to hold back the laughter welling up inside them. They couldn't hold out for long and soon deep laughter filled the room as they cracked up at the series of events and how truly hilarious it all was. Eventually, they began to calm themselves.

"Come with me. I'll find a pass key," Justin said.

They moved toward the door, but as Justin reached for the knob, a clap of thunder and lightning sent Loretta slamming into his embrace and noticeably shaking. Justin closed his arms around her, trying to quiet her fears, fighting the urge to do more.

Loretta found herself buried in Justin's embrace, feeling safe and warm. His hand in her hair and the other soothingly smoothing her back were one thing, but his deep-voiced, calming words in her ear were quite another. Her mouth at the base of his throat, she tentatively let her hands slip around him, bringing him closer. She felt his soft kisses on her cheek and she looked up into his eyes. His head began to descend and she stood on her toes to meet him. Tentatively, their mouths moved together and their tongues began the dance of the ages—slow, smooth and silently. A sigh escaped Loretta and Justin's moan followed hers.

Justin was holding on by a thin thread, but he loved the magic of their slow hunger building within him. His hand palmed Loretta's head, holding her to the commitment that had been in his dream, but he had to back away. That was easier said than done. Finally, he broke the sweet torture and held her head against his chest.

"Loretta," he breathed raggedly, "forgive me. I've tried not to touch you, but I want you so much."

"We're not children, Willis. You were dreaming about me and, in all honesty, I have to admit, I was dreaming about you, too," she spoke against his chest.

"I don't want to take advantage of you. You haven't explained, but I sense you're vulnerable at this point and I won't make promises to you I can't keep. We should—"

Loretta put her fingers to his lips, silencing him. "Make me no promises," she murmured, gazing into his eyes. The silence was deafening. "Just make love with me or . . . I'll go back to my room." She turned toward the door, but that's as far as she got before Willis pulled her back into his arms.

He lifted her and carried her to his bed. Setting her down on the floor, he stood back, removing her robe. It pooled at her feet. She looked up at him with trust and warmth in her eyes. His eyes raked over her and his hands slid under the thin straps of her silky nightgown. Loretta stood statue still, looking into his eyes as he slid her straps down her shoulders. Her eyes closed and her knees went weak as his warm, soft kisses moved over her enlivened flesh. Her head rocked back, as he stole her breath away. Across her breasts and down to her navel Willis moved, following the path of her nightgown. Her thighs felt his hot breath before she nearly shrieked with excitement. Her knees wobbled when he brought her to his mouth. She silently thanked Kayla for forcing her to endure the bikini wax. The storm outside paled by comparison to the storm he built in her. Her inner lightning streaked recklessly throughout her body.

"Willis..." she breathed and then lost it. The fireworks imploded and expanded, filling her body with a serenity she had never known before.

Later, Willis felt Loretta's third orgasm and heard her muffled cries. She had responded to him so timidly and sweetly at first, but now she was a raging inferno. Loving the feel and energy of her body, he delayed his own gratification through a will power he didn't know he had. When Loretta arched up into his body and gripped his back with purpose, he nearly lost it all. Still, he had the presence of mind to protect her. He made quick work of putting the condom in place before he lowered himself into position. By degrees, he slipped into her womanly heat, the feel of her almost eclipsing his ability to stay lucid. Her liquid fire engulfed him as he deepened his thrusts. He sensed she would feel this good, but his senses had not told him how good she could be. He had underestimated her ability to drive him senseless. No woman had ever taken him to the heights he now climbed in her embrace. Pure magic came to mind and he feared he would never reach the same highs with any other woman. He sucked in air through clinched teeth and shuddered with each stroke. Loretta matched each movement until his heart nearly leapt out of his body. Finally, his thin hold on sanity escaped when Loretta, once more, cried out in her ecstasy. His cries for divine intervention followed.

Loretta knew it must have been an out-of-body experience, because she had never felt anything close to the rapture now engulfing her. Tears sprung to her eyes and she wept.

The cool air took some time to reduce Willis' body temperature. Perspiration moistened every inch of him. His heart slowly resumed normal rhythm as he gathered Loretta's body to his. He felt her hot tears mix with his sweat.

"Oh, no, did I hurt you?" he asked with sincere concern. "I'm sorry, Loretta. I've never acted that way before."

Loretta couldn't speak immediately. She shook her head against his chest and held on to him tightly. "No, you didn't hurt me," she muttered.

Willis craned his neck to look into her eyes. "If I didn't hurt you, why are you crying?"

"Because I've wasted a lifetime without knowing what it felt like to be loved completely. It's so wonderful."

A grin curved Willis' mouth and then a smile. "Tell me about it," he said facetiously. "It's a new experience for me, too. I've never been where you took me. It's like the way you make me feel when I hear you sing. You take me to another place in time."

"Me, too. For the first time in my life, I've seen paradise. The problem is I didn't want to come back to earth," she said through her tears.

Willis caressed her face and kissed her lovingly. "Let's go back there again, together, now." They did, many times, throughout the stormy night.

Chapter Twelve

Loretta turned into the warm spot in the bed. A shaft of light cut across her eyelids, turning them into kaleidoscopes of colors and movements. Adjusting her head on the Downy-soft pillow, she wrinkled her nose and wet her lips. Her tongue felt the puffiness and the sweet taste of Willis. Reaching a hand out, as she had done many times during the night, she searched for the warm, masculine body, the bunched muscles, and the hairy chest that had been next to her. When she found nothing, her eyes opened and the sunlight blinded her.

Listening carefully, she wondered whether he was in the bathroom, but she heard nothing. She raised her head enough to peer at the clock and blinked her surprise at the lateness of the hour. She rarely slept this late, she thought, as she stretched her muscles. Immediately, she felt more of them than she thought she ever had. A smile bowed her kiss-swollen lips. Willis.

Lately, she sang songs that talked of how a man could make a woman feel. "You Make Me Feel Brand New." "You Make Me Feel So Young" "You Make Me Feel Like a Natural Woman." "You Make Me Feel Like Dancing." "You Make Me Feel Your Love." She wished to feel all of those things, but never, until last night, had she felt so good that it made her feel like crying. She did just that. She had cried with a joy, an exhilaration she never believed was possible. Willis. He made her feel emotions that were sometimes foreign and often frightening. Her capacity to respond to Randolph's lovemaking from the beginning was always limited, but with Willis, she let go and soared to levels of ecstasy she had never knew existed. He touched her very soul when he made love with her. She no longer questioned what it was to be orgasmic. It was an indescribable state of being, and she wanted to experience it again, and again. Not with Randolph, but with Willis.

It was early afternoon when Bonnie told Loretta she was wanted in the office. Loretta had looked for Willis several times after breakfast and after lunch, but had yet to see him. She was on her way to start rehearsals with the combo when Bonnie stopped her to deliver the message.

Immediately, a grin crossed her lips and she gave the much younger woman a big hug before starting for the office. She wanted to hurry. She knew Willis would be waiting for her. Her cheeks flushed with the thoughts of the night before they had spent together. Her steps were light, as if walking on clouds. Her spirits were high when she knocked on the closed office door, and was invited to enter. However, her bright smile faded when two men stood as she walked in.

"Oh, I'm sorry," she flushed. "I thought—"

"Loretta, please, come in. We've been waiting for you," Michael Rodgers said, offering a warm, welcoming smile.

Loretta's eyes flickered from the man she had seen before who met with Willis many weeks earlier, to the other man in the room. He was also tall, but had blue eyes and dark hair, his face matinee-idol perfection. A Matt Bomer clone. His tan was just turning golden as if he'd spent recent time cultivating it. He had an ingratiating smile and healthy looking white teeth. Distinguished, she thought, when she approached. He looked vaguely familiar.

Her eyes swung back to the man who introduced himself as Michael. She had a sense of something about him, but couldn't quite put her finger on it. He was certainly as handsome and virile looking as she remembered from seeing him months before, but he had an edge about him, a suave, more debonair carriage. Mentally, she had to shake the thought away.

"Uh, I'm sorry, did you say you were waiting for me?"

"Yes, Loretta. I don't know whether you remember me, but I'm Michael Rodgers. I want to introduce William Chandler, Esquire. Mr. Chandler represents Advantage Entertainment."

"William Chandler? You mean *the* William Chandler? I've seen you on television on *MSNBC*, *Face the Nation*, *Meet the Press*, the *Sweet Justice* show, and in movies, and high-fashion magazines. You even own several magazines, *Stallion* and *Risqué*. You represent some of the biggest names in the sports and entertainment industry today."

"I should hire you to do my promotions," he teased.

"He's here to make an offer," said Michael.

"An offer?"

"Yes," William said, and smiled ingratiatingly. "May I say we're thrilled Advantage will be producing your first recorded music, handling your bookings, and—"

Everything was moving too fast, Loretta thought. Entirely too fast. She raised her hand to hold back the race.

"Excuse me, but I don't understand. What recorded music? What bookings?"

Both men chuckled at her confusion. Then Michael spoke.

"Please have a seat, Loretta. We have much to discuss."

An hour and twenty-five minutes later, Loretta's eyes were bright. Her head was spinning. Her hand trembled when a pen was placed in it and an X marked the spot where her signature was to be affixed. Placing the pen on the desk in front of her, she sat back in her chair, and combed nervous hands through her hair.

"Gentlemen, please. Let me see if I understand what you've said." She took a deep, cleansing breath. "Your company, Mr. Chandler, Advantage Entertainment, is offering me an exclusive, multi-year contract for recordings, theatrical appearances, Broadway shows, movie roles, domestic and foreign tours, publicity, and promotion. You're including in this deal a four-bedroom apartment in New York City, a chauffeured car, clothing allowance at some of the most exclusive designer houses, housekeeping service—"

"A helluva lot of money, too," Chandler said and chuckled. "You've covered some of the perks, but, in the entertainment industry, there are many more that contracts simply fail to sufficiently cover. For example, a personal trainer, beauty and body salons, first-class tickets and accommodations for you and your family to join you when you're on the road, are covered. Social occasions where you meet and greet other celebrities can't be predicted, but the professional exposure is necessary to promote your career."

Loretta was in a stupor. "I can't believe it." She said in complete awe.

"Believe it, because it's true, Loretta. You have been singing music written for and by other people, but we have very good writers on our label who will write songs exclusively for you. There is also a hot, young songwriter and producer, Matt Kennedy, who we're trying to work into your schedule. He has written and/or produced five of the last top ten music videos in the past two years. He also has several movies he had to score the sound for. You have a very unique voice and raw talent we believe he can help shape into the world-class chanteuse he has been looking for. We want to expand the horizon of what you do so well. You're going to be a superstar as soon as your name is affixed to this contract."

"I have to talk with someone, don't I? I mean a lawyer or someone?"

Michael smiled at her. "That's already been taken care of by your agent, Kayla Hill. She's had the contracts reviewed by Attorney Chandler, legal counsel and partner in one of the most prestigious law firms in the country and she's signed the contract as your agent. You need only sign—"

When Loretta swiftly rose from the chair, both men abruptly stood.

"What is it, Loretta?" Michael asked, concerned.

"Uh, uh, I need to think about this," she said nervously. Suddenly, she needed to see Willis. "I'll have to talk with Willis. He manages the Inn. I don't want to abandon him."

"Oh, Willis, well," Michael began. "He left early this morning. Since the repairs on the Inn are well underway, he's been transferred to another location."

This information hit Loretta with the force of a runaway freight train moving downhill. She felt for the seat behind her and sat before her knees buckled. The men sat as well.

He's gone? Willis is gone?

That news stunned her as she sat immobile staring into near space.

How could he be gone? He had just been with her, making love with her less than twenty-four hours ago. She didn't know how long she sat there in the silence before her vision cleared and she focused on the Mont Blanc pen being held out to her. Mechanically, she took it and scribbled her signature on the contract. There was nothing else to do.

Justin raised the fine crystal snifter of brandy to his lips and slowly sipped. The sudden sting of the liquor didn't bite as much now as it had a few hours earlier. However, this was the second glass of brandy he had since coming in from his office. He was at home at a reasonable hour these days. Jessica seemed to appreciate that he stayed to have breakfast with her each morning and arrived each evening before the dinner hour. Other than the live-in cook, a housekeeper, and Carlos, his driver, and general dogsbody, it was just him and Jessica. He hadn't spent many nights at his suburban estate at Havenhurst as he did when he opted to stay in his corporate apartment above his K Street offices in downtown Washington, DC. Of course, the apartment was more convenient when he had an overnight guest. It had a stunning view of the Washington, DC, skyline and was one block north and west of The White House. He spent weekends, if he were not traveling on business, with a companion in New York or Chicago, the Bahamas or Atlanta. Depending on the season, he might take a woman with him on a long weekend to Los Angeles, San Francisco, or Toronto. Now, with the acquisition of the Delaware Hotel Group, he would be spending more time in Europe. There were more opportunities in Africa and Asia, particularly in Dubai, for consideration, as well as South

America. He would be visiting each hotel only sparingly until Jessica's baby was born. At this time, she needed him and he would not let her down.

Justin downed the last of his brandy and set the empty snifter on the highly polished Duncan Fife table at this elbow. The music changed and Loretta's dulcet tones floated on the air.

His jaw tightened at the thought of David Delaware putting his hands on Jessica. Springing from his chair, Justin mentally reviewed the plan in his head as he paced his den. If it were not for Jessica and her welfare, and that of the baby she carried, he would have, with malice and forethought, taken a gun to the head of David Delaware and his father, and pulled the trigger. However, Justin had always been a patient man. Calculated what had to be done, the risks involved, weighed the pros and cons, devised the solutions, executed the plan, and then evaluate the results. That methodical approach served him well in business, but never in his private life. Business plans were as easy for him to devise and execute as breathing in and out. Private relationships with women were still a mystery. A weekend affair or a night or two involved in some loveless sex was the extent of what his time and energy allowed...

Until Loretta.

Justin dug his hands into his pockets and moved away from the fireplace. *Loretta.* Her improvisations on the keyboard filled his spacious den. He really didn't need to hear her because she was never far from his thoughts. Pouring more brandy into the snifter, he wondered, not for the first time, how she was faring. Was she happy living in New York? Was she adjusting to the busy city, her busy schedule, the cold snowy weather? Had she met someone? Shaking his head to clear the unwelcome thought, he returned to his comfortable chair. He couldn't think of her or the night they shared over two months ago. Placing the crystal snifter against his forehead, he closed his eyes. That's all it took to recall that night. To recall her face, her sparkling eyes, her melodic voice. *Loretta.*

Leaving her that morning was impossible, but necessary. She felt so good, so warm, so right sleeping in his arms. During that night, he reached for her many times. It was as if he couldn't get enough of her, be close enough to her, or stay long enough inside her. She was right. They weren't children, but it felt like making love for the first time for him. All of the excitement was there.

Her inexperience astounded and enchanted him. She responded to him like a new bride, eager to learn and explore. He felt like a randy young teenager. Each time they came together that night, he thought he would die from the absolute pleasure. *Le petite mort.* He wanted her, needed her...was *in love* with her.

He could admit it to himself now. There was no question in his mind. He was in love with Loretta Louise Hill. Probably had been infatuated with her from the first time he saw her many years earlier.

Now, his desire for her had grown, but it couldn't be realized. He couldn't face her after having misled her for more than two months, loved her for only one night, left her without saying goodbye, and manipulated her life.

Their paths might cross again somewhere in their lifetimes, but he wouldn't be any better prepared for that day than he was right now. He would love her in his mind and in his heart, but from a distance.

"Daddy?"

Justin's head sharply turned. "Hi, baby," he said, his morose dissipating with his daughter's smile. He reached for her hands and brought them to his lips. His smile faded only slightly as his eye-level view of his daughter landed on her slightly distended abdomen.

Intellectually, he understood the baby growing in her womb was part of her. Emotionally, the fact the child was also a Delaware disgusted him. Taking his eyes from her abdomen, he smiled warmly up at her and received a kiss on his pulsating temple for his effort.

"Who are you listening to? I don't recognize her voice."

"She's a relatively new artist who recently performed for a few months at Oceans Inn in South Carolina. Her name is Loretta."

"She's really very good."

"She is, yes."

"You've been so distracted lately, Daddy, I was worried," she said, smoothing his shoulder with her free hand. "It's good to see you relaxing."

Justin held her other hand and guided her to sit on the ottoman after removing his feet. Leaning forward with his elbows on his knees, he continued to hold one of her hands while smoothing away the vertical lines in her forehead with his thumb.

"Nothing for you to worry about, baby, but we need to talk." He caressed her cheek. She was so young, so beautiful, and so vulnerable. It took all of his powers of restraint and a great deal of his energy to explain why her desire to marry into the Delaware family at this time would be ill advised. He convinced her he wanted to give her a spectacular wedding and in order to do it right, the event should be well planned. He spared her feelings as much as possible, but it was very difficult to convince her to wait until after the baby was born before announcing the engagement and wedding date.

Her questions, about the nature of his business relationship with the Delawares, were more difficult to deflect because of David

Delaware's influence over her, but he had succeeded. At least for now. The Delawares agreed David would slowly withdraw from her and sever the relationship entirely when the deal was signed giving the Delawares forty-nine percent of McCoy Holding International, the new corporate structure Justin created to cover his offshore interests with the Delaware Group. However, Frank Delaware would continue to allow Carla to run up gambling debts at any Delaware Resort until one year after their deal was in place. That was the best Justin could negotiate under the circumstances. He had stopped Carla's ability to gamble at any of his casinos, but he couldn't stop her from gambling elsewhere. The merger was set to be signed shortly after the beginning of the New Year. With any luck, that merger would never have to take place, but he hoped his daughter, if not his former wife, would be out of the Delawares' clutches by then and well on her way to distancing herself from David.

"You're not happy about David and me, are you, Daddy? Is it because he's Italian?"

"No, baby, I'm not prejudiced against Italians. I just want you to be happy."

"David will make me happy. After all, he's more mature and more settled than most of the boys I know."

"Yes, sweetheart, I know."

"Then what is it? Why don't you like him?"

"I don't know him well enough to say I don't like him. I suppose any man who wants to marry you will have to prove to me he is worthy of your time and attention."

"Oh, Daddy, David is just so wonderful. When some of my classmates and I went to the Italian Riviera last summer for school break, David was there on business at his father's hotel, which is located near your hotel on the beach where my friends and I were staying. We met on the beach and he and his business associates were so nice to us. They spoke Italian better than we did and knew the hot spots to visit. They took us everywhere. Even after their business was over, David stayed to show me some of the beautiful villages in the countryside. Everyone kept telling me how handsome he is and then just like that David said he was falling in love with me. He said age didn't matter, that he didn't want to stop seeing me. He is my first and only love, Daddy. I want you to get to know him," she pleaded.

Hell would freeze before that would happen, Justin thought. If he had his way, David Vito Delaware would go straight to prison or hell soon. He didn't really care which.

Chapter Thirteen

"Wow! Will you look at this view?" Elizabeth exclaimed, standing before the nearly full wall of windows. She would have gone out on the terrace if there weren't snow piled nearly knee deep. Loretta understood her daughter's awe. The corner condo unit took in the East River, the Queensboro Bridge, and a view of Central Park. Her three-floor condo had almost as much space as her former home in South Carolina and none of the responsibilities for the upkeep of the common areas. The building held all the amenities she could imagine, a concierge desk in the lobby and a five-star restaurant next-door.

Randy and Daryl joined their sister at the window, while Loretta continued putting the finishing touches on Thanksgiving dinner. Her main floor had an open-concept, full view of the more than one thousand-square-foot living room space, dining area, and kitchen. There was a powder room, library, and office on the other side of the first floor staircase. The building elevator opened directly into her condo suite, as well as the upper levels. Kayla came down the stairs from the bedroom she shared on the second level with Elizabeth and found a comfortable spot on one of the deep, plush sofas to put her feet up. Loretta was pleased at the interior décor she had chosen from a very high-end furniture company. The furnishings she selected made her space feel more like a home rather than a showroom. That helped her transition into this new life.

"Have you seen this view, Aunt Kayla?" Elizabeth asked.

"Oh, yes, I have. In fact, I helped pick out this penthouse condo with your mother. The view from the rooftop deck is what sold it for me and, considering the contract your mother has with her sponsors, she is guaranteed similar accommodations anywhere in the world. I'm looking forward to other spectacular views worldwide."

"I can't believe all of this is happening so fast," Elizabeth said, coming to sit next to Kayla.

"I couldn't believe the television hair shampoo commercial Mama is in where she's on the beach turning in circles and her hair is flowing in the breeze!" Randy exclaimed. "I had to remind the guys in my med school study group she's my mother before I have to knock some heads together. That commercial is hot!" he said with pride. "I've been told to get your autograph before I'll be allowed back in my dorm room."

"How about that commercial where Mom is singing into this old-fashion microphone and all you see are her lips and then her eyes. Talk about hot! I don't wear a lot of makeup, but I went out and bought it just so I'd look like my mama," Elizabeth said, laughing.

"I have several proposals on my desk for other commercials and upcoming awards shows. However, your mother is doing so well in this Broadway show, the director has scheduled her to be in the cast who will begin a European tour after the New Year. Then she's been offered a part in *Jelly's Last Jam*. Then *Ain't Misbehavin'*. She'll be tied up for the next two years."

"I have no idea why they think I can pull off a role that requires I learn how to tap dance and is clearly written for a much younger woman."

"Mom, you've got to be kidding. You look ten years younger and absolutely fabulous!"

"Libby's right. That's why I think I should travel with you as a part of your security team, just to keep the men away," Daryl said, as he turned on his crutches, hobbled to a chaise, and sat with his foot propped up on a pillow. He sustained a torn anterior cruciate ligament (ACL) injury that occurred during the last home football game before Thanksgiving.

"I wish you could, too, but not because I need extra security or a chaperone," she said, laughing. "You really need to take care of your body. You know what the doctor said."

"This holiday is going to be a real bummer. I can't get around campus on these crutches, so I was thinking about sitting out the next semester."

A chorus of "oh, no's" rang out.

"That campus is handicap accessible, Buster," Kayla exclaimed. "Plant your butt in a wheelchair or a scooter and let the good times roll."

Daryl laughed along with his siblings, his aunt, and Loretta.

"What's on your schedule for Christmas, Mom?" Randy asked.

"I'll be working over the holidays until I leave for Europe. I'm in the studio working on an album in the mornings and then rehearsals at the Théâtre in the afternoons. The cast has been very helpful in getting me geared up for this role. Then, of course, I have the show every night and twice on Saturday and Sunday."

"You were fantastic in the show last night, Mom," Randy said. "It was like that part was made just for you."

"Actually, I sang that part in college for our holiday festival. *Dream Girls* is one of my favorite plays."

"Your mother brought down the house back in the day, but she's even better now."

"It was fortunate Jennifer Hudson had other commitments and couldn't finish out the Broadway show and European tour."

"You'll wow them in Europe, too, just the way you're doing here."

"Thanks, Daryl. I'm looking forward to it. I've never been to Europe or Asia."

"Since we can't get together for the Christmas holidays, do you think I could go spend the holiday at the Oceans Inn Resort?"

The mention of the resort immediately brought Willis to Loretta's mind. She left a letter with Miss Nettie for Willis, but she hadn't heard from him. She wondered whether he received it. She hadn't made time to find out.

"Mom?"

"Yes?" Loretta asked, trying to pull herself away from erotic thoughts of Willis.

"Do you think I could go and stay at the resort for the holidays?"

"Uh, aren't you going to spend some time with your father?" There was a sudden quietness in the room. Loretta looked from her sons to her daughter and noted the bowed heads. They seemed to be looking everywhere but at her. "Okay, what's going on?"

Randy spoke up. "Dad is angry because we helped you move your things and won't try to intervene in getting you two back together. He said until we help him, he didn't want to have anything to do with us."

"We won't help him, Mom," Elizabeth said. "Randy, Daryl, and I agreed the divorce was the best thing that could have happened for you."

"We know everything that has happened is a big change for you. It can't be easy turning your life around after so many years with Dad."

"Both grandmothers are nearly apoplectic because you won't go back to Dad."

"Yes, I know. They've made their positions perfectly clear on the subject of my responsibilities to the marriage. I regret your father and grandparents have been putting pressure on you."

"We'll go to midnight mass and pray for the dearly departed," Kayla irreverently added.

It took a second, but then everyone cracked up at Kayla's deadpan delivery. The mood immediately lifted and Loretta announced dinner was ready.

She could have let her cook prepare dinner or taken everyone out to the five-star restaurant next door or the ones within walking distance of her condo, but this was something she wanted to do for her family. It was a joy to see them enjoying the meal she prepared with her own hands. She admitted to herself all the preparation was relaxing and familiar, but she still had a show to do tonight. She would have so little time in the near future to have her children together so each opportunity was a cherished event. They, and her sister, would be with her until Sunday after brunch when they would all leave.

Of her three children, Daryl was the only one who enjoyed cooking, so she agreed to see whether he could go to the Oceans

Inn Resort over the Christmas and New Year's holiday to work in the kitchen. She left the resort on good terms with the management and felt they would be amenable to her request. She would talk with Miss Nettie to ease the way and maybe learn whether there was news of Willis. At least Daryl would be doing something he enjoyed. Randy and Libby were making plans with their friends to spend the holiday skiing in Vermont. That would be her Christmas gift to them. She gave her Escalade to Daryl. The paperwork was filed. Kayla would be in Prague, but planned to take time after the New Year to catch her show in London, Paris, and Athens. Kayla didn't think she could make it to Italy, Spain, Portugal, or many of the other countries where the show was booked to perform.

They had their own priorities, but for Loretta, even though the future was bright and exciting, she longed to share her time with someone special. At home in Columbia, she had many friends and acquaintances, but no one special. However, because her extended family was there, she was never alone for long. Her parents and in-laws used to keep her busy with one society function or the other. They expected her to chair committees and organize events. Now, though she was surrounded by people and constantly on the go, without someone special, she felt very much alone and sometimes a little lonely.

Strangely enough, she missed one exceptional person most of all. She missed Willis.

"What's on your mind, Daddy?" Jessica asked.

Justin snapped back from his thoughts of Loretta and noted his daughter and his father-in-law staring at him. "What do you mean, baby? I'm just enjoying Thanksgiving dinner. The food is great, isn't it?"

"Mrs. Talbert did a good job, Justin," John Harvey agreed. "I certainly enjoy her cooking more than what my cook puts on the table."

"That's because your cook makes you stick to your diet, Granddad." Jessica laughed.

Justin appreciated John Harvey's attempts to keep Jessica's spirits high and to keep her entertained, while he worked secretly with the government authorities to keep the Delawares from using his business to launder money or for other nefarious purposes.

"This is nice music, Justin. One of your new artists?"

"Uh, no. Her name is Loretta."

"She used to sing at the Oceans Inn, Granddad. Daddy always listens to her music these days instead of his favorite classical music."

"She's very talented."

John Harvey acted as an unofficial bodyguard for Jessica, though Justin had a very highly skilled security company, Richardson Investigations and Security, at work twenty-four-seven to protect his daughter and even her mother. Instead of spending time with her daughter during the holidays, Carla was gaming at the casinos in Monte Carlo with yet another lover. At least this one had money and was a prince of an oil sheikh's family from Oman. The Sheikh also had visible security for his son, so Justin felt reasonably assured the Delawares had less of an opportunity to kidnap or harm Jessica's mother. Clearly, the Delawares knew Jessica was his Achilles Heel. He would do anything and everything to protect his daughter.

"So, I was thinking Jessica could accompany me on my trips to see the Inn's interior," John Harvey was saying when Justin again honed back in on the conversation. "What do you think, Jesse?"

"I'd like that, Granddad. I might as well since David is working over the holidays and can't get away. Is that okay with you, Dad?"

"Fine, Jesse. You'll keep your grandfather on his diet, I'm sure."

Justin and Jessica laughed at the mutinous, but funny scowl on John Harvey's face.

"Ms. Vickie will be there, too, won't she, Granddad?"

John Harvey's eyes lit at the mention of his longtime lover and head interior decorator, Victoria Lang. She was a widow with three grown children and four grandchildren. Victoria was spending Thanksgiving in New Hampshire with her family at a cabin she and her late husband built when their children were small. Traditionally, the family spent Thanksgiving at the cabin each year and the Christmas holiday with their respective spouses' families, leaving John Harvey and Victoria to discreetly slip away for some alone time in the tropics.

"Yes, she is arranging her schedule so she can have a firsthand view of the renovations your father has underway and match the furnishings and fabrics to the décor."

"Great! I really like Ms. Vickie and, since I want to study design and architecture, it will be interesting to watch her work."

"She's a great role model," Justin added. He was fully aware of his father-in-law's long-term affair with Victoria Lang. What he didn't understand was John Harvey's failure to ask Victoria to marry him, but far be it from him to suggest such a thing to his father-in-law when he hadn't seen fit to settle down with another woman after his disastrous marriage to Carla ended. The thought of settling down hadn't crossed his mind until recently when Loretta came back into his life. With her, he would have been interested in pursuing a more permanent relationship, but it was too soon for her. From what he learned, her husband divorced her while she was at the Oceans Inn Resort. If the tears Loretta shed were any indication, the dissolution of her marriage was not her idea. All indications were, however, that she was thriving in her new career. He read the rave reviews she received when she stepped into the *Dream Girls Retrospective* role on Broadway. He also couldn't turn on the television these days without seeing her in one commercial ad or another. There seemed to be more ads directed at the over-thirty, near-forty population. She was in a new convertible luxury car ad with a handsome man. He felt jealousy, envy, anger, sadness; all of the emotions blended when he viewed that commercial.

Loretta's voice was getting the recognition it deserved and so was she. In fact, she was slated to be on one of the late night talk shows and to give a performance at Buckingham Palace. It would be a long time before Loretta would have time to breathe and positively no time for a relationship with him. Certainly not now, when his life was on the line and he had to protect his family.

He appreciated Advantage Entertainment, which was owned by Vivian Alexander Montgomery, one of Kenneth Alexander's sisters, taking the contract to record and promote Loretta's music and career. It came as some surprise that Kenneth's family already knew Loretta quite well. They were from places near each other in South Carolina. In fact, he learned Loretta's son, Daryl, dated Kenneth's youngest sister, Aretha. He also found out Kenneth's father, Dr. Bernard Alexander, and Loretta were both educators, colleagues, and friends.

It was truly a small world. He liked working with someone he could trust, so he and Kenneth were working together on other projects.

This problem with the Delawares forced him to bring Michael Rodgers into his confidence. Since Justin knew the Delawares were watching him, Michael was the go-between with the government through his relationship with Kayla Hill. They were openly dating, while Michael passed messages between him and Kayla's government contacts.

The authorities were building an ironclad case against the Delawares as expeditiously as possible. Every contact between him and the Delawares was under electronic surveillance. His phones were tapped with his permission. His wristwatch had a high-powered microphone installed. As long as he continued to maneuver and manipulate the Delawares into disclosing their illegal plans and activities, the government's case was getting stronger.

He was, however, surprised Kenneth Alexander was involved and instrumental in getting the government's electronic surveillance set up at his homes and in his offices. The special electronic device Kenneth gave him looked like a smart phone, but it did so much more. It was not only a tracking device, but also a microphone with an incredible range and about the size and thickness of a credit card. He was pleased the security measures were doubled to insure his family's safety.

"Now you sit yourself down right chere, chile." Miss Nettie prodded the rail-thin Jessica. "You been on your feet a tad too long. That's why you're feeling skittish and a little light-headed. Daryl, honey, you bring Ms. Jessica a glass of water, please."

"I'll do it, Miss Nettie. Daryl's still having a little trouble walking," said Bonnie Shay, hopping up to do anything that would get her noticed by Daryl Mason.

"There's a good girl, Bonnie," said Miss Nettie.

"Thanks, Bonnie," said Daryl from his tall stool near the vegetable prep station. He really appreciated his mother for arranging this job for him during the holiday break. Miss Nettie was a taskmaster, but a very good cook. Not necessarily better than his mother, but she was teaching him things he didn't already know about Low-Country Cooking. They were even working on new recipes together with his mother.

It also didn't bother him the pretty, young, server, Bonnie Shay, was eager to snag his attention. If his torn ACL wasn't such a hindrance, he might have already taken her up on her offers to go out on a date with her. She was his age and cute.

He wasn't pressed, but a number of his female friends wanted to get maternal because he was injured for reasons that might be construed as incestuous. He smiled to himself. In high school, he had to be careful because his mother was the Head Mistress of the school he attended and his grandmothers, on both the Hill and Mason sides of his family, were socialites and high-society mavens. He didn't have that type of restraint to deal with in college in Atlanta. As a Morehouse student athlete, he had more offers to have sex than he knew what to do with. He hadn't taken advantage of many because he was still interested in getting with the incomparable Aretha Alexander. On her college tour, she visited Spelman University in Atlanta and he prayed she would decide to matriculate there. However, she opted to accept a scholarship to continue her education at Harvard University in Massachusetts. That put a damper on his ability to continue to date her, but she argued she lived all of her life in the south and wanted to live in the north for a while. Going to Harvard would give her that opportunity. He couldn't disagree with her reasoning.

She was his date for the Jack and Jill Cotillion, the Links Cotillion, and the other cotillions his grandparents forced him to attend. However, Russell Greene, whose sister, Stacy, was married to Aretha's brother, Benjamin, returned from Asia to escort her to her senior prom. Aretha was his date for his prom though. Daryl hoped to see her sometime during the holidays if he went to visit his grandparents, aunts, uncles and cousins, but he learned her family would be in New York visiting with her brother, Gregory. He signed his first contract as a professional basketball player for New York. Chosen fourth in the NBA draft, his rookie year was turning out to be as big of a success as his collegiate career.

Aretha and her family would be in New York to see Gregory play in a series of home games at Madison Square Garden and in the Meadowlands. He wished that...

"What are you about?"

Daryl looked up into the eyes of the most beautiful kind. "I'm, uh, I'm..." He had to swallow hard and take a breath before he continued. "I'm preparing the carrots for a salad."

"You're the cook?"

"Not quite yet, but I hope to become a chef one day."

"I've never met a man who wants to cook for a living. You're big and tall. You look more like a football player."

"I am a football player, but I was injured before Thanksgiving. I play for Morehouse in Atlanta."

"Don't be daft. I mean *real* football." At his confused look she said, "Soccer?"

"Oh," he said, his brows beetled. "No, I play American football."

"I've seen your American football, but World Cup ball is ace. I like soccer much better."

He noticed her European-tinged accented voice, her thin frame, and then the bulge in her belly. "You're not American?" was all he could think to say after the joy of looking at her pretty face and then the disappointment of seeing the baby bump.

She charmingly giggled. "Yes, I am. I was born in Washington, DC. You can't get any more American than that. I live with my mother in England sometimes. It's just that I'm at university in Switzerland."

"You're still in school? Like in high school? I mean, you're pregnant, right?"

"Blimey, of course, I'm still in school...well, I mean, I'll go back and finish after I marry my fiancé and our baby is born."

Daryl shrugged and continued peeling carrots, his interest in her deflating. If there were ever a poster child for birth control measures, she was standing beside him. She was pretty, but on the skinny side. He preferred girls with a little meat on their bones and more pronounced curves. He knew, at some point in his life, he wanted to marry and then have children, in that order, but no time in the near future was that on his radar. There was entirely too much life to be lived before he settled down—that is, unless Aretha Grace Alexander snapped her fingers. Then he would have to reconsider his plans. He didn't hold out much hope she would do that with Russell Greene always around her.

There wasn't much else to do and only a few people around to talk with, so Jessica pulled up a stool and sat beside the handsome young man to watch him work. She hadn't met many American boys her age. Most of the young men she knew were wealthy Europeans, Arabs, Asians, Africans, etc., who wanted to live on their families' wealth without lifting a finger to be gainfully employed. This young man, whose big hands were skillfully peeling carrots, intrigued her. He seemed to know, at his relatively early age, what he wanted. That was a new and novel experience for her.

"So are you going to school to learn to be a chef?"

"Uh, no, not yet. I first need a degree in business and management. Maybe even a masters' degree. Someday, I want to open a restaurant. Once I get my degree, then I'll go to culinary school. Maybe even at one of the famous Le Cordon Bleu schools, preferably in France. In the meantime, I'm gaining experience working here over the school break and recovering from my injury."

"You're keen. You seem to have your life all sorted."

He shrugged. "I can't predict the future, but for the time being, that's my direction. What about you? What's your plan?"

"Plan? I don't know what you mean."

His brows beetled. "Do you know what you want in life, what you want to do professionally and, if so, how you're going to get it?"

"Well, after I'm married, my husband and I will settle down and raise our family."

"That's it?"

"Well, yes," she said hesitantly.

"What about school? You do plan to finish school, don't you?"

"Well, of course," she said somewhat indignantly.

"So, you're going to live in Switzerland?"

She looked confused. "Well, we haven't talked about where we will live."

"You'll raise a family with more children?"

She pouted prettily. "My husband will be there, too. I won't be, like on the dole or anything."

"Okay. As long as you know what *you* want. What does your fiancé do? Is he in school, too?"

"His family owns hotels all over the world, but mostly in Europe, Asia, and Africa. He works for his family and travels a lot. He's not in school anymore. He's thirty-five."

Daryl shook his head as if to clear it. "Thirty-five? *Wow!* You're what, seventeen or eighteen?"

"You Americans don't understand European culture. He's Italian and in his country, men marry younger women."

"American men do the same thing, but it's not cultural. It's called having a trophy wife." He looked at this young woman and sighed. He didn't know her, but wondered how gullible she could have been to get herself into this predicament and think it was the norm. Yes, men married younger women, but this woman was still a teenager preparing to give birth to a child whose father was nearly old enough to be *her* father. He shook his head again and continued with his task.

Jessica suddenly felt foolish trying to explain her relationship with David Delaware to a complete stranger. An American at that. Her friends at school didn't understand either. They thought David was certainly handsome enough, rich enough, but too old for their crowd. They dated young men who were around their ages. She had to admit, at least to herself, she felt awkward at times with David around her friends from school. He was frequently impatient with the things she and her friends liked to do, but he rarely brought her around his friends. He was an executive who traveled a lot and was often away doing work for his family's business.

David also took his executive assistant, Helga Lustrum, with him when he traveled. The tall, willowy blond, with big blue eyes and an hourglass figure was his constant companion. Jessica didn't particularly care for her and she believed the feeling was mutual. These days, though she was younger than David's assistant, she felt dumpy around her because of her expanding waistline. David assured her his frequent absences of late had nothing to do with her changing body size. His statement, that he still cared as much for her now as the day they met, somehow rang hollow for some reason. She had not seen him for nearly a month. He was traveling in Europe and would not be back in the United States for some time yet. He promised he would try to make it back into the country for New Year's, but her hopes he would keep his promise were dwindling.

"Hey, where'd you go?" the young man asked, bringing her out of her reverie.

"I was just thinking, that's all. Do you live here?"

"If you mean in the Inn, the answer is yes, for now. I have to ride a chair around to work. If you mean where am I from, I was born in Columbia County, South Carolina."

"Is that where your parents live?"

"Well, yes and no. My parents recently separated and divorced. My father still lives there, but my mother moved to New York City."

"Oh, I'm sorry. My parents are divorced, too, but it happened a long time ago."

"I'm not upset about it or anything, so there's no need to be sorry. My brother, sister, and I think our parents should have divorced years ago. We're happy for our mom who is now doing some positive things for herself."

"I wish I could say that about my mother."

"You two don't get along?"

"We've never been close, but my dad is great."

"There you are, sweetheart," an older man said, coming into the kitchen accompanied by an attractive, middle-aged woman.

"Were you and Ms. Vicky looking for me, Granddad?"

"You just seemed to disappear while we were touring the grounds."

"I came inside because I wasn't feeling well. Miss Nettie made me sit down in here for a while so she could keep an eye on me. I lost track of time."

"You shouldn't be on your feet so much in your condition. Why don't you go have a rest before dinner?"

"Thanks, Ms. Vicky. I am feeling a little tired."

"Then come along. Your room is ready."

She got up from her stool and put it back against the wall. Then she turned to the young man. "It was good chatting you up. *Cheerio.*"

"You, too, I think," he said, with a wry smile, and watched her leave the kitchen. How sad, he thought, and hoped the pretty, naïve, young woman wouldn't be in for heartbreak in her near future.

Chapter Fifteen

"Oh, you were absolute inspiring!" Sylvia Alexander raved backstage in the Théâtre on Broadway after Loretta's show. "You've changed so much I can hardly recognize you!"

Loretta happily blushed as she accepted hugs and kisses from Dr. Bernard and Sylvia Benson Alexander, four of their five children, spouses, and grandchildren, who crowded into her dressing room. It was so good to see her close friends, again. She and Bernard were both South Carolina educators, though he was now a State Senator having turned over his school, Summer County Academy, to the more than capable hands of Jefferson Logan, a former American ambassador emeritus and diplomat. She was told when students from Columbia Academy learned she would be on sabbatical for a year, their parents transferred them to Summer County Academy as dormitory students.

"Mom is right, Ms. Loretta," Aretha Alexander, her friends' youngest daughter, said. "I've heard you sing before when you organized our chorale to perform for the Presidential Inauguration, but you sound so awesome on this stage."

"Thank you, Aretha. I hope you're keeping up with your music now you're in college."

"I sing in the Glee Club for pleasure, but I'm not doing concerts or entering piano competitions."

"If you change your mind and want to embark on a theatrical career, you let me know. You have an incredible voice and musical talent."

"Thank you, Ms. Loretta," she said, kissing her cheek. "Also, thanks for the backstage passes. I'm sorry I can't stay and have dinner with you and my parents tonight, but, please, tell Daryl I said hello and give my best holiday wishes to him and to the rest of your family."

"That will certainly make Daryl's day, Aretha. You have a safe trip back to Boston."

"I will," she said, as she and her brother, Gregory, left the Théâtre for the airport.

"We've got to go, too, and get these youngsters to bed," said Kenneth Alexander, the eldest son of Bernard and Sylvia, as he and his wife, JeNelle, a US Congresswoman, and their children each took turns hugging her.

"We're out, too, Ms. Loretta," said Vivian Alexander Montgomery, Bernard and Sylvia's middle child. She, too, hugged Loretta, along with Vivian's seven-foot-tall husband, Dr. Charles Montgomery, and their countless brood of natural born and adopted children. Hugs and kisses abound.

Later, at Jazzabelle's, a popular New York City restaurant, the late night Théâtre crowd was thick, but when Loretta entered with her friends, Bernard and Sylvia Alexander, and Bernard's brother-in-law and sister, Romelo and Olivia Dixon, she was met with a standing, rousing applause.

"You deserve every bit of this acclaim," Sylvia said, as they were seated in a VIP section.

They had a lovely visit over delicious New Orleans-style cuisine. Pleasantly sated, they sat over their after dinner coffees and aperitifs to continue their chat.

"You must be so busy," Olivia said.

"I am, yes. This happened so fast I still haven't had time to take it all in or even take a breath. One moment I'm preparing to start another school year at Columbia Academy and the next thing, I'm on a Florida beach singing before several cameras and my hair is blowing in the breeze for a hair shampoo and conditioner commercial. Later, after several other commercials, I found out the agency that represents me and handles my bookings belongs to your daughter, Vivian, Bernard. She and William Chandler are partners in her law firm."

"It does, yes, and they are, but because she's a sitting judge on the Federal Appellate Circuit Court for the District of Columbia, she doesn't exercise direct control of her businesses. Much of what she has, was inherited when she lost her first husband, Derrick Jackson. He died so suddenly many years ago, but his wealth and holdings were enormous. Her law partners continue to handle his and her estates. Gregory oversees it for her. I think Bill Chandler handles anything to do with entertainment and sports. Although her law firm is still called Alexander, Carter, Chandler, Charles, Lightfoot and Towson, PA, David Carter is the current managing partner in her absence."

"I remember her first husband, Derrick Jackson. He was such a great professional basketball player before he left the sport to become a medical doctor; a pediatrician, I think. That was such a tragedy when he died. As I recall, they were married the year Vivian graduated from law school."

"Yes, in September after her graduation and passing the bar. Establishing the law firm for Vivian with her closest law school friends as partners was Derrick's Christmas gift to her that year. He died the following April on the same day their son, Derrick, Junior, was born, April 1. In fact, he died in the hospital nursery holding their newborn son in his arms."

"They were adopting health-challenged orphans, too, weren't they?"

"Yes, but Vivian and her new husband, Chuck Montgomery, still adopt children who have been abandoned and have health problems. Chuck is an Emergency Room doctor. He built Physicians' Hospital and a general practice near their farm in a rural county in Maryland."

"I noticed Vivian's very pregnant, again."

"Yes, she is and so is our daughter-in-law, Stacy, Benjamin's wife. They're expecting triplets."

"They're both still in the military, right?"

"Yes, he's in the Air Force and she's in the Navy. They're both still stationed in Tokyo, Japan. Since they could not stay long in the states for both Thanksgiving and Christmas, Sylvia and I are going to visit them for a few weeks when the new babies come."

"You have family spread all over the globe."

"With Aretha in Boston, Gregory here in New York, Vivian in Washington, DC, Kenneth in California and Benjamin in Japan, Sylvia and I have accumulated a lot of flying time."

"It doesn't hurt that Vivian also owns Adventurer Executive Airlines. My contract specifies I use her ground and air transportation services exclusively."

Bernard smiled. "I didn't know that. It must have been something your sister, Kayla, arranged with Bill."

"It is, yes. She does a lot of traveling for the State Department and knows quality service when she sees it. I've been very impressed with the quality of service I've received."

"I'll mention it to Vivian."

"You two have every reason to be proud of all five of your children, Bernard. You, too, Olivia. You and Romelo have quite a wonderful family with your twin sons, their wives, and children."

"Thank you, Loretta. Our grandchildren are such a joy. We are very proud of both Donald and James and Cecil, and Janice, the women they chose as wives. You have every reason to be proud of yours, too, Loretta. From all accounts, Randy, Libby, and Daryl are all doing well."

"Yes, they are. They came to New York for Thanksgiving and we had a wonderful time. It's just that my parents and Randolph's are still angry with me and take it out on the children."

"What in the world for?" Olivia asked.

"The divorce," she said and laconically shrugged. "As you know, we're Catholic. Randolph is making it out to be my fault we divorced and I won't reconcile with him."

"Oh, *pisshaw!* He ought to just go somewhere and sit down with that foolishness!" Olivia fumed.

"I've heard that rumor, too," said Bernard. "However, no one who knows you believes it."

"Frankly, it's not anyone's business, but your own, Loretta," declared Romelo.

"Those who care about you are thrilled with your recent success and don't care about that other nonsense. Personally, I can't wait until you release your first recorded new songs written specifically for you," Sylvia added.

"I'm excited, too. I may even get to do a duet with your sister, Mariah, Sylvia, while I'm in France."

"That will be absolutely the best," Sylvia said enthusiastically. "Mariah hasn't recorded anything lately. She just finished a made-for-television movie where she plays the part of the incomparable Billie Holiday."

"I was in my early teens when Mariah was singing in her former husband's church choir. She was one of the first people to encourage me to sing and helped me to train my voice while I was still in high school and college. I hope my career in entertainment will be half as successful as hers is."

"We have no doubt it will. Sylvia and I plan to take a trip to Paris to visit with Mariah. Maybe we can arrange to be there while you are."

"Could you, really? That would be wonderful to see familiar faces in Paris."

"Benjamin and Stacy plan to see you and your show when you're in Japan."

"The hardest thing about all of this is that I don't have my favorite people along when I travel. With Randy in med school, Elizabeth in law school, and Daryl in his first years of college, they can't get away to travel with me."

"We're a phone call away, Loretta. You and I, our families, have been friends for many years. So, any time you're in need of friendly voices, don't hesitate to pick up the phone or turn on Skype. Our grandchildren have us on speed dial." Sylvia laughed. "We all hook up on Sunday for an hour or two. Nothing says you can't log in from wherever you are and visit with us."

"Thanks so much. I should do that with my children, too. I'm going to need the connection on this next journey in my life. I can't tell you how much it means to me to be with all of you. It is wonderful you made time to come to New York and see me. The four of you are such an inspiration; happily married for nearly forty years."

"Sylvia is my best friend and the love of my life. Maybe you'll meet someone on the next leg of your journey who will become your best friend and the love of your life."

Olivia placed her hand on Loretta's. "Always look forward, Loretta, but don't meet the new day with regrets. That's been Romelo's and my saving grace and, yes, we still love each other madly. Start fresh each day building toward a better tomorrow."

"Excuse me, Ms. Loretta? May I have your autograph?"

They looked up into the eyes of a middle-aged woman who stood by the table with a pen and show playbill in her hand. They noted others gathering behind a rope line her security team was establishing in the restaurant. This was a part of what William Chandler described as her obligation to promote her career.

Loretta smiled and took the offered pen and playbill. "What's your name?"

"Sara. Sara McPherson. You're such an inspiration, Ms. Loretta. When you were interviewed and sung that song, "It's My Turn," on the late night talk show, it was as if you were speaking the words in my heart. I've been a bank teller for a very long time. Because of you, I've decided to go back to school to finish my degree in banking and finance so I can move up in the company before I retire. My grown-up children think I'm crazy, but it's something I've always wanted to do. So, thank you, Ms. Loretta, for being a role model to women in the middle years of our lives."

"Thank you, Sara, and don't let anyone turn you away from your dreams. We dream girls have to stick together."

Chapter Sixteen

Justin paced the confines of the New York City Théâtre box-seat cloakroom as the aria on stage grew and other voices joined in. He enjoyed classical music and opera in particular. This was opening night for the opera *Porgy and Bess* with the incredibly talented Yvonne Kincaid in the lead role as Bess. He dearly wanted to return to his box seat before the end of the first act. He didn't like this cloak-and-dagger business one bit, but he understood and knew it was necessary to protect his family. Now the threat level had risen and things were spiraling out of his control.

"There has got to be a way to move this thing along without jeopardizing my family's safety," he said to no one in particular, though there were several people in the cloakroom.

Kayla Hill spoke up into the yawning silence. "You have specifically stated you do not want your daughter any more deeply involved. We have respected your position and understand your reluctance. She is a neophyte and would not do well as a covert operative. I must be blunt here, McCoy. Jessica is young, immature, and infatuated with David Delaware. We cannot attempt to interject one of our own operatives into the situation at this juncture, unless we put you and your family in a Witness Protection Program.

"As it is, your daughter talks with Delaware nearly every day. He asks her questions about you, what you're doing, how you feel about them being together. His interrogation is very skillfully done. We are sure he is being coached, but she doesn't realize he is pumping her for strategic information about you and your activities. He couches his questions as his attempt to get to know you better so he can ingratiate himself with you for her sake. He always talks about doing whatever he can to make everything easier with you for her. The problem is she believes him.

"Recently, she visited Oceans Inn Resort with your former father-in-law. Someone, perhaps one of your employees, may have mentioned to her you seemed interested in Loretta in more than a professional way. She told Delaware you used to listen to classical music all the time, but now you're always listening to Loretta sing and play the piano. In general conversation, your daughter mentioned to the Junior Delaware she hoped you were interested enough in Loretta to fall in love with her. She reasoned if you were, then you would understand how she feels about David. Then, according to her, you would know what it felt like again to be in love and this would make her relationship with David easier for you to accept."

"How naïve," Justin said, shaking his head in sorrow, regret, and frustration. "I really didn't think the music I listen to would register with anyone and certainly not my daughter. Obviously, I haven't done a good job of covering my feelings about her relationship with Delaware or even a passable job as a father either."

"Regardless, the very same day, Delaware's henchmen were dispatched to Oceans Inn Resort, posing as entertainment industry executives, to gather as much information as possible about Loretta."

Justin stopped pacing and stared. "You think they would try something involving Loretta, don't you?"

"It's possible, but that situation is under control. Loretta doesn't know Justin McCoy from a can of paint and I'm doing everything in my power to keep it that way."

Again, Justin stared. He should have been offended, but he understood her rationale. What intrigued him more at that moment was who was Kayla Hill, really. "You're more than what meets the eye, aren't you, Ms. Hill?"

"I'm what I need to be to monitor this situation."

"That does not answer my question."

"It wasn't intended to."

The two combatants stared at each other, frustration evident on Justin's face for everyone in the cloakroom to see. He didn't attempt to school his features.

"What do you specifically want me to do?"

"When the time comes, you are to move forward with the sale of a portion of McCoy Holding to the Delaware Group."

"The hell you say! Once that criminal element gets their hands on my daughter and my business there will be no getting rid of them! She would be at their mercy and I would be totally expendable after that."

"Oh, they'll get out all right. They'll be begging you to let them out so fast they won't leave skid marks on their departure. Then we'll have them exactly where we want them.

"This is the plan..."

"That was surreal," Michael Rodgers said later to Justin as they stood having a glass of wine in the Théâtre lobby at intermission.

"I'll say. Did you know before who you were dealing with?"

"Obviously not," said Michael straightening his neck in his tie. "I mean, I didn't even know the woman could carry a tune in a bucket, but she's got a hell of a set of pipes on her. I've known Kayla Hill is a government official for years, but I had no idea the parameters of her position. She has worked for the State Department for as long as I've known her. She and my mother are members of the same sorority and support the same women's organizations, causes, and agenda. That's how we met. My mother and Congresswoman JeNelle Towson Alexander hosted some charity ball to raise money for women's shelters. I was auctioned off along with my brothers, Ted, Bobby, and Ross, my cousins Mark Brooks and Rupert Townsend, and thirty-some other bachelors and bachelorettes. Kayla won a date with me. She out-bid several other women including someone I was seeing at the time. Our relationship has been a steeplechase ever since."

"You haven't mentioned her to me very often."

"She and I usually don't see each other that often; maybe four or five times a year at some remote or opportune location in the world as we did at the Oceans Inn Resort. She always keeps our relationship on the down low. I had no idea she would be there. Even after I ran that background check for you on Loretta Mason, I had no idea Loretta and Kayla are sisters. Her background information isn't listed anywhere. Even after I saw Loretta at the Inn, I didn't connect the dots until Kayla popped up. I didn't know anything about Kayla's family. She never talks about them or anyone else when we are together and I know better than to pry. Still, she has the uncanny ability to materialize out of thin air when I'm somewhere on a business trip. She never tells me she's coming or when she's leaving and she won't plan to get together before hand. Usually, she works with the diplomatic corps out of the State Department. She fluently speaks many languages. As far as I know officially, she's an attaché to the Secretary of State, a high-level diplomat, protocol escort for foreign dignitaries and primary contact. She never tells me anything pertinent about her tasks. I'm strictly relegated to booty-call status where Kayla Hill is concerned. She whistles and I come, literally and figuratively speaking. This? This open display of a real live date? It's not Kayla's style."

"If you ask me, Michael, there are still universes of information yet to be discovered about her."

"The only thing I'm sure of, where Kayla Hill is concerned, is I'm in love with her and I'm determined to one day be her husband."

"Yeah? Well, good luck with that."

"Yeah," Michael said, as he watched Kayla, Justin's incredible beautiful date, whose code name he learned was Satin, saunter toward them in the Théâtre lobby. Just as they arrived, the lights flashed signifying the end of the intermission. The final act of the opera *Porgy and Bess* was resuming.

Justin extended his arm to the young woman who was his blind date for the evening. It was all a ruse, however. Arriving in New York on opening night, his government handlers instructed him to walk the Red Carpet for the cameras and for those who were watching his every move. This date was a means through which Justin could meet secretly with the government officials handling the Delaware investigation. It was also used to downplay any idea the Delawares might have he was seriously interested in Loretta. He and Michael appeared to be out for the evening at the Théâtre and a late night supper; to give those of the Delaware Group who had him under constant surveillance the impression nothing was amiss.

Instructed to go about his usual routine, though he felt decidedly uncomfortable doing so with the knowledge Loretta's sister was his government handler. She didn't have a very high opinion of him as it was. Although he might see Loretta again, he was concerned about what information Kayla might be sharing with her sister about him.

The government factions, from the FBI, CIA, DEA, Interpol and other law enforcement organizations both domestic and foreign, banded into a strategic strike force that had the Delawares under intense investigation. The Delawares' strong-arm tactics were the catalyst for Justin to enlist the government's assistance with dislodging the suspected criminals from his business. His plan had been to inject a "poison pill" in his business to make it takeover-proof, but when the government agents and his own investigators, Richardson Investigations, explained certain facts, he had to alter his original plan.

He had to be very circumspect in his dealings with the Delawares because his family, particularly his daughter's safety, was paramount in his mind. He didn't take for granted how dangerous these people were and the dicey situation he was in. Francesco "Frank" Vizzini Delaware was the great grandson of Tommaso Cascioferro; Don Tomas, the boss of bosses, a man in his nineties in the Cosa Nostra in Palermo, Italy, who still ruled his family with a tight fist through his six sons, all of whom were in their seventies. One of his sons, Diego Valachi Cascioferro, was Frank's grandfather and would have been the perfect prototype for Michael Corleone. Diego positioned his grandsons, including Frank, in legitimate businesses with his handpicked Mafiosi to shadow and act as consiglieres (advisors). Frank's father, Pietro Delaware was handpicked to marry into the family because of the Delaware family's ownership of a legitimate, long-distance trucking business. Someone who disappeared in New York's Little Italy would be buried in the New Mexico dessert shortly thereafter. Although his marriage was arranged, Pietro did not stray because he had a healthy fear of Don Tomas and Diego. He was not a strong or fierce man, but his son, Frank, was. Don Diego Valachi Cascioferro made sure he molded each one of his grandsons to his exacting standards. Behind the scenes, however, the Mafiosi still controlled various illegal activities. The Delaware Hotels were a cover for laundering much of the money Don Tomas' family gained from extortion, prostitution, smuggling, loan sharking, the drug trade, human trafficking, and other disreputable dealings both in the United States and abroad. Frank was a highly educated and seemingly upstanding citizens, but he was not much more than a murdering puppet; his strings pulled by his grandfather and great grandfather through his consigliore.

Interpol and the CIA were involved because another Cascioferro, Salvatore Calabria was the leader of the most formidable criminal network known as Ndrangheta, the biggest cocaine smugglers in Europe. They had global connections in Argentina, Australia, Canada, and Columbia. With their connections built on blood ties through both religious and Mafioso baptism, they were nearly impenetrable. Daughters were compelled to marry sons of other bosses binding factions together through blood relations. That is what Frank Delaware was attempting to do through Jessica; bind Justin and his legitimate businesses to the criminal network by having David Delaware marry Justin's daughter.

The Delaware faction of the family was expected to 'make their bones' by killing someone, as a commitment to the family. That Frank Delaware enjoyed the killing aspect of his family tradition made him a favorite over his cousins in other parts of their family businesses.

Still, though the government believed they knew Frank's role in certain murders, they did not have sufficient evidence to arrest him or even take him before a grand jury. Witnesses and adversaries disappeared at his hotels never to be heard or seen again. The disappearance of Jimmy Hoffa was rumored to be among his more notable operations. Hoffa's interest in organizing hotel workers into a labor union was said to have offended Frank Delaware. Hoffa's disappearance solved the problem at all Delaware Hotels and Resorts.

Frank's young, teenaged wife, Anna, the very pretty daughter of a minor Mafioso, complained to her father she did not want to marry the then much older Frank. Two years after their wedding, Anna was overheard complaining, after the birth of David, she wanted a divorce and did not want to have any more children with Frank. A divorce was a no-no in Frank's family. Shortly thereafter, she, as well as her entire family tree, except her three younger sisters, ceased to exist. The younger sisters lived in Frank's home and each bore him many children against their will. The nearly sixty-year-old Frank kept them pregnant for the last thirty-plus years and heavily guarded, though he married none of his deceased wife's sisters. The three women were never overheard complaining nor did they wage a vendetta against Frank to avenge the death of Anna or their family.

With greater knowledge of the Delaware history and reach, Justin hoped these clandestine meetings would be over before now. Yet, the strike force wanted to not only haul in the Delaware crime family, but also the syndicate they were an integral part of all the way up the family tree to Don Tomas. Since the government was unable to indict Frank for multiple murders, several countries had to slowly and painstakingly gather evidence toward indictments for other criminal activities, including money laundering, human trafficking, and drug distribution. Yet, Justin felt there was much more going on behind the scenes than he was privy to. Hence, a date with this woman who was assigned to be his flavor of the month. She was certainly beautiful, but she had a certain edginess about her, a slick quickness. She seemed alert to the slightest change around them. He noted how she unperceptively and continuously scanned their environs. A quick look at Kayla Hill alerted him to the fact she, too, was much, much more than she appeared to be on the surface.

Chapter Seventeen

"Hello, again."

Daryl Mason looked up and did a double take at the intrusion. He was back at Oceans Inn Resort during spring break working in the kitchen. He was on his afternoon break while there was a lull in activity between the lunch buffet and dinner set up. "Hello," he gave her a distracted glance then returned to his friend's, Aretha Alexander's, blog about her biking trip through France. He wished he could have gone with her, but that other guy, Russell Greene, was always hanging around her. According to the pictures she posted on line, he was with her now. Just because Greene was some type of rising star in the art world and Aretha's brother, Benjamin, was married to his sister, Stacy, should not mean Greene got to spend all of Aretha's free time with her.

"What are you reading?"

"My girlfriend's blog," he said. Well, that was stretching his relationship with Aretha a bit. It is true she is a "girl" and they are "friends," but that was as close as they had ever gotten. He hadn't even received so much as a goodnight kiss from Aretha after he escorted her to the Jack and Jill Cotillion, other events, and his senior prom. He'd bet good American money Russell Greene got more than a peck on the cheek after he took her to her high school prom last year. Now she was off in freakin' France with him for ten whole days and nights!

"Who is the guy in all of the pictures with her? Is he a movie star? He's really cute."

"Nobody. Just some guy," he said morosely and shut down his iPad. Irritated, he started to get up and go for a walk on the beach. He didn't know whether Aretha got the special Valentines card he mailed to her place in Boston before she left for France. What he, and her gazillion other friends, got was a generic, on-line, Valentine's Day greeting!

"You didn't have to bite my head off," the young, more pregnant girl said. "You could have just told me to sod off."

He shook his head at his own rudeness. "I apologize. I'm not in the best mood, but I shouldn't take it out on you."

"Are you angry at your girlfriend?"

"Well," he hesitated a beat, "yes and no. I'm not angry with her, really. I just wish I'd known in advance she was going to be in France over spring break. I would have tried to arrange to be with her instead of here, but I found out about her trip too late to change my plans."

"She's your girlfriend, but she didn't tell you she was going to France?"

"Actually, I accidently found out. Her aunt lives there and my mother is also working there now, too. My mother mentioned it when we spoke yesterday. She said Aretha has a blog of her trip on line. That's what I was reading when you came in."

"From what I could see, your girlfriend is very pretty. She looks a little like the singer Janet Jackson when she was younger. Her smile is pretty like Ms. Jackson."

"Aretha's spectacular and absolutely brilliant, too." Daryl gushed. "She's always been a straight-A student and very accomplished no matter what she does. She's in her first year at Harvard University on a full academic scholarship. She plays the piano, sings, and knows how to fly a plane, too. Her brother taught her how to fly when she was just a kid. She got her pilot's license when she was thirteen. She's just as beautiful on the inside as she is on the outside. When the time is right, I want to make myself worthy to ask her to marry me."

"*Wow!* You really are gone over on her. I thought you had plans for your life and career. That's what you said the last time you were here."

"'Gone over on her?' I guess that's one of those European terms that means something like I've got a love Jones. If so, then I do, yes. I'm too young for marriage now and so is she. Maybe in ten or fifteen years, any time after we're in our thirties I plan to be established enough to step to her."

"'Step to her'? What does that mean?"

"You know, like get on one bended knee?" At her blank look, he said, "I forget you're not American, I mean you're not familiar with American terms." He shrugged. "It means we both have a lot to do before we'll be ready to settle down and start a fam..." he trailed off while looking at the young woman's distended belly. She was very pretty, especially her eyes. He could drown in them, but somehow he felt sorry for her. She was around his age, but by having a baby so young, in his opinion, she was cutting out a great deal of what life would offer a young, attractive woman.

"That's okay," she said as if reading his mind. "I understand not everyone is ready for the type of commitment David and I have."

"You're right. Good luck with that," he said rising from the table to stow his iPad and get back to work.

"You know, we never introduced ourselves to each other."

He turned back toward her and extended his hand. "Daryl Mason."

"I'm Jessica McCoy. My friends call me Jesse."

"Nice to meet you, Jesse," he said shaking her hand across the small, butcher-block table. Somehow, he sensed she was a little lonely and in need of company, so he sat again.

"I like chatting you up, Daryl. I'll be at the Inn for a week, while the new furniture is delivered and decorations completed for the spring grand reopening. Maybe we'll get a chance to talk again or have lunch or dinner together while we're both here."

"Maybe, but I'm here to learn and work with Ms. Nettie Baker. My mom got me this job as a waiter and as Ms. Baker's helper so I don't have a lot of free time."

"Haven't you gone out with the waitress, Bonnie?"

Daryl flushed. "Well, that's uh, different," he stammered, embarrassed. Yes, he went out with Bonnie Shay a few times to the movies and ended up spending the night in her bed at the three-bedroom apartment she shared with two other young women in North Myrtle Beach, not far from Oceans Inn in Atlantic Beach. He had to be at work at four o'clock the next morning and he hadn't gotten much sleep.

"How is it different? She tells everyone you are dating."

"We're not exactly...we're friends," he said, chagrined. Friends with benefits, he thought, but maybe he needed to clarify their relationship with Bonnie at the first opportunity. After all, Aretha Alexander is the woman he planned to marry. Until that day, he was just gaining experience along the way.

"Oh, there you are," Nettie Baker said to Daryl. "Time to start prepping for dinner. Bonnie said there are a lot of reservations on the books for tonight's dinner and show."

"On it, Ms. Nettie," Daryl said quickly rising, feeling saved by Ms. Baker's intervention. "I'll start the stock for the first course."

"There's a good boy," she said, taking the seat Daryl vacated. "How you feeling these days, Ms. Jesse?"

"I'm well, thank you. Do you know who is performing tonight?"

"I believe her name is Daphne Anderson," she distractedly answered while she consulted her lists of dishes and ingredients needed for the dinner buffet."

"Not Loretta?"

"Oh, no," she said while adjusting the menu to add pickled beets. "I'm sure Bonnie said a Daphne Anderson is scheduled to start tonight."

"So when will Loretta be back?"

"I don't think she's coming back to perform here. Why do you ask?"

"I wanted to meet her. Bonnie said my dad seemed interested in her on a personal level. He always plays her music at home."

Nettie turned away from her work on the menu to regard the girl. "Oh, I see. Well, don't pay that Bonnie any attention."

"She seems really interested in Daryl," Jessica interjected in an attempt at nonchalance.

Nettie, however, was a wise woman, not easily fooled. "I suspect she is. He's a big, strong, good-looking kid who has been raised right. Bonnie and Daryl's mother were friendly toward each other, but I don't see the relationship between Bonnie and Daryl going very far. Daryl will be back in college in Georgia in a little over a week."

"He will come back for the summer, will he not?"

"I suspect he will. At least that's his plan so far."

"Maybe his mother will visit him while he is here."

Nettie looked askance at the girl. "Why are you so keen on Daryl and his mother? You're about to be a mother and a married woman."

Jessica flushed. Something about the big, handsome football player, on first acquaintance, caught her interest. Maybe because her David wasn't around to keep her company. Actually, she was really beginning to like the Oceans Inn Resort for a number of reasons. The winter was milder here than in Switzerland and even Washington, DC. There was eleven inches of snow in Washington. With the installation of all of the new furniture and remodeling that went on, she was thinking about asking her father whether she could use the resort for her wedding and reception venue. It had a lot of old world charm with its antebellum appearance. It could have been the prototype for Tara in *Gone With The Wind*. She could envision having a period-style, destination wedding with everyone, including the guests, dressed in early eighteenth century attire. *David would look fantastic in a waistcoat and leggings*, she thought, and almost swooned. He was so handsome, virile with a great physique. He was her Mr. Darcy with his dark, curly hair he wore long. It would look rad tied back with a bow. It would make all of her girlfriends' pea green with envy seeing him there on her arm. Yes, that would be a cracking splendid idea. She would speak with her father at the first opportunity.

Maybe she and David could even settle down here. She was sure her father would let David manage the Inn so he wouldn't have to travel so much. She just had to pick the right time to ask for that favor, too.

Daryl was waiting for Bonnie to finish her duties as hostess in the dining room and working on creating a new recipe on his iPad when he heard a woman giggle. He turned toward the sound and did a quick double take. He stood from his leaning position against the front desk as he noticed his father approaching him with the singer, Daphne Anderson, on his arm.

Randolph was looking forward to getting Daphne out of her clothes as quickly as possible. He had taken the little blue pill an hour ago and was raring to go. That is until he spotted his youngest son standing in the lobby of the Inn. Of all the places in the world, why would he have to run in to him here and now?

"What are you doing here?" Randolph asked as he stood regarding his son.

"I work here," he said, looking his father in the eye.

"My, my, Big Daddy, is this your brother? He looks just like you," she lasciviously cooed eyeing him.

"Uh, uh," Randolph uncomfortably stammered.

"I'm his youngest son, Ms. Anderson," Daryl answered giving the woman the briefest of appraisals.

"His son?" she asked her face showing her surprise. "I know your brother, Randy, but I've never met you. My, you must be all of twenty years old."

"Not quite," Daryl answered, certain his father probably told this woman, who was in her twenties, he was still in his thirties. In point of fact, though he didn't look it, his father was over forty years old.

"Why are you working in a place like this? What do you do here?"

"I work in the kitchen as a sous-chef-in-training and, if we're really busy, as part of the wait staff."

"The kitchen!" he thundered. "This is more of your mother's silly influence, isn't it? You receive an ample allowance. I pay good American money for you to go to college and play football and you end up in somebody's kitchen?"

"It's honest work and I enjoy it."

"No Mason of mine is going to take us back to the days when kitchen help is all we could find to do! You will quit this foolishness immediately or you can find someone else to support you. You'll have none of my money while working in a hotel kitchen!"

"What's going on here?" asked Bonnie as she came quickly out of the dining room door. "I could hear the commotion all the way in the office."

"It's nothing, Bonnie. Let's go."

"Wait, Daryl," she said turning back to the man and the singer, Daphne Anderson. "Sir, is everything all right?"

"Who are you?" Randolph asked, eyeing the shapely young woman.

"I'm one of the hostesses for the dining hall. Daryl is my boyfriend."

"Boyfriend? Well, at least your mother didn't turn you into a complete pansy. You still have an eye for the pretty ladies."

"That's enough, Dad. I won't stand here and listen to you talk about my mother that way."

"Dad?" Bonnie asked. "Oh, I'm sorry, Mr. Mason. I didn't know Daryl is your son," she said, extending her hand. "Then your wife would be—" she abruptly halted her comment, uncomfortable watching Ms. Anderson possessively clinging to Mr. Mason.

He took her hand, rubbing his thumb over her knuckles. "We like to keep that information under wraps around pretty ladies, don't we, boy? Keeping it under the cover, so to speak."

"Let's go, Bonnie," Daryl said again, annoyed. He could hear the surliness in his own voice. He resented his father's intimation they would "tag team" women together. That's what he called it when he took Daphne Anderson, one of Randy's former girlfriends, to bed.

"Sure, sure, honey," Bonnie said hesitantly. "Good night, Ms. Anderson, Mr. Mason."

"Call me Big Daddy, sweetheart. All of my women do," he said, kissing the hand he had yet to relinquish.

"Uh, sure," Bonnie said, but Daryl had turned and walked away, leaving her to follow. She extricated her hand and hurried after him.

Daryl was waiting by the car door of his mother's former Escalade SUV for Bonnie to come out of the Inn. His father allowed his mother to give her car to him to induce him to spy on his mother. He accepted the car at his mother's insistence, but told his father he would not do his bidding. He was truly disgusted with his father for that and other reasons.

Whether anyone else noticed his father's boner, he wasn't sure, but he had. The woman he was with, Daphne Anderson, couldn't have been much older than his brother and sister, considering she and Randy seriously dated at one time. He didn't know why he kept expecting more from his father given his parents and heritage, but he was clearly an aging lothario too egotistical to respect what he had with his wife. Daryl didn't want to end up emulating his father in that respect. He would take Bonnie home, but he wouldn't spend the night.

The coast was finally clear, Jessica assured herself, before she left the secluded area moments after witnessing the incident between Daryl and his father. She was on her way to the kitchen to make a cup of tea when she heard the raised voice. She could have interceded, but Bonnie came out just in time to quell the disturbance. Then Daryl and Bonnie left and his father and Ms. Anderson went up in the elevator presumably to spend the rest of the night together.

Daryl was a big guy and looked the spitting image of his father. However, Daryl had a kindness about him she didn't detect in the older man based on her brief observation of them in the tension-filled scene. Yet, although his father was boisterous, Daryl remained calm and respectful and seemed even-tempered.

"What are you doing in here?"

Jessica jumped at the intrusion. As if she conjured him up, Daryl Mason stood in the half-light of the kitchen doorway. She was in such deep thought she had not sensed him there.

"I'm having a cup of tea. Would you like some?"

"No, thank you. If I was old enough I'd have something stronger."

"Tough going?"

"Yeah, something like that," he said as he came in, grabbed a bottle of water from the cooler, and then sat down at the butcher-block table across from Jessica. He was still reeling from the "tongue lashing" Bonnie gave him because of his attempt to clarify the terms of their relationship and his refusal to spend the rest of the night with her in her bed. "Tongue lashing" being a term of art she used to induce him to stay with her. He had his first ever blowjob in the front seat of his car. Yet he found the experience somehow incongruous with the fact the car used to belong to his mother, thereby rendering him incapable of rising to the occasion so to speak. Still, he found the energy to zip up and walk Bonnie to her door before he left to return to the Inn. He didn't hold out much hope he and Bonnie would remain friends after tonight. She accused him of thinking she was not good enough for him because he was in college, and, according to her, she barely finished high school. She had been working at the Oceans Inn Resort since she was fifteen as a waitress after school, on weekends, and during school breaks. He admired her work ethic and he told her so, but he also emphasized he wasn't ready for anything heavy to develop between them. That conversation went over like a lead balloon.

"You seem to have a lot on your mind for one o'clock in the morning," Jessica interjected. Daryl had gone quiet as she watched an array of emotions play across his handsome face. He developed a bit of a pronounced shadow of a beard that made him more handsome than without one. She could hear the bristles when he briskly scrubbed his face with both hands. His hair was thick and in need of a trim, yet it looked good on him.

She needed to stop looking at him like he was a dish of her favorite dessert.

"Yeah, it is late," he said again scrubbing his face. He was emotionally tired after the back-to-back altercation with his father and then the discord with Bonnie. "I think I'll turn in. I have to be up by four-thirty. Do you need anything else?"

"No, I'm finished with my tea and my little man seems to have settled down so I can sleep."

"Good," he said rising from the table. He picked up her teacup and put it in the dishwasher. Then he turned out all but the security lights. He escorted her to her room down the hall from his on the first floor. "Sleep well," he said on parting, leaving her at her door.

"You, too," she said to his departing figure. She really had to stop thinking about him. She loved David Delaware, didn't she?

Chapter Eighteen

Randolph purposely sat in the pretty, young hostess' section of the dining room having breakfast. Daphne was still asleep in her suite. He got up extra early to get his rocks off with her before the effects of the little blue pill completely wore off and then made a beeline for the dining room to seek out Bonnie. It would serve Daryl right if he took Bonnie away from him. Daryl, Libby, and Randy all sided with their mother against him. His parents were giving him grief about divorcing Loretta. He had to admit, at least to himself, it was not among one of his better ideas. In fact, it was a bit premature and impetuous.

His house sold above asking price after a lively bidding war with all of the furnishings included. His real estate agent confided the buyers were sold on the house and the landscaping because of the overall interior and exterior design and décor. That was Loretta's doing. The house was featured in magazines and on garden tours several times. Now he lived in a condo he had to hire someone to decorate. The place still didn't seem like a home. Somehow, it felt too sterile and impersonal. He also had to hire a cook and housekeeper. More money than he had to pay before and the services not nearly as good as what Loretta provided their entire married life.

Loretta was an excellent cook and never failed to be the perfect hostess for planning and executing his business events. The women he was sleeping with all seemed to be gold diggers or groupies who got off on sleeping with a famous athlete and didn't know jack about cooking or cleaning. They weren't interested in learning anything except how to spend his money. They always expected to be taken out for every meal, on shopping trips or for a good time. It was costing him a mint to entertain them, his clients, and potential customers.

He had a competent staff, but he was spending a lot more time and money going after the big whales like the McCoy Hotels and Resorts. He learned from Daphne last night the Oceans Inn Resort was a McCoy property. Something the hostess, Bonnie, said about Loretta caught his attention too. He was waiting for an opportunity to chat her up about what she knew about Loretta. If he managed to talk Bonnie into bed while Daphne was in rehearsals, all the better. It would serve Daryl right for defying him.

He had bigger problems to deal with than his wayward children. The economy had taken a hit and his business had fallen off in recent years. He was down to one-hundred-twenty-five employees. Natural disasters, like Hurricane Sandy, wreaked havoc on his underwritten policies and he needed an infusion of cash or his agents needed to pick up the pace to get through the remainder of the fiscal year without having to lay off more staff.

He used to be able to discuss these things with Loretta. Despite being lackadaisical in the bedroom, she had a good head on her shoulders. He couldn't talk with any of the women he was dating now about his business. His parents were right. Divorcing Loretta was not one of his best moves.

Just look at what she was doing now! He couldn't turn on the television without seeing her face. She even sang the *Star Spangled Banner* opening the Super Bowl! He was disgusted over the pitying looks he got from high-society people he used to call friends and acquaintances. Business contacts were actually calling *him* to talk about *her*! His own children wouldn't give him her contact information. However, if this Bonnie knew something about Loretta, then he would have another way to get in touch with her. If she had been working here and Loretta knew Justin McCoy, then he would have another way to approach McCoy without having to go through that Michael Rodgers character.

He looked up from his excellent Eggs Benedict just as Bonnie walked in and worked the room, chatting with people seated in her section of the dining room. He caught her eye and she smiled, moving in his direction. She was, indeed, a honey dip. He would have to take the little blue pill again today. He could already feel himself rising at the thought of sliding between her young, nubile thighs.

Chapter Nineteen

"Oh, that was such fun!" Loretta exclaimed, as she, Kayla and The French Mariah, Mariah Benson, sprawled on the upper deck of the huge, private yacht after dancing like teenagers to popular music. They were sailing off the coast of Le Havre, France. The day couldn't be more glorious. Bright sunlight, blue skies, deep blue waters, and not a cloud to be seen.

Bernard and Sylvia Alexander and Romelo and Olivia Dixon were still on their feet, dancing cheek-to-cheek to a much slower tune. Mariah's date and the yacht's owner, Christoval Oleg "Ollie" Ossian Aristotle, a Greek shipping tycoon, and his two equally wealthy friends, Octavio Kyriako Despines, who made his billions from his olive groves, and Andreas Leonidas Fotini, who had some of the best grape vineyards in the world, busied themselves getting drinks for the couples.

"I get a workout like that whenever Ollie is in Paris. He loves to dance and so do I," said Mariah, Sylvia Benson Alexander's older sister.

"He's truly an interesting man," Loretta commented.

"Ollie? He's the life of any party and a lot of fun, but he's a serial husband. He's been married and divorced more times than all of the Kardashians combined," Mariah said, laughing. "I enjoy him, but I would not take him seriously. He thoroughly enjoyed your theatre performance and wanted to help us show you a great time. Are you enjoying your surprise birthday party?"

"I was trying to avoid remembering this birthday, but I have to admit, I am, yes, thoroughly. Thank you and Ollie so much for arranging this," said Loretta. "Tell me, though, do you enjoy living abroad?"

"I do, yes. I absolutely love it. Don't misunderstand, I love my family and I miss them, but after my divorce, I needed a big change so I moved here. My parents, grandparents, and great grands were performers here in France with the great Josephine Baker. They lived here and toured all over Europe, Asia, and Africa until the war started. They and Ms. Baker closed up their homes and businesses here and went back to the states to live and work, but the American audiences weren't as receptive of them or Ms. Baker. So, when Ms. Baker returned to France to work with *la Résistance*, my people returned to South Carolina.

"My siblings and I were living with our grand Aunt Hanna Ivy while my parents and grandparents found work in places like Memphis, Chicago, St. Louis, Washington, DC, Baltimore, Philadelphia, and New York, but they didn't have much success until they started performing at the military bases.

"After the war, they returned to France, but it wasn't the same. Now, decades later, there is a tightly knit group of expats and entertainers who still prefer to live and work here in France. Many of the entertainment headliners from America and Europe like that I've kept my supper club decorated in the forties period and style. It's a little slice of history.

"That's how I met Ollie. He came in one night, with his entourage, without having made reservations. We were already packed to capacity. I couldn't accommodate him until after my last show. He paid every one of my staff and performers triple to stay and do a two o'clock show exclusively for him and his entourage that lasted until five-thirty. Then, he convinced my cooks to stay even later to make breakfast for everyone. We were all dead on our feet when he finally left at eleven o'clock in the morning."

"Ah, you tell the story all wrong, my love. I would have done anything to keep you talking to me. It was you I came to see, not your show, or your restaurant," Ollie said, presenting a drink to Mariah and kissing her tenderly. "The French Mariah is the toast of Europe, Africa, and Asia. I had to meet this fabulous woman. Now, I fear I will not live long without her as my mate."

"Stop with your foolishness, Ollie. You say that to all the women you meet."

"Tis true what you say, I do," he said, with his brows beetled in concentration, "but that is practice to find the right words to convince you to become my wife."

"Stop asking me and maybe I'll consider it." She winked.

Loretta sensed Mariah was only leading him on, but, after a disastrous marriage and divorce, Mariah was enjoying herself and her highly celebrated life as The French Mariah in France.

Though she loved everything about her hectic theatrical tour so far, Loretta still wished she could see Willis again. The tabloids had her paired with one man after the next because she was performing with them or because she was singing a duet with them for her upcoming album. The paparazzi dogged her heels here in France more than they did anywhere else. Although her security tried to keep them away, she knew photos of her and Octavio would end up in newspapers the next day. She worried Willis might see it and think badly of her.

"You look, I don't know, a little sad," Sylvia said, as she sat down next to Loretta in the seat Mariah vacated to dance with Ollie again.

She conjured a smile. "Not sad really. I was just listening to Ollie and, for some reason, I thought of someone I met nearly nine months ago back in late August. I was just wondering how he was doing."

"So call him, already, and ask."

"I can't. That would be too forward of me. Besides, I don't have his contact information. I didn't even find out his last name."

"He must have made quite an impression on you if you're thinking about him after all this time."

Loretta furtively looked around, leaned in closer, and whispered, "We had a one-night-stand," and then put her hand over her mouth and giggled like a schoolgirl.

Sylvia's eyes lit with merriment. "Oh, I see. Is that why he is so memorable?"

"Well, it's actually more than that, but we only had that one night together. The next day, he was gone and Kayla had me whisked away to start a new life. I didn't even have time to try to find out where he went. I asked one of the employees at the resort where I was staying to see whether she could find him and give a note from me to him, but so far I haven't heard from him."

"Maybe he didn't receive your note."

"Perhaps," she conceded, but she wondered whether he didn't really care enough to try to find her. She had to dismiss the silly notion she ever meant anything to him.

Justin put down the newspaper and took another drink of his scotch. Pictures of Loretta on one of Christoval "Ollie" Aristotle's floating bordellos were plastered all over the press and news media in Europe. He knew Ollie fairly well and he had been a guest on one or two of his yachts. Ollie stayed exclusively in McCoy Hotels or Resorts when he traveled. The photographer caught Loretta laughing with a woman identified as Sylvia Alexander, the mother of the industrialist Kenneth Alexander, Federal Appellate Court Justice Vivian Alexander Montgomery, and basketball phenom Gregory Alexander, known in sports circles as Alexander the Great. Wherever the multibillionaire went, the tabloids followed, even at sea, off the coast of Le Havre with guests aboard; there was no privacy to be had. Couple that with The French Mariah on board and there would be a media feeding frenzy and a blizzard of photos taken.

However, he had to admit he liked these glimpses of Loretta happy at last even if she seemed to be having fun with another man, Octavio, the olive oil merchant, who cornered the market in production for several years. For that reason he, too, was a focus of the press and news media.

Justin slipped the note Loretta wrote from his pocket. He read it countless times to the point the edges of the delicate stationary were fraying. He wanted desperately to go to her, take her into his arms, and love her endlessly, but that could never be. First, the threat was too huge now. He couldn't chance the Delawares would latch on to his interest in her and attempt to use her or threaten her safety to keep him in line.

Second, he didn't think she would forgive him for keeping his true identity a secret from her.

Finally, her sister, Kayla, had him by the short curlies. She didn't want him anywhere near Loretta because of his reputation with the ladies. She had a point. He did have a string of brief affairs with women, some much too young, like Daphne Anderson. Generally, he considered them flings, but he never cheated during his marriage. He had ample opportunities to be unfaithful to Carla, but he respected her and the sanctity of their marriage until the day he learned she didn't regard their wedding vows the way he did. That's when he became his father's son with a vengeance. Like his father and older brothers, he was willing to lay any woman with a heartbeat. His life was such a dichotomy from his early strict Catholic teachings before his mother died.

Apparently, Loretta's former husband, standout football player Randolph "The Bull" Mason, turned insurance company owner, was cut from the same cloth. Justin wasn't an avid sports fan, but remembered Mason when he played in the NFL. What he was surprised to learn was Daphne Anderson was, at one time, the love interest of the younger Randolph "Randy" Mason, Junior. She became the father's lover during the same time.

What Justin didn't know at the time was whether Randolph Senior had a hidden agenda and used Daphne as his intro or go-between to get the McCoy business or whether her interest in advancing her singing career was genuine. Justin knew she was lobbying for a contract to perform at his hotels, resorts, and conference centers. She certainly had talent, both in bed and out of it. She had a good voice, but he let his Entertainment Division executives decide whether to sign her to a three-year contract. They had and she was on tour at his hotels and clubs in the states. Her talent wasn't nearly as huge as Loretta's, but if she worked out, she would have her contract extended and be given a chance to perform at other larger and more prominent venues worldwide.

Of course, however, he would never be intimate with her again. The next question was whether to do business with her sugar daddy, Loretta's former husband. Michael Rodgers advised that Mason Liberty Mutual, Life, and Casualty was a reputable company with a good product line of business and personal insurance programs.

Generally, Justin took advantage of good business deals, but, in this case, he wanted what Randolph Mason once had more than he wanted the business Mason was offering.

He wanted Loretta.

She was the last woman he had been with in all the months since they parted and, as he slipped her note back into his pocket, he believed she would be the last woman he loved for the rest of his life.

"So, what do you think?" Jessica finished explaining her plan to her grandfather and Ms. Vickie over dinner at the Oceans Inn Resort.

She was so pumped, she failed to register the distress on the older couple's faces.

"Well, honey, you're right. This resort would be a wonderful place to have an eighteenth-century-style, destination wedding," Victoria Lang interjected into the yawning silence. Under the table, her hand gripped John Harvey's tightly bunched thigh muscle to calm the rage she knew and felt was building at the thought of the Delaware's continuing to blackmail his former son-in-law into letting them launder money through his company. "Perhaps we could talk more about it after the baby is born."

"That's just it, Ms. Vickie. I want to be a June bride. It takes time to plan an event like this, doesn't it? I mean, I want my girlfriends from school to be my bridesmaids. That's at least twelve of them who would need to plan to come here for three or four weeks before the wedding to have their dresses fitted and attend all of the pre-wedding parties. Then, of course, David will need even more groomsmen..."

"Wait, honey," Vickie interrupted. "You're talking about a large number of people. Wouldn't you want a more intimate wedding; maybe just your family and David's?" She silently shuddered at the thought of the Mafia descending on the quiet, seaside community of Atlantic Beach.

"Oh, no. I only plan to do this once so I want it to be spectacular. Then I want Daddy to let David take over the management of Oceans Inn. We could settle down here and raise our family."

"Excuse me," John Harvey said abruptly, rising from the table and briskly walking away.

Jessica frowned after him. "What's wrong with Granddad?"

"He's just heading to the men's room. That's all."

"Oh…" Jessica continued discussing the dream ocean-front and garden wedding she wanted.

"Of all the—" John Harvey fumed, rending the air blue with his vitriol while angrily pacing the men's room floor. If he had to sit there and listen to his naïve granddaughter another moment, he would have exploded. There were too many similarities between his daughter's character and his granddaughter's. They both were flighty, erratic, capricious, wayward, and impulsive. "Women!" he raged.

"Yeah," Daryl said aloud unintentionally, as he stood before a urinal. Bonnie let him have it right in front of the whole kitchen staff as soon as she spotted him and had been dropping little bombs all the damn day. Apparently, his father had asked her out on a date, behind Ms. Anderson's back, and Bonnie had accepted.

"What did you say, young man?"

"Uh, nothing, sir. It's just that a female friend, correction, former friend, has been riding my back all day and now she has done something incredibly stupid. You were saying some things I was feeling. That's no excuse, though. I shouldn't have been listening to your private conversation with yourself." He shook himself off, zipped up, and flushed the urinal before stepping to the sink to wash his hands.

"I've seen you before talking with my granddaughter, haven't I?"

Daryl looked at the man's reflection in the mirror. "You have, yes, sir. Your granddaughter is Jessica McCoy, right?"

"Yes, that's right. You are employed here?"

"Yes, sir, from time to time."

"You're not a part of the permanent staff?'

"Oh, no, sir. I'm a student athlete at Morehouse College in Atlanta. I only work here during school breaks."

"A fine institution, Morehouse."

"Thank you, sir. I agree with you."

John Harvey thought the young man very respectful and somehow humble, but with a joyous smile on his face. This was the type of young man he would rather see with his granddaughter, instead of that conniving Delaware whelp. Then he hit upon an interesting thought. "So you plan to come again for the summer season?"

"Yes, sir. I plan to be here as soon as classes end in May until I have to report for football practice in August," Daryl said, towel drying his hands and tossing the paper in the trash.

John Harvey extended his hand. "What's your name, son?"

"Daryl Mason, sir," he said, accepting the older man's hand for a shake.

"I'm John Harvey Hamilton."

"Yes, sir. I know. Your company, Hamilton Textiles, designed and built the new furniture for the resort. Everyone thinks the new color scheme and decorations are perfect for this type of inn."

"Thank you. I agree. I look forward to seeing you during the summer."

"Oh, here comes your grandfather now," Victoria said, and noticed the little smile on his still handsome face. "We were beginning to wonder why you were delayed."

"Oh, no reason at all. So, Jesse, I've been thinking maybe you should stay here at the resort and get to know the place on a more intimate basis. You know, get to know the staff and employees. You could be a big help with the grand reopening plans. That way, you will better visualize how your wedding would fit here or if not, have plenty of time to think of somewhere else you might want to hold it. You know your father has resorts and hotels all over the world. If you're planning to have a big, splashy wedding and reception, you may need a larger venue. Of course, your mother will want to weigh in on the plans."

"I hadn't thought of that. Staying here is a good idea because Daddy is so busy these days and Mother would definitely want to be involved. After all, her society friends and their families will be on the guest list. I admit, I really like it here, but I could take time to do a virtual reality tour of Daddy's other resorts and David's, too."

"That's true," Vickie chimed in, not at all sure of why John Harvey's demeanor changed so drastically, but liked the direction of his thinking.

Chapter Twenty

"So, what do you think?" Mariah questioned her younger sister, Sylvia.

"I think your daughter would make it work. Satarah has great ingenuity and intestinal fortitude. Now she's divorced from JoJeff, it would be a good place for her and the boys to make a new beginning."

Just then, Loretta walked into the first floor, glass-enclosed, garden conservatory in Mariah's beautiful palatial Parisian home.

"Oh, am I disturbing a private conversation?"

"Oh, no. Please come in and have a seat. How was your nap?"

"Fabulous. I needed it after Kayla's shopping adventure, but, if you want to spend some alone time together, I could find something else to do."

"Don't fret, Loretta. Olivia, Mariah, and I were discussing signing over property that belonged to our great grandparents to Mariah's daughter, Satarah Whitfield. She divorced her husband, Jonathan Jeffrey Whitfield, after he ran off with her older sister, Carlotta, and left their six-week-old twin boys behind for Satarah to raise. Jonathan and Carlotta took every dime they could lay their hands on and the only family car.

"My daughter and Jonathan were living in a little guest cottage behind the house where I used to live with my former husband," contributed Mariah. "Now he's turning Satarah, his own daughter, out with the twin boys because she doesn't have all of this month's rent money. My former husband is the devil incarnate though he calls himself a minister!" she fussed. "I wish I had seen this mean streak when I was fifteen years old and hot to trot after him. He was twenty-six and seemed so worldly to me. Well, after my shotgun wedding, Carlotta and then Satarah were born. It's Satarah who he has put out on the street."

"How is she supposed to survive with no resources and twin boys to take care of?" asked Loretta.

"Satarah graduated from my nursing school, so she has options," said Sylvia. "She's a qualified Nurse Practitioner and has been for many years. She won't take handouts so my daughter, Vivian, will talk her into accepting a small business loan to start renovations on the mansion on the property to turn it into a bed and breakfast."

"We just won't mention to Satarah the money is actually coming from me through Vivian's bank," said Mariah.

"All of our other sisters and brothers agree the property should be signed over to Satarah because no one else has the time or inclination to take on the responsibility this undertaking will require."

"Satarah is the perfect one of all of our children, the cousins, to take up the challenge to turn the house into a model of historical significance," Sylvia commented.

"She also needs somewhere to live now," said Mariah.

"That's a fine idea," said Loretta. "I don't know why I didn't think of establishing something as a legacy for Randy, Libby, and Daryl. I'll have to discuss this with Kayla when she gets back."

"Continue to do well in your new career, Loretta. You've got time yet to determine what you want to leave as a legacy for your future generations."

"Thank you for saying that, Sylvia. Regrettably, Randy and Libby have been so disillusioned by what they witnessed in our household, I'd be surprised if either of them decided to marry and have children. Daryl is the only one who may contribute to future generations and that's only if he can convince your daughter, Aretha, to take his interest in her seriously."

Sylvia laughed. "He and any other young man will have a long row to hoe and a short time to get there if they are interested in getting my Aretha Grace anywhere near an altar. Bernard and I would welcome Daryl as a son-in-law, but she is our wanderlust child. She intends to see the world and experience its wonders for a very long time. She has already signed up to work with the Peace Corp in Asia this summer."

"I've always sensed Aretha Grace will do great and amazing things with her life. She has such great talent for so many things. She will never live a mundane existence. Daryl has no idea what he's up against," said Loretta.

"True that," added Olivia, but never said she sensed her niece was already clandestinely working through the aegis of the Peace Corp to serve and protect. Her son, Donald, she believed, though she could not prove it, was intricately involved in the struggle to protect and serve on a global basis. She believed her other son, Donald's twin, James, knew some of it and she suspected he may have even participated in some way, but again it was only her mother's intuition at work. There was nothing overt or concrete she could pin her beliefs on. Yet, every time she watched the news reports of some failed terrorist attacks, attempts at genocide, or something as mundane as mobsters in the United States going to jail, she had the unsettling, but somehow proud, feeling her Donald was intricately involved.

"What's on your mind, Olivia? You seemed a million miles away."

"Oh, no, I'm just thoroughly enjoying my travels. Although, I do miss my grandchildren. The next time Romelo and I travel abroad, we have to bring them with us."

"I would love to see more of Jonathan and Jeffrey, too, but until Satarah feels more comfortable with her future, she won't bring the twins for a visit."

"I'll keep a close eye on her, Mariah. I'll do whatever I have to do to make sure she doesn't hurt herself if she falls."

"I know you will, sis. Sometimes I wish my Satarah Josephine wasn't so stubbornly independent."

"She takes after you in that regard, Mariah. You wouldn't let anyone help you when you divorced and moved to France to reopen our great grandparents' home and businesses here. Still, look at what you've accomplished. This house is constantly referenced in architectural magazines and your club is packed every night. Our family's sweet-grass basket business is flourishing. You're importing more and more Gullah goods from our family members for sale here every year."

"I started out with my family's moral support, but after what Carlotta did to her sister, JoJeff's infidelity right under Satarah's nose, and now my former husband piling on by kicking our daughter and our grandchildren out of the house unless Satarah pays him more rent. It's going to be much harder for Satarah Jo than it ever was for me. My ex-husband lied to me and said, while I was away with the church choir one weekend, Satarah ran off at fifteen when she was pregnant with JoJeff's baby. I believed him and I was heartbroken. However, the truth of the matter was, as soon as my back was turned, the scoundrel actually took our daughter out of town to live with a minister friend of his and then forced her to give up her baby for adoption. He lied again, told our daughter I was ashamed of her, and didn't want her under my roof anymore. Nothing could have been further from the truth.

"I didn't have to get over any family deceit to get where I am today. Satarah's road will be harder."

"I know how you feel, Mariah," said Loretta. "My former husband is making things hard for our children, particularly Daryl, because he's interested in becoming a chef. So to hell with our old exes. We're capable of giving our children the moral support they need and deserve."

"So this is your last day before the end of spring break?"

Daryl turned around at the question posed at his back. "Good morning, Ms. Anderson," he said and turned back to his work, preparing the ingredients for the lunch menu's second course: French Onion Soup. The onions were making his eyes water.

"You need not be so formal, Daryl. It's not like we don't already know each other. It's just that we never met before the other night."

"Yes, I know, but I have a job to do here."

"How is your brother?"

"He is fine," he said, annoyed with her continuing presence. "Look, Ms. Anderson, we aren't friends and never will be. You once dated my brother and now you're sleeping with my father. Let's not pretend we have a basis for conversation."

"Well, we will have when I marry your father."

"Yeah, like that will ever happen," he lowly grumbled.

"You don't think your father will ask me to marry him?"

"I have no idea what my father may or may not do. It seems he's prone to make bad decisions recently in his declining years."

"Your father is a strong, virile man. Now he's divorced and available, he's in the top fifty wealthiest bachelors in South Carolina. I like men who are seasoned and know how to show a woman a good time."

"Good luck with that, but as I said, I'm working here."

"I hear your mother got this job for you and she's on a world tour. You can't pick up any entertainment industry trade paper or magazine and not find her plastered everywhere. I've seen her national commercial ads on television, too. According to *Entertainment Nightly*, she's in Paris now working on an album with the famous French Mariah and a made-for-television movie, isn't she?"

"Is that why you insist on interrupting my work? You're looking for inside information about my mother?"

"Well, I'm just curious, that's all. I mean, according to her bio, she was discovered working here and Advantage Entertainment snapped her up from right under McCoy Entertainment's nose. Everyone in the industry knows Advantage is among the top talent representation companies in the world. They only pick the cream of the crop to represent. It's just curious McCoy Entertainment didn't sign her to an exclusive contract before Advantage even got wind of her. I know Justin McCoy personally. I'm under contract to McCoy Entertainment to perform at his resorts in the United States. He doesn't strike me as a man who lets an opportunity get past him. I think your mother must not have been as spectacular as everyone seems to think she is. Certainly, your father divorced her at the first opportunity. He, like Justin McCoy, is a very astute businessman."

Daryl turned toward the woman and folded his arms across his chest. "Frankly, Ms. Anderson, I, and legions of others, don't give a *damn* what you think." He didn't raise his voice, but something in his demeanor must have alerted her that her immediate departure was warranted.

"*Wow!*" said Jessica, suddenly standing at his back.

Daryl looked over his shoulder, dropped his head, and sighed. At this rate, he would never get his work done on time. "Good morning, Jesse, is there something you needed?"

"Well, I heard today is your last day before you return to college. I wanted to make sure to say goodbye before you left. Here is my contact information," she said, offering a business card, "in case you want to keep in touch until you return in the summer."

"Thank you, Jesse," he said and held up his gloved hands. "Would you put your card over there?" He nodded toward his backpack.

She did as instructed and then returned to watch him work as she usually did whenever she could catch him working in the kitchen. Sometimes, when they had a big group in the dining room, they pressed him into waiting or bussing tables. People seemed to like him and always chatted with him in the dining room. He got really big tips as a result and the young women always wanted to sit in his section of the dining hall. He worked really hard from early morning to closing. Admittedly, she enjoyed his company, too, probably more than anyone else she met after returning to the states, and definitely more than she should. She began to look forward to seeing him each day and had to search hard for something to say to him to get him to talk with her. If he were waiting tables, she would purposely sit in his section. Unlike other boys her age, he didn't seem impressed with who her family was or with her particularly. That, in and of itself, was simultaneously interesting and disconcerting.

"Ms. Anderson said your mother is in the entertainment industry?"

"She is, yes."

"So she worked here as an entertainer?"

"Yes, she did."

"Did she know Loretta?"

Daryl raised his head; his brows drew together when he looked at Jessica. "She *is* Loretta," he said. "That's her name. Loretta Hill Mason."

"Oh," Jessica exclaimed, surprised. "I didn't know. I knew everyone thought she, that Loretta was, I mean, *is* a very talented songstress and pianist, but no one—I mean, I never made the connection. I thought your mother worked in management or something and that's how she was able to get this job for you."

"My mother was the Head Mistress of Columbia Academy, an exclusive private prep school, but she decided to take a sabbatical after she and my father divorced. Her popularity just blew up all of a sudden. Now she has launched an entirely new career as a performer. She's in at least five commercial ads on television and performing on tour in a revival of a stage show. My mom is also doing a made-for-television movie. She has offers to do the title songs for some upcoming, feature-length films and she's scheduled to do two Broadway shows in the next few years. I'm very proud of her and her success."

Is this the woman Bonnie said her dad seemed interested in? The music he seemed to prefer to listen to now? She is Daryl's mother? Jessica's thoughts whirled, as Daryl continued to work and simultaneously talk about his mother and the many wonderful things she did. She thought, if that were so, her father would have helped her career, Jessica was sure of it. She listened as Daryl talked about her in such glowing terms. Jessica had no warm and fuzzy feelings about her own mother and she had been away at school nearly all of her academic life.

She was just getting to know her father. That is the type of man she was learning her father's character to be. She even Googled her father. People in business called him The Rejuvenator because of his uncanny ability to turn a sow's ear into a silk purse. Just look at what he had done at the Oceans Inn Resort. According to the articles she read about him, this was the first resort her father purchased because he worked here every chance he got when he was in college and grad school, just like Daryl is doing. Even back then, her father said he saw the potential in what this place could be and he was right.

The former owners let the resort decay and run down so her father said he was able to purchase and renovate it for pennies on the dollar of its true worth. He even put in long days of physical labor in his youth to help remodel the Inn. This purchase led to the well over one hundred other McCoy Hotels, Resorts, and Conference Centers he now owned. With the merger of the McCoy chain and the Delaware Group of properties, McCoy would be among the top twenty-five largest hotel chains in the world. Yet, what she overheard Ms. Anderson say to Daryl was very curious, indeed. She would have to do some research on Loretta Hill Mason and maybe try to find a way to get her father and Mrs. Mason back together, again. If her father was truly interested in Mrs. Mason on a romantic level, that would be so radically kool! She would have to tell David about the good news of her discovery when she talked with him.

Daryl took off his baseball cap and looked around to make sure everything in the kitchen was clean and orderly. He sniffed the air that still held a hint of the lunchtime French Onion Soup he helped prepare and smiled to himself. Ms. Nettie let him slip some cooking sherry into the soup base of her recipe. Everyone raved about the flavor, but Ms. Nettie would not reveal the ingredients to anyone, except him. She told him his cooking sherry addition made all the difference in the flavor. That would forever remain their little secret.

He already said his goodbyes to her and to everyone else, including a wrathful Bonnie, loaded his belongings in his SUV, and prepared himself with ice-cold bottles of water and veggie snacks for the long ride ahead of him back to campus, but he was still reluctant to leave. The remodeled kitchen was where he truly believed he should be, regardless of his father's negative sentiments. Creating gastronomical masterpieces was in his blood, learned at the knee of one of the best chefs he knew, his own mother. He loved everything about the process, including finding unique seasonings to give a dish something extra special for the palate. Presentation was important, but if the food didn't please the taste buds, then it was just so much pretty garbage. He wanted to learn how to create food combinations that not only looked good, but also taste phenomenal, too. He believed he could start to do that here and then hone his skill at one of the best culinary schools worldwide. He was glad he would have the opportunity to come back here over the summer. He felt at home here, among people who appreciated what he was trying to do. He no longer felt welcomed in his father's house.

Thankfully, his mother assured him if this was what he wanted for his life's work, she would support him no matter what. Although his full four years in college were already paid for, she told him he didn't have to rely on his father for financial support. Though she insisted he complete college and even graduate school, she told him she now had more than enough resources to help him reach for his dreams in the culinary industry. He would always have a home to come to, she said, regardless of whether she was in her New York condo or not. She had given him and his siblings keys to her condo during Thanksgiving.

Still, he was born and raised in a family where people were taught to stand on their own two feet, watch their manners, and respect their elders. He liked Atlanta and even New York City to visit, but he would not want to live in either place for long. Truth be told, he liked it here at the resort by the Atlantic Beach seashore best of all. It was a nice blend of southern charm and country living, with just enough urban amenities in Myrtle Beach and Charleston to make it interesting.

The new resort management team gave him a hefty monetary bonus as a going away gift and, as an inducement to return, they were saving one of the two-bedroom employee cottages on the resort grounds for him to use over the summer as a part of his compensation package. He could make enough money during each school break to cover his expenses so he wouldn't have to rely heavily on his mother or his father. He was pleased with that plan and called Randy and Libby to ask them to come for a visit during the summer when they had a break in their schedules. They both said they would find time to, at least, come for a week. They were working on trying to plan it so their mother would be able to join them here. Still, she much preferred they join her in Europe. She was reluctant citing her tight schedule, but she agreed to consider it.

Daryl looked around, again, to make sure he hadn't forgotten anything and spotted Jessica's contact information card on the counter. She was a pretty girl, and, under other circumstances, he might have wanted to get to know her better, but she was getting married and having a baby. Other than their ages, they didn't have anything else in common. She probably wouldn't be here when he returned in the summer anyway so he didn't see any reason for them to keep in touch. The likelihood was they would never meet again.

He picked up a stack of recipes he created and stuffed them in his backpack. He slung it over his left shoulder, raked his fingers through his long hair, fit his cap backward on his head, and dug his hands in his pockets. He walked away, leaving Jessica McCoy's card behind.

Chapter Twenty-One

"So, how did the meeting go with Randolph Mason?" Justin asked, as he poured a drink for Michael Rodgers. They were in his penthouse apartment atop his business offices in downtown DC. Since Jessica was under close surveillance with her grandfather at the Oceans Inn Resort in South Carolina, he didn't bother to travel to his estate home in nearby Prince George's County, Maryland. Usually, he elected to stay in his four-thousand-square-foot apartment. She and her grandfather would be back in town in a few weeks. While she was away, he preferred the penthouse for convenience rather than rattling around alone in his huge mansion.

His attorney's, Bradley Taylor's, law offices were in the same block as his DC headquarters offices. They worked well together for many years as they were doing almost daily now with the acquisition/merger of the Delaware Group properties. Some of the finest restaurants lined the K Street corridor, mere steps from his office building or at his hotel next door.

He went to the theatre several times a week. There were new shows in town at Ford's Theatre, The Kennedy Center, Warner Theatre, and other venues all the time. His love of live theatre started when he was still in his teens. That's where he first saw Loretta in a beauty and talent competition for Ms. Palmetto State.

Washington, DC, was such a vibrant place, but he knew he would love any place just as well if he could only have Loretta at his side. He wanted news of her so he invited Michael to dine with him. Their seven-course dinner would be delivered shortly.

"Mason was disappointed he wasn't going to have the opportunity to pitch the insurance portfolio directly with you, but I assured him you generally didn't involve yourself in decisions at this level."

"Which is true. You're usually the one I rely on for internal decisions of this nature."

"Only after you've thoroughly reviewed any proposal," Michael said and laughed as Justin handed his drink to him. "You don't need me to put a stamp of approval on plans submitted. Especially not when I could be wrong, as I was when I advised against revitalizing the Oceans Inn Resort. Since the grand reopening, there's been a steady stream of bookings. It's running at about ninety-seven percent of capacity. I have to admit, your daughter contributed some very valuable ideas about what a younger clientele would appreciate in terms of services and amenities at the beach. Her suggestions appeal to the young twenty-to-thirty age group. She helped design chic social media ads for the young European market as well."

"Yes, she did. Now, what do you think of Mason?"

Michael released a frustrated breath. "You know I'm trying to steer you away from discussions that might involve Loretta, don't you?"

Justin grinned. "We're as close as brothers. If I didn't know your tricks by now, I'd be up the proverbial creek. Kayla is keeping the pressure on you to keep my mind off Loretta, isn't she?"

"She threatens sexual terrorism if I don't keep you from checking up on her sister. I've got your back on anything you go after, but when it comes to me, Kayla, and sex, my brother, you're on your own."

"Kayla Hill is a real piece of work," he said, shaking his head in sympathy. "How did Loretta's kid, Daryl, do at the Inn?"

"All reports say he did a great job. Ms. Nettie highly praised him. As instructed, I arranged for him to get a good sized bonus with his last paycheck and he'll have one of the cottages when he returns in May."

"John Harvey is impressed with him, too. He thinks Daryl Mason is a good influence for Jessica."

"By all accounts, the new management team agrees with John Harvey's assessment of Daryl Mason, though he did have a little dust-up with one of the hostesses, Bonnie Shay. Seems Bonnie was demanding more than Daryl was willing to give on a romantic level. She got a little promotion to front desk duty to keep her away from the kitchen, dining room, and Daryl."

"Smooth move, Michael."

"It was relatively easy. He's a big, strong, good-looking kid who should be conceited about who he is and who he comes from, but he handles himself like a gentleman. I looked into his college athletic and academic performances. He's a standout football player who has all of the right moves to make it in the NFL, but, according to one of his coaches, who happen to be a fraternity brother of mine, he doesn't have the fire in his belly to play professionally for long. He prefers being a cook, works between classes in the student cafeteria and he's good at it. He's well-liked by his teammates, professors, and others. When he can make the time, he volunteers at a youth mentoring program for young males. He's an honor roll student athlete."

"I would expect nothing less from a kid whose mother was a private school Head Mistress. What about her other two children?"

"Solid academic performers, both of them. The oldest boy, Randolph, Junior, is in med school, starting his residency at John Hopkins and her daughter, Elizabeth, is in her second year at Duke Law. Both, like Daryl, are good-looking, extroverted, honors' students. All three are very close to their mother, but disappointed in their father.

"Randolph, Senior, for lack of a better term, is somewhat of a cock hound. He had both Randy, Junior and Elizabeth out of wedlock and presented them to his new, unsuspecting bride shortly after they married. His trysts are legion and legendary. As you already know, he even seduced his son's girlfriend and he's still sleeping with her from time to time. Rumor has it he even took Bonnie Shay to bed.

"Though Richardson Investigations did pick up on some intel that Randolph's parents and in-laws are a part of the old South Carolina landed gentry. They are very influential in South Carolina society and politics. They are not pleased with his decision to divorce Loretta. They have been putting pressure on him to reconcile with his wife."

Justin's head came up. He took a long sip of his drink while eyeing Michael. "Is she receptive to his attempts at reconciliation?"

"Not according to information Richardson's agents gained from a friend of Elizabeth's. Apparently, the three children have a pact to do nothing to help their father reunite with their mother. They won't even give Loretta's contact information to him. Kayla is working through her usual mysterious ways to keep their parents and Loretta's in-laws at arm's length.

"Yay, Kayla," Justin said, with tongue planted in cheek, raising his glass in salute.

The deadpan delivery made Michael laugh.

Chapter Twenty-Two

Carla was feeling more weary than she wanted to let be known to her slightly younger, energetic lover. Every day, it seemed there were more crow's feet and age lines on her face. She didn't like the idea of getting older and would fight it with every face-lift and Botox treatment she could manage. The long flight from Monte Carlo aboard one of Sheikh Abdullah Ali Al Junaibi's jets while he worked her body was getting harder to endure. He was not a gentle lover. She wasn't as young as she used to be, but she would never admit that fact out loud. She proclaimed her age to be in her mid-thirties, though that was getting harder to sustain with a pregnant, nineteen-year-old daughter.

It took a while to clear US Customs with Abdullah's large entourage of over one hundred, so she was not in the best of moods already, but the U.S. State Department minions were doing their best to move things along.

She and Abdullah were booked into the top five penthouse floors of the McCoy Grand Hotel on K Street. He was somewhat of a daredevil and got some kind of perverse pleasure from knowing her ex-husband owned the hotel where they were staying. For Pete's sake, thought Carla, Abdullah did not even know Justin.

The Sheikh and his attorneys had business to tend to with the State Department. So, when the government cars escorted the three huge limos he had brought on the plane with him away, she arrived at Justin's offices only to be told he was out to dinner. It took no time for her to find out through social media he was spotted at one of his favorite restaurants within walking distance of his office and his K Street McCoy Grand Hotel. Her funds were depleted after gambling in Monte Carlo so she needed Justin to fill in the shortfall. She was getting nowhere with convincing the slightly younger Sheikh to pop the question and whisk her off to the altar. His family was among the wealthiest in the world, but they believed in marrying within their own culture. He already had several wives who were a part of his traveling entourage. However, she made sure he spent his nights with her. She knew he would continue to lavish her with expensive and beautiful gifts, but his father, Sheikh Al Ghalbi, was at that moment completing arrangements for his son to wed yet another virgin, the daughter of some important wealthy Arab potentate.

Carla had seen the young woman, Fatima, who was betrothed to Abdullah and who was Jessica's age. She was, in fact, at the same private school in Switzerland with her daughter. It was, indeed, mortifying to have to compete with women half her age for a man's attention. Her efforts to wed the Sheikh were dwindling. That was why she was searching for Justin. She needed to step up her plan to remarry her former husband before the Sheikh was required to wed this most recent woman. Fatima was too beautiful to compete with and men went crazy when they knew they could get their hands on a virgin.

If she could find a way into Justin's heart, again, she wouldn't be so careless when she took lovers to her bed behind his back. He loved only her to distraction once, perhaps with the exception of some woman he saw perform and was infatuated with before they married. If her plan worked, he would love her, again, or whatever passed for love. She really didn't care.

She knew he would do anything for their daughter. At the moment, she was disgusted with Jessica for getting herself pregnant. She was too young to be a grandmother. Though David Delaware was indeed eye candy, and Carla wanted a taste of him, herself, she settled for his father, Frank Delaware, because of his wealth and the easy access to an extensive line-of-credit he permitted at his casinos. She was working her way into a marriage proposal from Frank Delaware until the night she met Abdullah at one of Frank's casinos. She occasionally still slept with Frank, not because he was a great lover, but because of his air of danger. She liked living on the edge. She would miss that when she married Justin, again. He wasn't a bad lover, just not an adventurous or edgy one. He would not be prone to tie her down and spank her or let her be the dominatrix she enjoyed the way Frank did. Still, Justin was a steady, dependable source of cash and Jessica was her intro into his bank accounts.

As she entered the restaurant, she tossed her hair, plastered on a beatific smile she was hard pressed to feel, and prepared to work her magic. That was until she saw her husband-to-be sitting at a table in the VIP section with one of his Vice Presidents, the incorruptible Michael Rodgers, and two unusually striking women.

Kayla casually put her hand to her ear and attempted to listen to the alert. She locked eyes with Satin who she knew was listening to the same report. Carla Hamilton had just left the

McCoy offices and, like a heat-seeking missile, was honing in on her target—Justin McCoy. Kayla's operatives reported Carla landed at nearby Dulles International Airport with her current lover, Sheikh Abdulla Ali Al Junaibi, and were ensconced in the McCoy Grand a few doors away from the restaurant. While the Sheikh was on his way to a business meeting at the State Department, accompanied by his attorney, Carla was looking for McCoy at his offices. Shortly after the report was relayed, Carla made her grand entrance at the restaurant with the flair of an experienced diva.

Carla spotted Bradley Taylor, Esquire, Justin's lawyer and friend, sitting with a young, pretty woman he introduced as his protégé, Amanda Nelson. *Yeah, right,* thought Carla. Bradley was a handsome, very wealthy, middle-aged man she considered making a play for primarily to gain information from him about Justin's business.

More than six months ago, Frank Delaware expressed an interest in doing business with Justin and offered her a million dollars if she could find out what his near-term plans were and facilitate a deal. She didn't have that type of intro into Justin's business dealings, but for that type of payoff, she would make the effort.

However, if Bradley sought the company of much younger women, she wouldn't attempt to infiltrate Justin's business through him. It would serve Justin right if she did. It was frustrating receiving only one hundred thousand dollars a month as a stipend from Justin. Still, if she could get a million out of Frank for brokering a deal between him and Justin, maybe she could get two million. Her spies informed her Justin offered five hundred million for the Delaware properties. Two million would be a pittance to Frank if she could make the deal happen. She had done all she could.

For now, she would keep her options open where Bradley Taylor was concerned. However, again if he was seeking the company of much younger women, she was unwilling to compete, but he did have a very handsome and equally wealthy son, Brent Taylor, who practiced sports law. She had seen him at a soccer tournament in Spain. However, in addition to Brent, Bradley had three other grown children who would likely be giving him grandchildren at some point in the future. Ugh! What a singularly disgusting thought that was, so she continued to work the room, purposely avoiding former lovers, as she cautiously made her way to her ultimate destination.

"Your former wife just entered the room, McCoy. She's making her way in this direction at your nine o'clock."

Justin didn't turn; his back was to the room. "I thought you had her under guard in Europe."

"She's under loose surveillance, not guard, except what you provide through Richardson. She arrived here a few hours ago with Sheikh Abdullah Ali Al Junaibi. He and his attorney are meeting in my office at the State Department with one of my senior staff members as we speak. He's looking for more US investment in Oman. He hired a local law firm, Kitt, Kenmore, and McAllister, PA, through the Minister of Commerce. Capri McAllister is a founding partner, an excellent lobbyist and attorney who has her fingers on the pulse of both Houses of Congress and most of the federal agencies. She's a dynamic negotiator who never fails to get the job done. Quite a rising star in the international arena as well, I understand. On a personal level, she's been dating Attorney Lex Brockington for several years."

"Brockington Foundation," Justin offered. "I've met his father and grandfather, but not him. Why is this relevant?"

"The Brockington Foundation has been seeking a way into Oman and ultimately into Oman Oil to foster their philanthropic endeavors worldwide. Sheikh Al Ghalbi, Abdullah's father, is a major player in Oman Oil and OPEC and the Foundation is looking to make a substantial investment in Oman. A *quid pro quo*. The Arab Spring is a key catalyst, driving the creation of jobs through increased export of local goods and services. Sheikh Al Ghalbi has his fingers in the Petroleum Development Oman Company, the largest employer and producer of oil and gas in Oman. The government of Oman is seeking partners for the development of its manufacturing industry in Duqm."

"Then it's your job to facilitate that connection."

"Exactly. However, your former wife's involvement with the younger Sheikh could be a fly in the ointment, so to speak, because of her connection to both Sheikh Abdullah Ali Al Junaibi and Frank Delaware. If Delaware turns his interest toward Oman Oil as a money laundering cover, that could potentially spark unrest in that part of the world. Reluctance on the part of the Sheikh could cause a rash of disappearances among the Sheikh's family. Italy does not want an Italian-Arab conflict breaking out and neither does the US. Your former wife, who is nearly at the table, could be the linchpin in starting or halting another war. Brace yourself."

"Justin, darling." Carla swooped in, placing a kiss on his lips. Though he did not respond, she slipped him a little tongue nonetheless.

Justin stood, using his lap napkin to wipe her lipstick from his mouth. "Carla," he acknowledged, expressionless.

It was always disconcerting Justin had absolutely little, if any, interest in her these days and as she looked around the table at the strikingly attractive women seated there, she could understand why. With the number and variety of women Justin had to choose from, her only advantage over them was the fact she and Justin shared a child.

She turned to the younger of the two women seated to Justin's right. "Move," she instructed in a tone of voice that brokered no argument, but the young woman only smirked and gave her not a bit of the attention she demanded. Clearly, the woman was not intimidated in the least by Carla.

Carla turned back to Justin, expecting him to dislodge the woman from her seat, but he only shook his head.

"Ladies, if you will excuse me for a moment," Justin said, as he touched Carla's elbow and swept his hand out to lead the way through the center of the restaurant toward the front lobby.

Carla knew everyone in the restaurant must have been looking at her being ushered away. She was absolutely mortified, but perhaps if she could convince Justin to leave with her she could save face and use it to her advantage.

"Carla," he said, leading her to a relatively secluded space in the restaurant's elegant lobby, "why are you here?"

"I haven't seen you for some time. Whenever I come to your office, that dragon who guards your door says you're unavailable. I had to hear it from our daughter you spent a considerable amount of time last fall in South Carolina, of all places. What could possibly interest you in that area of the country?"

"That's not important. What is important is you haven't answered Jessica's phone calls, e-mails, or text messages."

"Why should I talk with that impudent child who allowed herself to get pregnant and refused to get an abortion as I instructed her to do! Now it's entirely too late! I refuse to accept this situation! I'm still too young to be anyone's grandmother!"

He sighed frustratingly. "That's between you and Jesse, but I believe you're making a big mistake. She needs us to be there for her, particularly at this time when the baby is due in a few weeks. I hope you change your mind and try to be the mother to her she needs.

"I have people waiting. Why have you tracked me down? What do you want?"

"I want you, Justin," she said, moving into his personal space and fiddling with his tie. "I want to be with you, again, the way we were when we were first married. Maybe then, you, Jessica, and I can be a family, again. You remember how happy we were, don't you, darling?"

He took her hands off him and looked into her eyes. "I remember I came home early from a business trip eager to surprise my loving wife only to find you in our bed with the man who became your second husband."

"Why must you bring up old stuff?" She huffed and pursed her lips. "You were working crazy hours and always on the go and I was left alone too often with your daughter. She's nearly grown and married now, so I could travel with you instead of staying cooped up at home with nothing to do. I hear you're buying the Delaware Hotels," she interjected lightly, but failed to notice the subtle change in Justin's demeanor, "so I know you'll be spending a lot more time in Europe, Asia, and Africa. I could be an asset to you because I have such great friends and connections there. As your wife, I could open important and influential doors for you. I could introduce you to my dear friend Sheikh Abdullah Ali Al

Junaibi. He is looking for more American investments for his country. Perhaps you could build another hotel or two in Oman."

"I open my own doors, Carla, so stay out of my business. I am only interested in you reconnecting with Jessica, not with the development of a marriage between us."

"Are you into that young woman with you tonight? I know you date these women just to make me jealous. It could be so good between us, again. I would even permit you to see other women, discretely, of course. We could have an open marriage. One where we could share the women you find interesting."

"Not interested."

"Justin," Michael Rodgers interrupted. "We'll be waiting in the car. The show starts in twenty minutes," he said, as he escorted Kayla and Satin toward the entrance.

"I'll be there shortly," Justin said, and then turned toward Carla. "I have to go. See the maître d' if you need to call a cab."

"You're just going to walk away and leave me standing here in front of all these people?"

"Uh, yes, Carla, I am. As I said, I have people waiting. Don't try to make this encounter something it isn't ever going to be, again."

He walked out the door and climbed into his limo, while she stood with her mouth agape.

"We'll just see about that!" she hissed. She didn't have many options for someone to take care of her in the style to which she had become accustomed. She reached into her slim purse, pulled out her cell phone, and speed dialed a number.

"Jessica, darling. It's Mummy. How are you, my pet? I understand you've been trying to reach me. Where are you?"

"Hello, Mother. I am well. I'm at home in Maryland with Granddad. Why do you ask?"

"I just spoke with your father. He suggested we get together for a family reunion. It's good Father is in town. I think I'll just run out there and have a nice long visit, but I don't know the address. Would you give it to me?"

"Dad did not mention you were going to be in town."

"You know how busy your father is. It probably slipped his mind."

"Well, he has been rather distracted lately."

"We're just the ones to get his mind back on track, aren't we, darling? We'll make a plan when I arrive. This will be so good for all of us to have our family back together again."

"We could also talk about my wedding, too, couldn't we?'

"Yes, of course," she said, but rolled her eyes at the thought. Not that she wouldn't like to have a man as sexy as David Delaware at her fingertips. Frank might even like to watch. She brightened considerably at the thought of sleeping with her daughter's fiancé, while his father looked on. She jotted Justin's address in her iPhone. "Mummy will be there shortly, darling."

Less than an hour later, Jessica and Carla sat in one of the salons in Justin's Maryland mansion talking while John Harvey sequestered himself in the den to do paper work.

"Is that why your father spent so much time in South Carolina? Because you want to have your wedding at some remote country inn?"

"No, Mother. Daddy was renovating Oceans Inn Resort. After I came home from school before Thanksgiving, he came back to be with me here in Maryland."

"That doesn't sound like something your father would do. He has minions who do that type of work and handle such menial tasks."

"Well, of course, it is the first Inn Daddy bought."

"Yes, yes, I know. Your grandfather gave him his start in the business, but Justin doesn't go on extended trips like that. He was there for more than two months, you say?"

Jessica shrugged. "I suppose. I was still abroad, but that's what Bonnie Shay told me. She also said he seemed interested in one of the entertainers."

Carla perked up at that bit of news. That sounded more like Justin, so she Googled the resort and found a picture of Daphne Anderson as the current headliner. She remembered the Anderson woman and thought she had been successful in warning her off Justin. Maybe she would have another little talk with her. She would not permit another woman to come between her and Justin. Something about the one he was with at the restaurant tonight told Carla she might take a little extra effort to dislodge. Perhaps she could ask Frank Delaware for a little help with the woman in exchange for inside information. Justin's trysts usually didn't last long and the Anderson woman wasn't the first one she had to deal with, but she was not in the mood to be patient and wait it out. She quickly had to get herself positioned to become Mrs. Justin W. McCoy, again. Her daughter's wedding would provide a golden opportunity to separate Justin from any of his sex interests and she would have him all to herself for two whole weeks of activities leading to the wedding day. Hell, if she worked it right, they could make it a double wedding.

"Are you listening, Mother?"

"What is it, Jessica? I really want to shower and change for bed before your father comes home."

"It's just that I'd like to have this woman, Loretta, perform for the wedding."

"Loretta? I've heard that name before. Loretta? Oh, yes, now I remember. She was in the Society pages with Ollie Aristotle, I believe, but isn't her style a little passé for the younger crowd? I thought you'd want someone like Lauryn Hill, NSYNC, or those Spice Girls to perform for your wedding."

"Loretta is fresh and everyone who saw her on Broadway says she's sensational. They are raving about her in Europe, too. I think she would be perfect for my period-style wedding."

"Well, whatever you want, darling. Your father and I will make sure she performs."

"I'll take care of that. I don't want to bother you or Daddy with every little detail. He's been so busy lately. He sent a message to me a little while ago. He has early meetings so he won't be coming out here this week."

Carla was fit to be tied. "Did you mention I was spending a few days here with you to your father?"

"No, it was such a surprise you were in town, it slipped my mind. It's getting late, Mother, and I feel a little tired. I think I'll go up to bed."

"Yes, darling," she absently said. "You run along. Now that we've talked, I think I'll go back into town. I have friends I want to see." Oh, yes, she would arrange to see Frank Delaware ASAP and ask for a favor or two. She would have to plan to spend several days and nights with him to get what she wanted from him, but ultimately she would be rid of that too beautiful young woman who was Justin's current fling and maybe Frank would get rid of that Anderson woman, too, for tickles and giggles.

"Yes, Mother," Jessica said, leveraging herself up to waddle to the elevator. It was entirely too difficult to climb the stairs in her father's home anymore. When she entered her bedroom, she went immediately to her iPad to see whether David left any messages for her. He was so busy, too, these days. It had been months since he was in the states and came to see her. Although they spoke almost every day, he had not found time in his schedule to visit. Of course, he said he had a lot of work to do before the wedding, but he would be there when the baby was born, and two or three months later, they would marry.

He did agree a period, destination wedding was a great idea and promised to have his guest list ready before the baby was born. He admitted he didn't know anything about the 1800s in the American south, but wondered how her father felt, considering slavery was in effect during that period. That question had caused her to blanch. She hadn't considered that and didn't know how her father would feel, considering he was born and raised in the south, but she would talk with him when he could make time for her. She liked he had not given her a budget for the wedding and festivities and left the details up to her.

Since she wasn't ready for bed yet, she checked Daryl Mason's social media pages. He had many friends, most of whom were women. There were candid shots of him on campus at Morehouse or on the campus of some other universities in Atlanta. He always looked like he was having fun with his friends. He had a very nice, genuine smile. His hair was growing long and it almost reached his shoulders. He looked oddly handsome with long hair. It went with the perpetual five o'clock shadow and the baseball cap he wore backward for some reason.

She sighed, touching his image with her fingertip. She had not heard from him, though he and Miss Nettie were in constant touch about recipes. He did accept her friend request, at least.

She had not heard from many of her friends from school either. They were busy with classes and trips to new and exciting places. She was busy, too, she assured herself. She helped with the spring reopening of Oceans Inn Resort. Daddy said she did a really great job so he said she could help his Research and Development Department plan other events. She liked working with her father and with Michael Rodgers, too. He was as old as her father, but he was really good-looking. Almost as handsome as Daryl Mason.

She really had to stop this silly infatuation she developed for Daryl and concentrate on her upcoming wedding to David. She looked at Daryl's image again, and then shut down her iPad for the night. Maybe she would ask David to come soon for a visit. Then, she wouldn't think about her friends having fun without her or the fact she never heard from Daryl.

Chapter Twenty-Three

Loretta was opening her mail that accumulated in her absence when Kayla dragged herself into the family room across from the kitchen where Loretta sat at the breakfast bar. "It's really good to be home among my own things," Loretta commented.

"I know. When I'm on the road too long I sometimes lose track of what country I'm in. This Secretary of State always likes to stay on the move."

"How do you keep up with your friends as much as you travel?"

"Friends? What friends?" Kayla laughed. "You're my BFF, Mouse, and we talk every day."

"I mean like male friends. You know, like Willis."

"Willis who?"

"You know, the man I introduced you to at Oceans Inn."

"You mean male friends as in to sleep with?"

"Yes, you do remember him, don't you?"

"I do, yes, but I never slept with him."

"Oh?" Loretta said surprised. She turned on the bar stool to regard her sister. "I thought when you weren't sleeping in my room at night you were with him."

"Uh, no. He's not my type."

"Oh," she said again, even more surprised. She turned back to review her mail.

"What made you bring him up?"

"Uh, nothing. I mean, I was just curious."

"Mouse, do you have feelings for him?"

"Well, he is a really nice man."

"He's handsome, too, right?'

"He is, yes."

"If you could, would you want to see him again?"

Her demeanor brightened considerably, Kayla noticed. That, coupled with the fact Michael confided his belief McCoy was in love with Loretta for more than twenty years, had her considering maybe there was something to their relationship. She was doing everything in her power to keep them apart, but she would keep an eye on her sister until after this crisis was over. Just because she wasn't interested in love or marriage, she didn't want her sister to be alone or lonely for the rest of her life. One bad marriage shouldn't stop her from finding someone special.

"Well, this is interesting," Loretta commented.

"What is?" Kayla asked from her reclining position on a chaise.

"An invitation to sing at a wedding."

"That's not unusual. I have a stack of requests in my home office to have you perform at private events. Most are not convenient with your current schedule. How did this one get directly to you and not through me?"

"Miss Nettie Baker included it in her usual letter to me. She, Daryl, and I keep in touch about recipes. This is a request to sing at the McCoy-Delaware wedding at Oceans Inn Resort."

Kayla was up off the lounge as unobtrusively as she could manage. "Let's see that," she said, plucking the "Save the Date" missive from her sister's hand as Loretta read the letter from the Inn's cook.

"Well, it says here the renovations on the Inn are completed and Miss Nettie says the kitchen is great. She hopes I'll find time to come for a visit even if I can't make time to perform at the wedding.

"You know Daryl will be working there over the summer. He, Randy and Libby want me to come for a visit, too. What do you think, Kayla? Do I have time to fit a visit to the Inn into my schedule?"

"I thought you wanted them to join you for a European vacation to France, Spain, and Greece."

"Well, I do, but that might be difficult for Daryl. He's really excited about working this summer at the Inn."

"I'll have to talk it over with Advantage Entertainment. You're scheduled to start rehearsal for *Jelly's Last Jam* next month."

"I don't want to disappoint the children, Kayla. This past year has been challenging for them. Randolph is still being difficult and so are our parents. My in-laws, too."

"I think a trip abroad would be good for all of you. Do something different for a change. I might even find time to join you. I have a lot of vacation time stored up and I have great contacts in all the places you want to visit."

"I just got back from Europe, Asia, and Africa, remember?" Loretta said, laughing.

"Your children have never visited Europe. This would be a perfect opportunity to show them the sights."

Loretta listlessly shrugged. "I'll talk it over with my children and see what they think. Then, depending on what they want to do, I want you to negotiate up to two weeks for us to travel to Europe or to have a holiday at Oceans Inn Resort. I really want you with us no matter what we decide to do. So work us into your vacation schedule. Okay?"

"Okay, Mouse," Kayla said, tightly hugging her sister. She fervently hoped the McCoy wedding would never take place and Loretta would not be drawn further into this dangerous situation. She had conspired to keep her sister in the dark about Willis' identity. Any newspaper with his likeness her security team assured never reached Loretta. If Loretta searched electronically, the equipment she had installed on Loretta's iPad would corrupt anything to do with McCoy. The same was true of television programs. What she had not counted on was the low-tech means through which her sister communicated with her friends at Oceans Inn Resort. A postage stamp was a deadly weapon in the wrong hands. Rather than continue to invade her sister's privacy, she was stepping up the plan to facilitate a much more rapid conclusion to this crisis. This was no longer business; this was personal.

Being under guard twenty-four-seven was often annoying, Justin thought, but it had its benefits too. He got used to Satin pulling a gun from her thigh, back, or shoulder holster and checking his condo before he entered. Although there was a guard in his apartment twenty-four-seven, with Carlos, he was always required to wait with another agent for Satin to return from checking all four thousand square feet. Tonight's benefit was learning by intermission that Carla was at his home in Maryland with her father, John Harvey, and their daughter, Jessica.

Video surveillance carefully concealed throughout his home caught Carla invading his home office, master bedroom suite, and trying, without success, to get into two of several safes he had installed in his home. Her arrival also allowed the government agents to identify Frank Delaware's thugs. Havenhurst was a gated, secure seventy-two-hole championship golf course community where wealthy homeowners paid dearly to protect their privacy and property. Fort Knox had less security than Havenhurst Estates so when Frank Delaware's men were turned away at the gate, facial recognition equipment captured their likenesses and criminal connections were established.

It also saved Justin from walking into a honey trap Carla was setting for him in his master suite. Ordinarily with Jessica at the house, he would have returned home after his evening out. Carla correctly assumed he would not have brought his evening's companion anywhere around Jessica. Of course, Satin was not one of his lovers, but a highly trained government security operative. What Carla had not counted on was his decision to stay in town at his apartment.

As planned, he used the front entrance to his building instead of the garage to allow photographers to capture pictures of him escorting Satin. The assumption he left the press and Delaware's henchmen to draw was she would be spending the night.

It was true Satin spent nearly every night in his condo, but never in his bed. She and three other agents took turns providing protection, while he slept and dreamed of Loretta.

Chapter Twenty-Four

Randolph Mason considered it a personal coup to get by Loretta's concierge and security to access her condo in this high-toned New York building. While he was in the lobby waiting to be cleared, he saw no less than three multi-millionaires he would dearly like to sell policies to. It took willpower not to approach them and whip out his business card, but they were not his target; his wife was. He worked damn hard to find a way to contact her. Bonnie Shay provided the information by looking it up in the Inn's head cook's address book. He regretted not getting a taste of the cute hostess, but her only interest was in gaining a favorable reunion with his son, Daryl. It cost him no little amount of shame to realize the woman preferred his son over him. There was really no accounting for taste in this younger generation.

As the elevator climbed to the top three floors, Randolph slicked back his hair, straightened his tie around his neck, and blew into his hand to check his breath. He was reminded that Daphne told him Oceans Inn Resort was one of the McCoy Industries' hotel properties and from what he learned, his wife was as thick as thieves with the owner, Justin McCoy. He was determined to convince his now very wealthy wife to marry him again. At least that would get his parents, siblings, and in-laws off his back. He even had a cashier's check in his pocket that represented what his attorney told him was her right under the law. He considered it too generous by half, but his attorney advised that Loretta's lawyers were partners in one of the most prominent law firms in the country. If she wanted to, Loretta could take the matter to court and would probably win. That included a share of his business she helped build while they were married. He didn't have time to negotiate the issue so he simply wrote out the check, choking on the amount with every stroke of the pen.

Well, getting Loretta to come home and take up where they left off would save him a lot of extra costs for cooks and housekeepers, etc., and as a deduction on his taxes, too. Yes, this could be a win-win situation for him.

When the elevator doors began to open, Randolph plastered on an ingratiating smile and started to step forward. The next thing he knew, he was getting an up-close and personal view of the warm, Italian-marble floor with his hands and ankles securely tied.

"You can lift him up now, guys," a familiar voice said.

He lifted his head enough to see a pair of pretty, bare feet with pink painted toenails, shapely ankles, and legs in palazzo pants before he was again upright. The behemoths at his sides lifted him as if he were a sack of feathers, not a nearly three-hundred-pound, toned, former football linebacker who used to sack quarterbacks on a regular basis. Loretta stood before him, shaking her head with her hands on her impressive hips.

"Well, hello, *Randy*. How has your day been so far?"

"Retta, tell these cretins to release me this instant! I'm your husband, for Pete's sake!"

"Yet you come to my home posing as my son?"

"Retta, please. Can't we talk privately without these...these..."

"Oh, you mean my security team?"

"Well, yes," he said somewhat contritely.

She pursed her lips and shook her head again. "Release him, Scott. I'm not in danger from my *former* husband."

"You know what Kayla said would happen to any of us if anything happen to one strand of hair on your head, Loretta."

"You don't relish having your balls scrambled with eggs and fava beans and with a chilled glass of Chianti, huh?" she teased.

Scott trembled, and then paled at the thought.

"Let him go. I'll handle my sister's wrath."

"I should have known that witch had something to do with this," Randolph grumbled. "She's always been jealous because I married you instead of her!" Randolph fussed, as her security team released him.

"Oh, for Heaven's sake, Randolph, cut the crap. You were offended because Kayla never had any interest in you," she said and walked away to sit in the living room area. She propped her feet up on the L-shaped sofa and then picked up the script she was studying before Randolph's arrival. The terrace doors were open to the breeze. Randolph stepped cautiously toward them and peeked out, but not down. He was terrified of heights, she remembered. He even had to be medicated before getting on a plane.

Loretta watched him for a moment before slipping her glasses back into place. She wondered, not for the first time, why she let herself stay in a bad marriage for so long. Catholic doctrine aside, she didn't deserve the treatment she received at Randolph's hands. True, he was never *physically* abusive toward her or the children. As big as he was, he didn't have that in his DNA, but he had always been an arrogant and egotistical man. She guessed he needed those traits to survive in a family of high achievers, on the gridiron, and to succeed in the insurance industry.

His oldest brother owned an aerospace engineering company. His only sister was a university president and his other younger brother was a bank president. Randolph was very successful primarily because his celebrity opened doors for him. He was bright and eager, but no rocket scientist, like his brother or other highly intelligent, high-energy siblings. He sat on several boards for that very reason. People liked to boast they were acquainted with him; a professional football star and they fed his ego.

He wasn't a mean person, but she questioned whether she was mature enough to agree to marry him when she was only twenty years old. She wondered whether she would have felt quite the same about him had she waited and lived her life as a single woman for a while instead of letting both of their mothers rush them into marriage.

It was all water under the bridge at this point, but she could honestly look at him, as she was doing now less than a year after he cast her aside, and say she had fallen out of love with him ages ago. What they had in the later years of their lives together was a marriage of convenience.

"Why are you looking at me like that, Retta?"

"No reason, particularly. Why did you go to all of this subterfuge to see me, Randolph?"

"I'm willing to take you back, so I think we should get married again."

The laugh bubbled up and was out before she could control it. She was laughing so hard she feared she'd wet herself. As Randolph stood there looking curiously at her, she laughed more. "Excuse me, a moment," she said and escaped to the powder room. When she returned, Randolph had settled into a comfortable position on the sofa and picked up her script to peruse. She took it from his hand and marked her page before sitting and crossing her legs at her knees.

"No," she said to his earlier statement. "I loved you once, but you must have played football too long without a helmet, if you think anything would induce me to marry you, *again*. I am sincerely happy I am not still married to you."

"Then the rumor is true. You're seeing another man."

"Oh, for Heaven's sake, Randolph, I don't have to be involved with someone else to reject your suggestion. If you're referring to Octavio Despines, yes, we dated a few times, but we're just getting to know each other as friends."

"Octavio? Who the hell is he?"

"Oh," she said and blanched. Reporters captured pictures of him escorting her to dinner and other events in Paris, London, and Tokyo. They successfully avoided the press in Bonn, Madrid, and Milan. "He's a nice man who enjoys the theatre."

"I'm talking about Justin McCoy. I understand he seemed very interested in you on a personal level."

"Well, that's a new one. I have absolutely no idea who you're talking about. I've been supposedly coupled with so many men I've lost count. The number gets more outrageous every time I pick up one of those tabloid newspapers in the grocery store with my face on the cover. One even suggested I've discovered the Fountain of Youth and I'm keeping it a secret from the rest of the world."

"I heard this about you and McCoy from a reliable source at the Oceans Inn Resort."

The mention of the resort threw her off her stride. She immediately thought of Willis, but she quickly recovered.

"Where you spent time with Randy's former girlfriend, the singer, Daphne Anderson, I suppose?"

"Well," he hesitated. "If you come home and introduce me to the owner of the resort, I'll stop seeing Daphne."

"No deal, Randolph. I don't know the owner of the Oceans Inn resort and as for Ms. Anderson, good luck with that. I can only wish you the very best for your future." She rose from her restful position. "Now, if you don't mind, I have to get ready to go to rehearsals. Scott," she called out.

"Yes, Loretta?" he answered and appeared with her other security man. "Mr. Mason is leaving." She offered her hand to her former husband in a gesture that was achingly impersonal. "Goodbye, Randolph. I don't suggest you attempt to contact me again."

"Wait, Loretta, we're not done. I mean, we should talk about this, don't you think? I even have this check for you," he said, fishing it out of his chest pocket and handing it to her.

She took the check and shrugged at the figure. A year ago, she would have fainted away at the amount. Now she had three times that in her petty cash fund. She handed it back to him. "Donate it to the Columbia Academy in the Hill-Mason family names. I'm sure they could add a wing on the library or a new dormitory with it."

Randolph dejectedly moved into the elevator and, as the doors began to close, he saw not one iota of love present in Loretta's beautiful eyes. He wasn't giving up yet. If he couldn't get to Justin McCoy through his wife, then he would have to figure out another way to go to the top.

McCoy? McCoy? Loretta thought, as she showered in preparation for her afternoon rehearsals. She wondered whether there was a connection between the McCoy Randolph mentioned and the McCoy who wanted her to perform at a wedding. She didn't think it was important enough for her to bother herself further, but it was certainly curious.

Still, every time she thought about or heard the name Oceans Inn Resort, Willis came to mind. Especially that one, gloriously-magical night she spent with him. Many times, she wondered where he was, what he was doing, and whether he thought of her. She still missed being there by the ocean even in hurricane season.

She finished dressing and was out the door into her chauffeured car in less than thirty minutes.

Kayla, as her agent, declined the invitation to sing at the wedding, but she was still working on clearing her schedule for two weeks so she could spend some quality time with her children. Although they usually spoke several times a week, she still missed seeing them. She hoped they could spend a leisurely time at the beach during the summer. Even if Willis was not there, she still had fond memories of them together sharing a light, late night repast and conversation. It occurred to her that Willis mentioned he had a daughter, Jessica, but he didn't mention her age. Strange that she should remember that now when she should have her mind on preparing for her new role on stage.

The car pulled to the curb and Scott got out to open the rear door for her. As usual, there were fans waiting at the stage door for autographs. She chatted with them as she signed the little bits of paper, but then Scott caused a break in her routine and quickly ushered her through the stage door. There seemed to be some type of urgency to his routine as he hurried her through the backstage halls to an area other than her dressing room. She noticed he had drawn a gun and had it pointed down, but he was scanning the darkened corridor, rapidly speaking into his cuff. Shortly, they were joined by more of her security team. Since her celebrity reached world-renowned proportions, her team increased. There were incidents where she had been approached by people who were not operating with both oars in the water, so to speak, and other instances where her residence was breached while she was on tour. Emotionally challenged people killed without warning. Witness Sandy Hook, the Boston Marathon, Congresswoman Gabrielle Giffords, and too many others, especially in Orlando, Florida. As a result, her security was tightened.

She was drilled on the proper procedure when Scott or any of her other security team members alerted to possible danger. They were as unobtrusive of her personal space as possible. She was very grateful for their sensitivity and didn't bother him with inane questions, but swiftly moved at his direction. She knew the risks to her own life and to the lives of those who protected her.

0

"Mata Hari, Delta, here."

"I've got a situation."

"Go."

"Stuck in the freakin' Isles with SecNav! Need The Stallion to intercede. Satin is already in the mix. Must activate Wind Breeze and Explorer One."

"Operation: Tiny State?"

"Affirmative. Tiger Cub and Scout found four worms in the apple. Bird clear for now. Pushing up the party date.

"Done. Granted on Wind Breeze; negative on Explorer One. Replacing with Sapphire.

"Reading five-by-five. Out."

<h1 style="text-align:center">Chapter Twenty-Five</h1>

"Hello, Ms. Allen, is my father available?"

"No, I'm afraid, not, Ms. McCoy. He asked me to tell you not to worry if you called, but the IRS, FBI, and the CIA came in to headquarters today and confiscated McCoy corporate records. Your father is meeting with his lawyers."

"I don't understand! What's going on? Why would the government be interested in my father? He operates hotels! He's not a criminal!"

"Not to worry, dear. Your father will handle it. Right now, the agents are shutting down our computers and confiscating those records and all telephone records as well. I have to go now. The agents want everyone to clear the building. I'm sure your father will contact you as soon as he can."

They simultaneously hung up.

"Granddad! Something terrible is happening at Daddy's office!"

"Yes, not to worry, honey. I've been called by my executive assistant. Several government agencies have raided all factions of McCoy Industries."

"Why? What do they think Daddy has done?"

"That's not clear at this time, but your father's attorneys are working on it. You go up and take care of your daughter. She should be waking up shortly, shouldn't she?"

Just then, the nurse brought little two-week-old Anna Marie Delaware to Jessica to feed.

"You do it, Nurse. I have to make a telephone call," she said and sprinted to her bedroom suite. "David," she urgently said as soon as he answered, "Something terrible is happening!" and proceeded to tell him everything she knew about the government's raid on her father's businesses. "Hello? Hello? David? Are you there, David? Hello?"

Dial Tone.

"And we're off! Operation: Tiny State is underway!" exclaimed Kayla. "And just look at them run"

Justin took a deep breath as he stood in an operation's room that looked like the inside of some futuristic space station at some undisclosed location and watched the raid simultaneously unfolding live in several different countries and the United States. Screens and monitors stacked at least twenty feet high surrounded the room as if this were the inside of a world globe. A man, who was introduced only by his code name "Delta Dawn," to Justin's eyes looked a lot like Kenneth Alexander, but wasn't, sat in a chair that floated like an untethered drone around a football stadium during a game. He was clearly the boss orchestrating activities, though the teams in place seemed to have worked together for quite a while and performed the plan like a well-oiled machine. Satin seemed quite at home, as did Kayla, who he heard call herself by a code name Mata Hari, as they carried on separate conversations in headphones and voice mikes with operatives and fed updated information to the reader boards that circumnavigated the room.

What he did know was this was not a State Department operation. He could have believed it was the FBI, CIA, or even the NSA, but it seemed too over the top for that. There were always rumors in the security and law enforcement community that hinted of an elite worldwide organization so secret it didn't have the benefit of initials. He believed he was standing in the midst of that operation. Why he had been given this glimpse of the operation, he did not know. What he did know was he would be eternally grateful for everything they were doing to save his life and his family. These people put their lives on the line every minute of the day without question or forethought. He would never complain, again, about how his tax dollars were being spent.

Justin had long felt there was more going on behind the scenes, to which he was not privy. This operation proved his point. However, as he watched the activity, he believed this was only the tip of a very big iceberg.

Indeed, the plan worked just like it should. He hated using Ms. Allen and his daughter as the linchpins, but it was, nevertheless, his idea to do so. No one had talked him into it. He knew if his daughter believed he was under serious government scrutiny and couldn't get to him, she would turn to her grandfather and then David Delaware.

He was right on target with that belief. Jessica had more than enough panic in her voice David wouldn't question the validity of what she told him, but would immediately run off to tell his father their operation was in jeopardy through their connection with McCoy Industries. If the government got a hold of Delaware's records, their entire syndicate would be in the crosshairs of the governments of many countries within hours. It would be a disaster to Don Tomas of epic proportions. Meticulous surveillance identified and neutralized the Delaware clan. They were moving on Diego Valachi Cascioferro quickly and efficiently and heading up the family tree to the ninety-plus-year-old Don Tommaso Cascioferro himself. By the time David raced to his father's compound, federal, state, and local agents were already crawling all over the property.

David Delaware saw, from what he thought was a safe distance, his three aunts/stepmothers and his hoard of half siblings led into awaiting big, black, unmarked SUVs. He had slept with each one of his biological mother's sisters—his aunts—on a regular basis behind his father's back and threatened to take his half-sisters to his bed, too, if they spoke a word about it to anyone. He was sure most of the babies they carried were his and not his father's. He saw tears on his aunts' faces, but they seemed to be smiling. Still, from a distance, he couldn't be sure. He was sure of one thing: his father wasn't with them. If he had gotten there before the authorities, he would have taken his three aunts and left the children behind. It was too late now, but he would find them. They knew too much about the murders Frank committed. They were loose ends that needed to be snipped. David discretely left and headed for the first of several safe houses they had established in the hope his father was at one of the locations safe and secure.

What he didn't know was he was being tracked via satellite and drones every mile he drove.

He and his father would have to go underground to regroup and determine whether this government raid was as bad as it seemed. If so, his father's decision to embed a lucrative, legitimate business, like McCoy Industries, would be considered a life-ending event by the Tommaso Cascioferro, Don Tomas' family. He and his father would be hunted down like dogs by not only the governments of several countries, but also by their own family members. They were marked men and royally screwed. Their only hope of survival might be to try to make a deal with the government and go into a witness protection program or face certain death. David knew if the Cascioferro family was brought down, other competing Mafia families, not just the Italians, but the Russians, Irish, Spanish, and others would be circling like buzzards, waiting to swoop down and move on all of the Cascioferro family's businesses and interests the governments didn't confiscate.

First, though, he had to find his father, and together they had to find a way to get out of the United States and into a country that did not have an extradition treaty with any of the countries where they would no doubt be arrested and brought up on criminal charges. They would literally have to escape with the clothes on their backs. He pulled into a shopping mall parking structure and drove around until he found a car with out-of-state tags. He quickly switched the tags and got back on the road.

After hours of careful driving to insure he wasn't pulled over for speeding, he pulled into the country two-lane road that led to the safe house—a modern, two-story log cabin at the top of a rise. There should have been guards down at the gated entrance, but he dismissed the thought as he drove around to the back and opened the garage. He found two of his father's cars and breathed a sigh of relief to see them parked there. He touched each hood to find them both cold. The cars had been there for quite some time. He wondered why his father hadn't called him to tell him about the raid and to come to this particular safe house.

He went in through the back and noted the dirty dishes in the sink and on the counter, but he didn't hear anything other than the sounds of the deep woods. He started through the expansive dining room and noted a metallic odor in the air. He had smelled it often enough that his heart began to jackhammer in his chest. He sprinted toward the living room and came face-to-face with a most gruesome sight—four bodies lying in pools of congealed blood on the floor—none of whom was his father. He pulled his gun and began to search the rest of the house. After a thorough search of the first floor, he headed upstairs, hoping to find his father safely ensconced in their panic room that led off from the master bedroom closet.

David cautiously opened the door to the master suite and could go no further. There, surrounded by pillows, was his father with his eyes open, filmed over, a single shot dead center in his forehead and his mouth agape, sitting up naked in bed. His throat was slashed and his tongue pulled through the slit—an Italian necktie. Face down in his lap was a naked woman with a gunshot in the back of her head. He didn't have to guess who she was, he had seen her often enough in the videos his father secretly made of his sexual encounters.

This woman was Carla McCoy, Jessica's mother.

David filled with rage as his eyes filled with tears. His father didn't have to die. It was all because of that damn McCoy family: Justin and Jessica. He bit his fist hard, drawing blood in a sign of vengeance. He would find them, torture them unmercifully, rape her until she pleaded for death, and then eradicate them both and the child he sired as well. There would be no more McCoy or McCoy Industries. He would plan and he would strike back at them for causing this scourge to fall on his family's name. For now, he slid to the floor and let his grief overtake him.

Chapter Twenty-Six

The single car pulled away from the mausoleum and headed for the exit to the cemetery. Jessica sat between her father with her head on his shoulder and her grandfather holding his hand. They were the last to leave. The few others who attended the burial left, following the hearse and the priest.

Carla Hamilton McCoy Greer Byrd's casket remained closed during the short service in the mausoleum. No one needed to know the once beautiful face was so shattered as to render her unrecognizable. The hollow point bullet wound to the back of her head had shattered her face. When the CSI investigators found the bullet, it was grotesquely lodged in Frank Delaware's testicles. The local police had not been kind or sensitive in their ribald comments that old Frank had *cum* and *gone* at the same time.

Victoria Lang met the car when it pulled under the side portico of the McCoy mansion at Havenhurst Estates. She and her children journeyed to Maryland for the funeral, but few of

Carla's acquaintances put in an appearance, sent flowers or even a card. The Sheikhs were noticeably absent. Not even her former husbands sent acknowledgements of her passing. Those who attended were friends of her father or Justin.

While Victoria took John Harvey's hand to lead him into the house, Jessica moved to take her sleeping daughter into her arms from the nurse. Slowly, she followed her grandfather inside. Michael Rodgers passed her as he came out of the house and got into the back seat of the idling car where Justin still sat alone.

"Thank you, Carlos," Michael said to Justin's driver, who turned off the ignition and stepped out of the car, closing the door behind him. He didn't move away, but stood stone-faced, with his back to the car and his hands clasped before him.

Michael sat quietly beside his brother from another mother, his boss, his friend, and waited through the silence.

"I keep wondering whether I'm the reason she's dead," Justin said, pinching the bridge of his nose between his closed eyes. "If I hadn't gone after the Delaware Hotels would she still be alive?"

"We will never know what led to her death. The Delawares targeted you and McCoy Industries specifically to infiltrate and use for their money laundering operation. They brought the deal to you, initially, as a straight sale of their properties and then when they had your agreement to buy their hotels and resorts, they changed to what probably was their game plan from the beginning. They wanted a major interest in a legitimate business. They were targeting Carla long before they even approached you. Any wealthy socialite would probably do because somewhere in his or her family there would be clean money. Business deals of that nature are brokered every day. You know that, as well as I do. When you threatened to sever the deal, they went after Jessica. You had no reason to suspect they would come after you through your family. We discussed it and believed they would come after you through a hostile takeover attempt to get your hotel chain."

"I knew they were dangerous people to deal with. Slade Richardson personally advised caution, if I chose to accept their proposal."

"They certainly were, but their strings were being pulled by those up the chain in their own family. No one, not even Richardson, predicted Don Tomas would order a hit on his own grandson and his family. Plus, he used Frank's own consigliore to do the deed. Richardson's operatives followed Frank, Carla, and his bodyguards to this safe house. When the second contingent of Frank's men showed up, Richardson's operatives thought they were there to provide further security for Frank. The government agents instructed Richardson's people not to breach the cabin until they arrived. They had no reason to think Frank's men were there as a hit squad. They did the deed and then paid with their lives.

"All of the wheels started turning when David tried to reach his father after talking with Jessica. Then he called his grandfather and caused a chain reaction. We still don't know what happened to David. He is the only one who is unaccounted for. Richardson's people said they didn't know what had happened until after David came roaring out of the security gate and sped away leaving it wide open. That's when they went in before the local, state, and federal agents arrived and found the massacre. David dumped his car and he's not been spotted since."

"The good thing is, according to all of the newspaper accounts, except for Carla's murder, Operations: Tiny State is a complete success. Everyone in the syndicate is in jail or under indictment. The cases appear to be airtight. Most of the criminals are trying to make deals for turning state's evidence and asking for witness protection. Everyone, except David Delaware."

"We don't know for a fact he's not dead, too, and his body just hasn't been found yet."

"Or ever. I just have no answers for Jessica. She's shattered after reading the newspaper accounts and seeing the exposés on television. Reporters have been trying to get statements from her. Apparently, her school chums have spilled their guts about Jessica's relationship with David and the fact she had his baby."

"That will die down soon enough."

"I know, but it's hard to watch my daughter and my father-in-law suffering."

"You know it will take time for all of you to heal from Carla's senseless murder. She was a victim who happened to be in the wrong place at the wrong time."

Justin briskly rubbed his face. "Did the tabloids have to make this tragedy worse by printing stolen crime scene photos that show Carla giving Delaware a blow job at the time they were murdered? Jessica should not have had to have that image of her mother in her head. I tried, but I couldn't protect her from so much of what the press and news media published. On top of that, she learned about David's criminal connections and the fact he was already secretly married to his so-called executive assistant, Helga Lustrum, who was also found murdered at David's home. Now Jessica wants to petition the court to legally change Anna Maria's name from Delaware to Hamilton-McCoy."

"She's hurt right now."

"I know, but I'm going to have someone look into it for her and get the paperwork started. I don't want Anna Maria growing up with the Delaware family stigma weighing her down. I hate to do this to you, again, but I'm going to take care of a few things, help John Harvey settle Carla's estate, and then I'm going to take him, Jessica, and Anna Marie away for a while. That means I'm dumping on you, again."

Michael cut his eyes at Justin, and he noticed.

"No, I'm not going to contact Loretta," he said, reading Michael's mind. "Right now, John Harvey, Jessica, and Anna Marie need my undivided time and attention. I am, however, going to ask Victoria Lang to join us. She's been a real trooper through all of this."

"I can handle McCoy Industries while you're away, but things are clicking on all cylinders for me with Kayla right now, so don't put a monkey wrench in the works by contacting Loretta. I won't be a happy camper if you do. Now, let's go inside. You do have people waiting to offer condolences."

With that, Michael tapped on the window, Carlos opened the car door, and they went inside the mansion.

Chapter Twenty-Seven

"With the power vested in me, by the State of South Carolina, I pronounce you, John Harvey Hamilton, and you, Victoria Lang, husband and wife. Mr. Hamilton, you may salute your bride."

Cheers went up and applause rose from the small group of family and friends gathered to witness the intimate ceremony at the Oceans Inn Resort. It was a bright, warm, cloudless summer day. The resort's jazz combo played age-appropriate music. The glass-enclosed, small, party room held the fifteen or so guests in cool comfort. In attendance were Victoria's adult children, their spouses, and her grandchildren. Justin stood as John Harvey's best man and Victoria's eldest daughter as her maid of honor. Two of the youngest granddaughters were flower girls and a youngest grandson was the ring bearer. Victoria's teenaged granddaughter entertained Anna Maria while Jessica spent her time helping to coordinate the event.

Everything was set and the luncheon would begin soon. Jessica had worked harder than ever to orchestrate the event. After they began their European tour, shortly after the funeral, Victoria had actually gotten down on bended knee and popped the question at Mariah's, a sensational restaurant and night club in Paris, France. The diva herself was actually there that night and after John Harvey, laughing heartily, accepted Victoria's marriage proposal, complete with an engagement ring, The French Mariah serenaded them, along with everyone in the restaurant. Both John Harvey and Victoria had happy tears in their eyes. That's when Jessica convinced them to let her plan the wedding at Oceans Inn Resort scheduled for late summer. They agreed and Jessica went to work on the next phase of her plan.

"Hello, again," Jessica said to Daryl's back.

He was arranging the platters on the buffet table for the wedding guests. He turned and almost did a double take. "Jessica?" he asked, not quite believing the vision of loveliness standing before him. He always thought of her as a pretty girl, but a little too shallow and on the too slender side for his taste. Now she looked spectacular and filled out the summer frock she wore to perfection. He knew little or nothing about women's fashion, but he'd bet his next weeks' paycheck what she wore had a designer label attached. He knew he was staring, but couldn't quite reconcile the pregnant young girl he met last year before Christmas with the young woman standing before him.

His reaction to her was exactly as she hoped. He looked positively poleaxed. She had carefully applied her makeup to perfection and had accented her perfectly tanned skin with the ideal shade of coral dress for the wedding. It took a lot of maneuvering to arrange for Daryl to be one of the servers for the wedding, but, if being the daughter of the owner didn't get a few perks from the Inn's management team to arrange that little detail for her, nothing could.

Still, she had to admit, he looked absolutely as delicious as the buffet he was setting up. His hair was longer and tied in a ponytail at the nape of his neck. His face sported the five o'clock shadow that made him too sexy when he finally smiled at her. Her heart did a little jump and flutter when he looked into her eyes with what she hoped was renewed interest.

"Hello. I mean, *wow*, Jessica, you look...I mean, how are you?"

"I am well, thank you. How have you been, Daryl?"

"No complaints, but I, um. I read about...I mean. I wanted to offer my condolences to you and your grandfather."

"I appreciate that. It's very kind of you. Uh, how is your family?"

"Fine, everyone is fine. I mean, my brother, sister, and mother are doing great. In fact, they just arrived yesterday for a visit. They're actually staying here at the resort."

"That's wonderful. I've read so much about your mother and her success. I hope I'll have the chance to meet her, and your brother and sister, too, of course."

"Actually, you might get a chance shortly. She and my sibs are meeting me next door in the dining room for brunch."

"Do you think they would mind joining us? I mean, my dad is a huge fan of hers."

"Well," he hesitated, looking around at the mingling guests. "I don't know. This is a private party. The management specifically asked me to handle the setup and wait at table. I don't think I should intrude."

"Oh, it would not be an intrusion. It would be a huge favor to me. In fact, let me introduce you to my father, grandfather, and my new grandmother," she said, taking his arm and steering him toward her father. "Of course, you must meet my beautiful Anna Maria. Dad, this is a friend I met here last year. This is Daryl Mason."

Although reluctant to step away from his duties, Daryl didn't want to be rude and let Jessica steer him toward her family for introductions.

As soon as Jessica got them talking, she slipped away to complete her plan.

Justin turned and surprise registered on his face. He could see some of Loretta's features...and it caused him to ache to see her lovely face again. He accepted the hand Daryl extended and chatted pleasantly with the young man, but he would be hard pressed to repeat what they said to each other. He was awed by Daryl, recalling all of the positive things he learned about him and Loretta's other children and somewhat relieved when John Harvey and Victoria joined the discussion. Apparently, John Harvey had already met Daryl. They proceeded to introduce Daryl to Victoria's children and grandchildren.

However, as if he had conjured her up, Justin just stood and stared, as his eyes tracked Jessica as she approached him with Loretta in tow flanked by a young man and woman.

He couldn't take his eyes off her, and he hoped to God what he saw in her beautiful eyes was real. She was as happy to see him, as he was to see her. His heart wanted to explode with joy.

Then there was a deafening roar in his ears that sounded like his own voice shouting that momentarily eclipsed his heart and then everything seemed to happen in slow motion. Instinctively, he simultaneously grabbed Loretta and Jessica, and wrestled them to the floor. He saw the fear and panic etched in the faces of those he loved dearly, but he also saw the horror of blood splatter over their faces and clothes. Then the scene went into real time for him when he heard the screams, Anna Maria's wail, and the gunfire. He now knew what cordite smelled like washed over by a metallic taste in his mouth and nostrils, but he couldn't feel anything and could barely see anything as his eyes began to blur with Loretta screaming for him to stay with her. Not to leave her. He wanted to tell her he didn't want to go, but he could not seem to stay. Then the sound stopped and everything went black.

He didn't understand why he was looking down on himself, with Loretta on her knees, crying, and pleading and Jessica shell-shocked. Blood covered her pretty, peach-colored dress. As she moved to grab his hand to her cheek, he saw blood fountaining up from several wounds in his body. As he pulled further away from the scene below him, pandemonium seemed to have taken over. There were bodies sprawled on the floor. People were crying and screaming, but oddly, he could not hear their voices. He could only see the sheer terror on their distorted faces. Then, in his peripheral vision, he saw David Delaware's lifeless eyes staring up at him as he floated further above.

Moments later, he saw Kayla Hill with her SIG Sauer out in a two-handed grip. She kicked an automatic weapon away from David's hand before she bent to check his neck for a pulse. By then, he was losing sight of the room and just seemed to be floating in deep space before everything, again, faded to black.

Epilogue

A storm passed over the Grand Strand and Oceans Inn Resort the night before and left quite a bit of debris on the beach. Still, Jessica sat next to Daryl, while he played silly little games that made her baby show her biggest two-budding-front-teeth smile. Her long, dark eyelashes swept her chubby cheeks. With the sun high and bright, they sat on a blanket under a large umbrella, facing the Atlantic Ocean.

Jessica wrapped her arms around her knees, pulling them to her chest. Her feet were bare and she wore a T-shirt and a pair of shorts. Her fair hair was long and loose, being whipped in every direction by the frisky breeze.

With raised knees, Daryl cradled the grinning Anna Maria against his thick, finely sculptured thighs. She used his flat, muscular belly as a springboard to push off as she bounced, giggled, and laughed at the silly sounds he made strictly for her amusement. He kept up the play, as her beautiful eyes widened with joy and awe. Her hair was thick, ink-black, and silky, but refused taming, so Jessica left it loose. When Daryl buried his face in Anna Marie's tummy, she managed to grab his baseball cap off his head. The awe on her small face, with big, dark brown eyes, was priceless as she transferred her interest from Daryl's cap to his perfusion of hair the breeze caught and blew in all directions around his head and shoulders. She captured a thick hank of his hair in her tight fist and pulled it with surprising strength toward her pink, rosebud mouth.

When Anna Maria began to cloud up, Daryl placed her on her back on the blanket between his outstretched legs and reached for the diaper bag. Her little legs kicked energetically, catching him square in the crotch. Jessica couldn't contain her laughter at Daryl's pained expression. He reached out, palmed her face like a mask, and playfully pushed her over sideways on the blanket. Her cheeks warmed from her still uncontrollable laughter. He continued changing Anna Marie's smelly diaper. It was a good thing they were outside and the breeze was brisk because her poopy diaper was ripe.

"What in the world have you been eating, Anna Banana?" Daryl teased, as he efficiently finished the smelly task and passed the offensive diaper over to Jessica for disposal. "I'm going to have to teach you to eat foods that don't turn into a toxic waste dump."

"She doesn't eat solid food yet, silly. She only drinks breast milk and eats baby cereal."

He looked over at the impressive pair of breasts on Jessica and shook his head. "Maybe I better teach *you* what to eat, so Anna Banana doesn't give off skunk bombs."

Jessica pursed her lips and rose in one fluid motion to dump the wrapped diaper in a beach trash barrel. Daryl watched her walk away with no little amount of chagrin. She had *really* filled out in all of the right places, he thought.

"When are you leaving to go back to school?" Jessica asked when she resumed her seat on the blanket beside Daryl, who fed Anna Marie her bottle.

"End of the week. I promised both sets of my grandparents I would stop by Columbia for a visit before I went back to campus in Atlanta. I know they just want to pump me for information. Now that my mother is all right, again, they're restarting their campaign for her to come home and reconcile with my father."

"You don't think she would do that after what happened to her, do you?"

"Yeah, no, they can stick a fork in it. It's done."

Jessica released a pent up breath she didn't realize she was holding. "So you'll be back for the holidays like last year?"

"If the management will have me, I will, yes. Of course, I have to see my favorite girl, Anna Banana," he said, raising the sleepy child to his shoulder to burp. He continued to rub her back until she released several, successive, loud burps. Her tiny rosebud mouth curved into a beatific smile in her sleep.

"As a part of the Oceans Inn Resort's management team and your favorite girl's mother, we will welcome you back with open arms."

Daryl didn't want to look into Jessica's beautiful eyes at that moment. He still had so many years ahead of him to reach his goals. The inducement to reevaluate his plan and including Jessica and Anna Maria in the mix was strong, but he had to be stronger for all their sakes. "I appreciate that," he said, cradling the sleeping baby and looking only at her pretty face.

Jessica looked away from the sweet scene of Daryl and her daughter. With her legs pulled into her, she propped her chin on her knees. She had probably gone too far with the "open arms" comment, but it was exactly how she felt. She had lost so much in the last six weeks to two months that she clung too tightly to those she had left.

Fortunately, her grandparents, John Harvey and Victoria, were back on their feet, again. Their bullet wounds were not as severe as those sustained by others. Bonnie Shay may have to spend the rest of her life in a wheelchair, though. She had been spying on Daryl when she accidently bumped into David Delaware on his way into the small party room of the wedding. He pushed Bonnie down and kicked her so hard, he broke her hip and caused a spinal cord injury. She was recuperating in a convalescent home.

However, that act of violence saved other lives. Kayla Hill was on her way to join her family for lunch when she saw David violently kicking Bonnie. She pulled her weapon split seconds after he opened fire, spraying bullets on those who were inside the party room. The glass enclosure shattered raining debris down on everyone.

What Jessica orchestrated, timing her grandfather's wedding to coincide with Daryl's family's visit, had been such a grand idea at the time. Now, it was an unmitigated disaster. She still paled at the thought of her father...

"Jessica? Jessica?" a voice brought her out of her reverie.

She scrambled up and flung her arms tightly around her father's midsection.

"Careful," Justin said, holding his daughter as tightly as he could in his arms.

She quickly released him, mindful of his still healing body and flung her arms around the woman at his side—Loretta.

"How was your walk?" Jessica managed, while briskly wiping her tears and helping Daryl set up the beach chairs for his mother and her father.

"I'm getting better every day, baby. Don't look so worried. Loretta won't let me overdo it."

"Ms. Loretta, you need to take it easy, too. You were seriously injured."

"I'm fine, honey," she said, her palm caressing Jessica's worried expression. "Your father is right. He's under strict orders from me not to overdo it. Our walk on the beach today covered approximately half a mile. He's getting his muscle tone and stamina back."

"I have no choice in the matter. I want to be able to dance between the raindrops with my beautiful granddaughter...and at my upcoming wedding," he said, his eyes shining as he looked at Loretta.

"*Wow!* Congrats, Mom! That's great!"

"Willis, I mean, Justin, isn't taking *maybe* as an answer," she grinned, "so since we shared a room together in the hospital for nearly three weeks, proper decorum dictates I marry the man I'm sleeping with." She giggled. "I don't know whether I will ever get used to calling him Justin though."

"Frankly, I don't care what you call me as long as you call me your husband. I'll be thrilled when you are actually in *my* bed and I am not comatose during the majority of that time. When I finally opened my eyes, I saw you. When you sang just for me, I knew I was in Heaven."

"It's like that young, active duty military couple we met last year. Do you remember them?"

"I do, yes. You told me then it's good to be at the beginning of something. I agree and here we are about to start something new." He smiled and kissed her while their children looked on.

Further up the beach, two people walked with bare feet in the surf that edged the shore. Their journey had gone well over a mile, most of it in silence.

"When are you leaving?" Michael finally asked Kayla.

She shrugged. "I'm on mandatory downtime, but it shouldn't be much longer. What about you?"

"I need to get back before next week. Justin is back on his feet, again...oh, hell, Kayla! Please don't force me into an inane conversation about corporate tasks. I need to know how you feel. What can I do to help you?"

"What? Because I shot a man to death?" She shrugged, stopped walking, and turned to face Michael, while the warm surf continued to wash over their bare legs and feet. "You should know by now killing David Delaware wasn't my first experience with violent death. I'm a trained operative in every form of hand-to-hand combat and weaponry." She put her hand to his troubled face. "I can press your neck here and cause your death. I'm very good at what I do, Michael, because I've been doing it since I graduated from college over twenty years ago. I'm not the type of woman you should know or be involved with. Yes, you can dress me up and take me out to high society social events and I'll know exactly which fork to use for the escargot. I won't embarrass you in polite company, but I'll probably be in surveillance mode most of the evening. I may be gone for weeks or maybe even months on end undercover in some country with a name that ends in 'stan.' I will never take on membership in the Rotary Club or the Daughters of the American Revolution, though I will have fought for this country in ways I can't talk with you or anyone else about except those who stand shoulder-to-shoulder with me in the battle between right and wrong.

"I can come to your bed and work your body like it's my regular nine-to-five. That's nine at night to five in the morning, but by six, I may be on a flight to do something that would offend your sensibilities.

"In other words, Michael Rodgers, I can be your lover and your friend in ordinary ways, but in my current life, I'm too dangerous to love."

About the Author

Ann Jeffries, the critically acclaimed author of the Family Reunion—Wisdom of the Ancestors Series, is a native of Washington, DC. As an only child, she enjoyed the benefits of a private school education at Allen in Asheville, North Carolina, and a public education at the University of Maryland. Ann began writing fiction for her own amusement.

Ms. Jeffries is the recipient of many awards for leadership and public service. A keynote speaker at colleges, universities, conferences, and conventions, she has extensively traveled the North American continent, Asia, and Europe. Among other endeavors, she is an entrepreneur, an avid supporter of public television, a genealogist, and a voracious reader.

Her pride and joy are her family, particularly her Fabulous Four grands. She lives in Maryland and South Carolina.

Follow Ann on her website: www.annjeffries.net, Facebook @Ann Jeffries, on Twitter @Ann Jeffries and her publishing house site: www.newviewliterature.com. Her novels are available in both e-book and paperback. Her autographed copies can be found through annjeffries.net and also un-autographed on Amazon.com and barnesandnoble.com.

From the Author

Greetings all—

It was a long, tough, dangerous road, but we were able to get Justin Willis McCoy and Loretta Hill Mason together after more than twenty years. Stay with me because we still have a journey to make to get Michael Rodgers and Kayla Hill on the same page for more than just a one-night stand in *Too Dangerous To Love* and there's Kayla's nephew, Daryl Mason and Jessica McCoy to consider down the road in *Dancing Between The Raindrops*.

However, next we have to find out more about Sylvia Alexander's niece and The French Mariah's daughter, Satarah Josephine Whitfield, her twin nephews, and a stranger to her community of Summer County, South Carolina, during a record-breaking blizzard. Let's see what you think of firefighter Douglas Edward Johnson and Nurse Practitioner Satarah Josephine Whitfield in *Touch Me In The Morning*.

Contact me at:
www.annjeffries.net *or* annjeffries@newviewliterature.com

To be continued...
Much love and many hugs!
Ann Jeffries

www.ingramcontent.com/pod-product-compliance
Lightning Source LLC
Chambersburg PA
CBHW022015120726

47902CB00012B/261